T0194112

WHAT HE LEARNED

Elliott M. Abramson

iUniverse, Inc.
Bloomington

WHAT HE LEARNED

Copyright © 2013 Elliott M. Abramson

iUniverse books may be ordered through booksellers or by contacting:

iUniverse
1663 Liberty Drive
Bloomington, IN 47403
www.iuniverse.com
1-800-Authors (1-800-288-4677)

ISBN: 978-1-4759-7686-1 (sc)
ISBN: 978-1-4759-7685-4 (hc)
ISBN: 978-1-4759-7684-7 (e)

Library of Congress Control Number: 2013902977

Printed in the United States of America

iUniverse rev. date: 2/28/2013

CHAPTER ONE

"Sept. 3, 1988

"I'M STARTING THIS JOURNAL hoping it will help me get some control. I'm forty—eight already and beating myself: I'm teaching young law students how to defeat and frustrate my deepest ideals.

"A growing, incontestable knowledge of futility, (it's no longer merely a suspicion,) is overwhelming whatever inspiration a codger like me can still summon.

"Anyway, in here I can write anything I want, refer to all my favorite plus and minus touchstones.

"That founder of Existentialism, playwright, novelist, philosopher, Jean Paul Sartre, (maybe, also, too 'collaborative' with the Nazis, in Paris, during World War II,) titled his autobiography LES MOTS, The Words. I wish I could express the tremendous power and glory of words by using words. Les mots, les mots, les mots; the words, the words …

"In that youthful spring of inspiration, WALDEN, Thoreau, old Hank David himself, one of my very favorite scribblers, wrote: 'I learned at least this by my experiment: that he who advances confidently in the direction of his dreams and endeavors to live the life he has imagined will meet with a success unexpected in common hours.' Now *that's* a

1

use of words! Some writing, huh? But, it's either one of the most flagrant crocks, (as in crock of shit,) as my students would so delicately put it, or the words which must be rung daily to help one make it through the jagged crevices of this tough life. Since I've just had practice at deploying quotation marks, how about Beethoven's 'I am overwhelmed by the petty details of life,' to chasten Thoreau's pealing optimism—if that's what it really was, rather than just a gifted recluse whistling against the ever deepening darkness.

"What the hell am I talking about here? And why, whatever the hell it is, am I talking about it to myself?

"If Anna were still alive I wouldn't be doing this. But after three years, I've even lost the habit of talking as though she were listening.

"But, as I was saying, I do have to talk, if even to myself, because maybe it can help me get a grasp. (Is the contemporary phrase 'Get a grip'?) I have to feel that I'm moving towards *some*thing, not just plodding, drifting. Toward something 'good,' in fact, if that word still has any meaning.

"That other insightful Frenchman, seventeenth century this time, Blaise Pascal, who knew that 'The heart has its reasons which reason cannot know,' also wrote his PENSEES. (Thoughts.) More accurately, PENSEES SUR LA RELIGION ET LES AUTRES SUJETS, ('Thoughts on Religion And Other Subjects,') but PENSEES is how it's usually referred to and will do. I certainly don't have his philosophical acumen, but I must be entitled to *my* pensees, right? Aren't we all? We all suffer. But it has to be the obligation of those privileged to suffer the least to help relieve the suffering of others. Especially those who are most assailed by the world. Or as it is put in the title of a song by that master composer of human tragedy, Gustav Mahler, "I Am By The World Abandoned."

"But the enormity of this task is staggering and depleting, even, of idealism. The profound poverty, the savage illnesses, the piercing pain in the world is rife. The most organized, most massive, most dedicated effort can have only miniscule impact. Not to mention the puny efforts of a single person, doing a single thing, in a given place, for a short time. The universe dwarfs and swallows what any individual can do and breeds despair in the hardiest, most determined of the well—meaning and beneficent. So what can I do? Montaigne's, (those French are smart,) motto was 'What do I know?' He went right past 'What can I do?'

"An iota of good accomplished still leaves all the rest undone. Thus the sense of overwhelming futility. No matter how much anyone does, even all of us, astounding misery will remain. I once heard that great anti—war activist, Daniel Berrigan, admonish, in reference to such a despairing posture, 'Of course you'll fail. But that gives you not the slightest dispensation not to completely spend yourself in trying.'

"In addition to the moral compulsion to do what one can, little as it might be, if one is built that way, there should be satisfaction in what's accomplished, regardless of the distance to go. Or, as Emily Dickinson poeticized, 'If I can keep one heart from breaking/I shall not have lived in vain.' And there are those encouraging aphorisms from the Hebrew tradition: 'He who saves a single life, it is as if he saved the entire world' and 'The task is long, the day is short; let us begin.' Unfortunately, however, it's the spirit deadening knowledge that the saving of a single life, or the mending of one heart is so sub—microscopic in the calculus of the total need that too often blunts the power of these inspirations and makes them ring hollow. Sometimes, even, with terrible cacophony.

"But words are a solace, both because they can be comforting and because they can be inspiriting—they have the potency to inspire—tirelessly and timelessly. And they can make us feel like we have the power to wrestle the universe into some submission. With words we can describe and prescribe. State a problem precisely and tell how it can be solved; how a certain aspect of the world, as it is, can be fixed, resolved into a better state. Words can enlighten, even goad, others as to how an undesirable situation can be addressed and ameliorated. Words can make history. (Notwithstanding that Norman Mailer once wrote: 'Men make history with their actions not their sentiments.') For words, if trenchant and powerful enough, can instigate revolution, not to mention mere change. Nevertheless, words are a source of despair too, because so often, irrespective of their logic or cogency, deafness is their sole audience. Indeed, too often it is exactly their logic and cogency in behalf of upending established power which guarantees non-attention, surely non—compliance. So , another paradox—the paradox of the futility of the power of words.

"Words are also limited in their reach. Their chief appeal is to others in love with words. Most people seem fairly immune to words, even the most beautiful and the most beautifully shaped and arranged of them. It's just that most people are not poets or aficionados of poetry. But, of course, great words are carried forward, by those who do respond to their greatness, to others who so respond … and they are "popularized" and their ideas, their kernel truths, slowly spread, wider and wider and wider. Which is why those who love words, or it's at least one reason why those who adulate words, continue to mold and shape them, work and create with them. Didn't Archimedes say 'Give me a long enough lever and I will move the world'? Words are levers which can move the world, even if it will not be moved.

"Sometimes a mere phrase or fragment is immeasurable in its beauty. John Ruskin, the great English art and social critic, entitled a set of four essays on political economy, published in 1860, 'Unto This Last.' That title derives from the biblical parable involving he who comes last, late in the day, to toil in the vineyard. He is, nevertheless assured that 'I shall give unto this last as I gave unto thee.' It is an admonition to, and an inspiration for, our lives. A title that evokes tears. It reminds me to never give up the struggle to continue seeking that the last be not last always, and not always have the least. I hope I will never stop believing that it is appropriate to give unto the last as the others, more privileged, were given. 'I shall give unto this last as I gave unto thee.' Surpassingly beautiful words. Les mots, les mots.

"Clement Attlee, in tribute to the wartime rhetoric of the man whom, in 1945, he defeated to become Prime Minister of England, said of Winston Churchill: 'Words at great moments of history are deeds.' What a magnificent tribute! All the more so for its pith. It expresses a monumental respect for words. I've tried to articulate that kind of respect for many types of words—not just those uttered at the barricades of history. Sometimes words at very quiet, seemingly insignificant times may swell and eventually instigate, history. Words convince to sentiments which can harden to conviction which, finally, flame into action.

"(Incidentally, speaking of Churchill, I just love his 'We make a living by what we get, but we make a life by what we give.') I can write what I want in here—regardless of how unconnected.

"To return to the real of now—maybe I'm just nervous about having to face classes again, next Monday, after three months of just more or less meandering mentally. Reading, flipping the newspapers, watching baseball on t.v., napping, etc., etc. I don't like to admit this, even to myself, but I'm afraid that I've gotten to just plain dislike too many of the students. Maybe I'm just jealous that they're students, and young. Maybe I know too much."

He must be so tight, so tense, he thought, because he had to resume teaching tomorrow. It was always daunting, to start anew as it were, even after being at it for over twenty years. While it was considerably boring to teach, essentially, the same material again, at the same time you were still nervous about proving yourself, yet one more time, to still one more group of first year students to whom it all was both fresh and intimidating.

Well, at least it was better teaching here, in Chicago, at a second rate law school than at the third rate one he'd started out at in Oregon. Those farmers didn't really get his jokes, playful barbs or serious cynicism. Here the kids were at least street smart. (At least there were streets.) They caught on pretty well—they knew when his tongue was in his cheek, when the "insult" was only banter, when the "compliment" dealt back—handed rebuke. Nevertheless, each September you had to show, all over again, how good you were, how much teacher knew, how they should have a tinge of fear of him, but only a tinge that could eventually melt into respect. How even, bottom line, (as they themselves were wont to bark,) they should even consider liking him.

But why blame the tension and edginess on anticipating 9:00 A.M. tomorrow. It's not as though he often didn't feel just as uncomfortable when there wasn't anything specific that he could finger as breeding anxiety. Maybe he should see a doctor about the plethora of tension. But that, probably, would only fester more tension. All the questions of the M.D. would be acutely suggestive to him. Then, days later, the tests. The interminable waiting for the phone to ring with results. The knell of doom.

Maybe playing the piano a bit would calm his nerves. Music could be a great solace. A few years ago he'd gone to Orchestra Hall, on

Michigan Avenue,1 to hear a pre—concert talk by the great British mezzo—soprano, Janet Baker.(Dame Janet, as she is now.) In the course of the talk she'd remarked, "Music is solace, music is peace, music is healing." He needed to practice anyway.His next lesson with Anatoly, the Russian émigré virtuoso, who couldn't get quite enough solo engagements to drop giving lessons to inept law professors like Martin, was only a few days away. Martin loved music, but he couldn't perform it himself with any real competence. Ironically however, his ear and sense of rhythm were so faulty that he actually liked some of the sounds that he, himself, made at the keyboard. They were better, in any event, than the squeaking, screeching, piercing sounds he made practicing the violin as a kid in Brooklyn.

He would try the Chopin Prelude he'd been working on. "Born Chopin player" Anatoly had dryly remarked, during a recent lesson, after Martin had been fumbling at the brief piece for months. He started making the raindrops of Chopin's lament and yearning fall. There were two "Rain Drop" preludes, actually.Naturally, Martin was working on the easier one. Easier but no less affecting. Enormous poignancy lay in the simplicity.The music, even as made by Martin, did start to smooth the jagged edges. It seemed always to be able to confer some serenity, however unraveled he might be feeling.

Also, practicing, with Anatoly's admonitions and urgings in mind, usually brought to memory one of the émigré's amusing asides. He'd been taking lessons from the Russian ogre for seven—eight years now, so Martin had, good—naturedly enough, been the butt of a substantial amount of mock abuse. One of the vignettes he loved to recall to himself, as well as to tell to others, (Anatoly stories were always hits as fillers for conversation lulls—especially with people Martin was meeting for the first time,) went all the way back to the second lesson with Anatoly. It was right after Martin had rendered "Mr. Frog is Full of Hops." Very nonchalantly the virtuoso had let drop: "Wrong notes in right hand, wrong notes in left hand. No sense of rhythm and absolutely no feel for the music at all. Otherwise was good."

The Prelude ended so quietly, it was marked triple pianissimo, so resignedly. Now Martin was more tired than depressed. Maybe tomorrow wouldn't be so bad his head whispered, although his heart still beat anxiously.

"September 8

"Well it's begun, and I feel better for that. 'The anticipation is worse than the reality' is a truism which proves out over and over again. So how come so many anticipate so much so anxiously so often. (Seems like Churchill continues on my mind.) And, incidentally, just because it wasn't as bad as I imagined it would be, in my worst moments, doesn't mean that it wasn't bad. But, admittedly, no worse than usual. The students are in their typically bewildered first semester state and can't conceive of how they'll ever penetrate the mysteries of my questions, the arcana of what I seem to be talking about. Their 'answers' have about the usual degree of obtuseness for this stage of the game. Although sometimes I could swear the obtuseness increases each year. They seem to have no understanding, whatever, that by reading carefully, critically, questioningly you might learn something or, at least, put yourself on the verge of learning something. (John Dewey, that acute philosopher, inter alia, of education, once wrote that the purpose of education is to prepare one for more education.)

"Oh, of course they're not all that way. Some show quite a bit of cleverness and capacity, even at this early point. They're more fun to teach. But teach what? To transform their cleverness to guilefulness—to how they can best exploit and/or screw innocents. Teach them to argue any question, no matter how clear cut legally, not to mention morally, from both sides—even the third and fourth sides—as though each position were as strong and sound as the other. Some questions just don't have two sides. But the so-called adversary system of representation has no berth for this most elemental of human truths. Everyone, the fable goes, is entitled to representation. From competing deception and prevarication truth will emerge. How euphemistic and convenient it all is as far as ensuring that lawyers' pockets will continue to be well represented.

"Most of them are here to learn these flagrant rationalizations—and as soon as possible. They're paying plenty for my pearls of wisdom is how they look at it. And they want the wherewithal, the techniques, the vocational skills, the dodges which they can deploy to get it back, and a lot more, too, and as soon as possible. 'More' seems to be their ensign, the basic ethos, just about the ultimate end of life itself. Some are better, genuinely compassionate, and with some social conscience. Not many.

7

"Oh, by the way, I'm not so deeply immersed in parsing legal niceties, when I'm striding around on the slightly raised platform, (just slightly, but raised, nevertheless—to establish hierarchy,) perched at the front of the classroom, which holds my 75 eager imbibers of Contract Law, that I fail to notice that there are usually several quite nice looking women amongst the assembled. (And now the classes are almost fifty per cent women.) Most of them are not really beyond girls, having been undergraduates just a year or two ago, but 'girls' is now verboten terminology. As it should be. I have no problem with that. In fact, it is a few years ago already that I won the Progressive Langauge Award, from the school's Women's Law Caucus, for using 'she' as frequently as 'he' in presenting illustrations and hypothetical problems in class. They're young women, but women. Yet, still, surely, girls in the sense that I'm more than old enough to be their father.

"But not all of them. There are usually one or two in the 35—40 range, often divorcees who've just about finished raising their children and now want a professional career. Perhaps while searching for the second Mister. At least they think they do. I noticed a wholesome appearing, near fortyish brunette, with bangs and very large brown eyes in the third row , this year. Not that I've really been interested in such things since Anna died. But, apparently, I still do notice them. Maybe, in fact, I'm beginning to notice them more."

Martin could never force himself into the classroom before the designated starting time of 9:00 A.M., 3 P.M., whatever it happened to be. Usually he tried to not even leave his office before starting time. He always wanted to enter the classroom at least several minutes late. That way, if he felt he just *had* to end the class exactly on quitting time, if it was psychologically imperative that he get out of there at the earliest possible moment, he was, when he started espousing, already, a small part of the way toward salvation. It was always better once it actually began, but on some days, before it actually did start, he felt he just wouldn't be able to endure it for the full fifty minute hour.

He'd gotten into the habit, when entering the large classroom,(it could hold 100 students "comfortably," if necessary, to look over to see if Jenny Hauser, Ms. Hauser as she was in his mind and ruminations,(just as every other person in the class was 'Mr.' So and so or 'Ms.' Such and such,) was in her seat That way he could enjoy the lustrous brunette bangs and the fine, just short of ravishingly beautiful features without her knowing that he was indulging. It certainly wouldn't do to gaze at her , as he paced the front of the classroom, any more, or any more intensively, than he looked at any of the other students. A moment here, then on to the next face over there, and, then, to that one up there, as he shot out questions to be answered by any of those signaling themselves as volunteer guinea pigs by raised hands. Or by that unlucky soul that Martin would sometimes ruthlessly call on to respond to a particular question or problem—notwithstanding that such laggard was not, by raised hand, or otherwise, indicating his or her uncontrollable enthusiasm to dazzle Professor Steen, as well as the class at large, with command of the most subtle intricacies of Contract Law.

Martin had the idiot—savant knack of learning the name of just about each of the seventy—five students in the class after only a few weeks. By that time, through recognizing the hand—wavers and by calling on the others he'd asked most, if not all of them to identify themselves several times. This easy facility with their names gave him the power to call on any of them, by name, whether or not the victim wanted to be sacrificed, (without even having to sneak a peek at the seating chart,) while he was in full pacing mode on the platform. Or when he descended therefrom , as a real lawyer might pontifically put it, to approach the first row or two of student seats.

They sat in long rows of table desks , about ten rows on each side of a wide center aisle, in the amphitheater like room. The chairs were of a hard plastic type substance, garish orange, and were attached at their bases by rods to the long table desks. Each seat was mobile, however, to some extent, moving side to side a bit and also back and forth.

Martin fidgeted with laying out his books and notes, as well as the cumbersome seating chart, (he kept it there just to let them know that he could quickly summon a particular potential target's name in case his memory failed—which of course it virtually never did,) for a minute or two after stepping onto his little platform. And he pushed aside the portable "podium," centered on the table which ran along his platform so that there would not be any "object" between him and contact with the class.

All these preparatory gestures were also designed to allow the hum of conversation generated by seventy—five nervous people, waiting for what was making them nervous to begin, to subside into a more or less expectant silence. He didn't like to rap a piece of chalk on the blackboard or table top to encourage quiet since he felt that the authority of his obviously being ready to begin should be sufficiently compelling to claim the horde's attention. If just being there, all set, didn't hook enough serenity sometimes he would start to speak in a low voice, in tones that couldn't be heard by most of the congregants, until the buzzing stopped. Martin seemed to remember having read, somewhere, once, that this was an effective ploy which orators would use to draw in an initially indifferent group. Most times these non loss of face approaches crystallized the necessary silence, but not always. Occasionally he'd have to tap the chalk more insistently against the slate of the blackboard or on the formica table top. That only made him more irritated.

Today, since it was still early in the school year, very early, they came to attention fairly quickly. They still thought every one of his words were important—or were still too petrified not to think so.

"As you'll recall, when the last class ended, I mentioned that we'd begin, today, with Problem 2 on page 49. Now that you've had an entire week—end, plus, to think about it, what's the answer? Is it an enforceable contract?"

Exactly no hands shot up. And it wasn't because the problem was so hard. He knew damn well that although he surely had told them how the class would begin today, that they really didn't much care what a professor was mumbling at the close of a class, once the ringing bell had proclaimed release and relief. Even if it had been a successful class,in which they'd been largely, even highly, interested, by the time the fifty minutes had elapsed they just wanted to get out of there; they didn't want to even try to absorb any more. They'd worry about the next time next time. No one thought that she'd be the one actually called on for the problem the prof was rambling on about, anyway.

"Mr. Jensen," Martin called, looking at a ruddy cheeked, blonde young man on Martin's right—hand side of the room.

"Sir?"

"Now, Mr. Jensen, you tried to avoid being called on by looking down, by evading my gaze. So, naturally, I'm going to call on a suspicious character like that.If you looked straight into my roving eye I might have thought that you had put in some small modicum of preparation and didn't need to be hounded." This drew a nervous titter from other delinquent parties—and the non—guilty ones, too, he imagined. Everyone was nervous.

"Well, in any event, Mr. Jensen, regardless of how we've come to be speaking to each other, what about problem two on page forty—nine?"

"Problem two, on, uh, page forty—nine?"

"Yes, Mr. Jensen. You were here last session when I said that we'd begin today with that problem, weren't you?"

"Yeah, I guess so."

"You guess so? I seem to distinctly remember you being here. Don't you? Or am I delusional?" More titters.

"Oh, yes sir," he said, with a little more brio in his voice, "I was here."

"Well?"

"Well, sir, the thing of it is, I guess I didn't really try to work on the problem."

"A big week—end, huh? Well, from my point of view, the thing of it is that when I clearly tell you that we're going to start the next time with a certain problem I expect you to be ready to start with it."

Martin now stretched his arms out, in the general direction of the entire class. "Am I asking too much? I'll tell you, let me not recriminate here. Maybe you could just enlighten me—why is it that when I go to the trouble of specifically telling you that we'll begin with a specific problem you're not ready with your analysis of it?"

He paused, and then repeated: "Am I asking too much?"

Seventy—five heads more or less hung down and seventy—five pairs of hands did a lot of shuffling of books and notes.

Martin was just about to recapitulate the problem when the door at the back of the room opened and Ernest Stolzer, almost ten minutes late, started shuffling, as unobtrusiveyl as his gangly frame could, to his assigned seat. Martin couldn't resist invoking a line he remembered one of his college professors using to lash a flagrant latecomer.

"Mr.Stolzer, I'm just terribly sorry that we don't have ushers to show you to your seat."

The tallish, rather spare Stolzer began to redden as he continued his expedition seatward with more than moderate laughter from the class as background music.

This incident seemed to dissipate some tension and induce a more genial atmosphere. When Martin returned to problem two a few hands went up even before he started paraphrasing it. And by the time he'd finished describing it there must have been at least ten volunteers willing to grapple with it. From a mélange of three different responses a not entirely shallow analysis was woven. And the rest of the period went acceptably, about average, if not particularly shiningly. After the amount of time Martin had been teaching, the norm, uninspiring as it might be, became comforting in its fashion.

CHAPTER TWO

"September 22

"I REALIZED, FROM THE phone bill that I paid tonight, that I have more friends in New York than I do in Chicago. Not that I have so many in the Big Apple. Only two or three I speak to regularly. But that's at long distance rates and, en tout cas, as the French say, (I love to pull out mon francias every once in a while, at least, so that I don't *completely* forget it,) more than the one or two I have here.

"Not that I want more friends here. It can get to be a real pain. They can want you to accompany them to places to which you don't really want to go. They ask you to their homes and, then, it too often turns out that guilt impels you to reciprocate when taking the trouble is maximally inconvenient. I can cook, sort of, to sustain myself, but I certainly don't want to entertain. This whole problem gets even more prickly when your friends turn out to be married couples.

"So, I spend lots of evenings, or good parts of them, with classical music. That's usually at least comforting, and sometimes even exalting—you get to soar. Naturally, being a professor, I also read a lot. All sorts of things. Even a thorough going—over of "The New York Times" takes an hour and a half, at least. More, much more usually, especially because of the 'Book Review,' for the Sunday edition.

"You might say that the paper is part of my daily beat. I don't work on one, as a reporter or anything, obviously, but, actually, I do work on one. I read the "Times" virtually every day of the year and often underline phrases, sentences, paragraphs of articles. Sometimes I read an article just because I should—because one, (especially an academic!) 'should' if one is to be well informed. Many of the 'political' articles are in this category. But I'm also genuinely interested in quite a few different things, sports, 'arts,' particularly music reviews, obituaries, the editorials, on some topics at least. I read most anything which pertains to such stuff. Even, for example, the Chess column, because I used to play some when a teen—ager. Sometimes I'll go through an article or Op—Ed piece because I realize that a friend, even just an acquaintance or colleague, would be interested in it but is unlikely, or at least not a sure thing, to come across it himself. Some of the articles are joint purpose: I'm interested and someone I know would be too. When it's one that I want to bring to someone else's attention I underlie salient points. Sometimes I'll also add marginalia comments addressing the person to whom I'm going to mail the article. Other times a single article will be interesting to several people and I have to resort to my home Xerox machine. In the most complex situation I have to make several copies and personalize marginalia commentary to the various individual recipients.

"This routine is a means of communicating with others and, perhaps, extending and elaborating continuing 'discussions' with them. It's a mechanism for expressing ideas, making points, (debating or otherwise,) alerting others to information which might be interesting, useful, comforting, maybe, even, deliberately unsettling or provocative to them. I suppose, to be candid, (and why wouldn't I be candid in my own journal?) a great deal of the push to do this 'work,' and some days it can consume two, three, even more, hours, comes from it being a way to clothe one's sermonizing, a natural proclivity for a teacher, in 'acceptable' social interchange. A methodology to keep on proselytizing for changes in this sordid world. From time to time, de temps en temps, I can prod some strong reactions from those I assail this way. Eminent economist, ambassador to India in the JFK administration,

Harvard prof, J. Kenneth Galbraith, once wrote: "Those who afflict the comfortable serve equally with those who comfort the afflicted." Anyway, a means of keeping the avenues of communication pregnant with suggestion.

"I also work on the paper by being stimulated— provoked or goaded might be more accurate— to respond to an article, or, more likely, an Op—ed piece, with a letter to the editor. Sometimes I might try my own op—ed concoction—even one that doesn't respond specifically to anything I've read in the "Times." But these seem exceedingly difficult to get published, anywhere. But especially in the "Times," or "Washington Post," or "Los Angeles Times." Unfortunately, it's not too much easier with simple letters to the editors of major papers like these. I've had letters published in the "Times," occasionally, over the years, but I'd be very surprised if I was wrong in strongly feeling that they have a system precluding the publication of another letter by the same letter writer within a specified time frame, e.g. three months or, even, six months. Too bad for me who would *love* to have the forum of a newspaper page in which to be able to frequently spiel my 'ideas,' feelings, notions, reactions, apercus, etc., etc. I would really cherish such a podium, in lieu of the one, with very limited reach, I do have, from which to urge the world to cleanse, improve and fix itself. (The great Victorian art critic and prophet, John Ruskin, as a three or four year old, is reputed to have simulated the posture of a minister, shaken his fist and cried 'People be good.')

"To be able to sermonize the world on a regular basis, to have the capability to admonish it to improve by moving in the right direction, (i.e. the one I know to be correct,) is just about my dream role. Continual moralizing. Constant value instruction. Your usefulness never ends until the world is perfect. Not a likely near term outcome. That would be a reason to get up every day. (The great sports announcer, Red Barber, for many years the voice of the Brooklyn Dodgers, perennial runner-ups, once wrote that a person should always have some uncompleted work to wake up to every day.) But I've never been able to find the venue, (to use terminology from my profession—I can't seem to shake it,) from which to communicate with the many as opposed to the few. Therefore I've done the next best thing—communicated with a few. Although as many as possible.But there's no moving the world with a sparse audience, even supposing those to be well—intentioned. Often a much too hardy assumption. Basically, it's just about always immovable. Nevertheless, if one can only chip away, then one must chip away. So one chips.

"However, one of the problems with 'working on the paper' is that it is a voracious time—consumer. There, is, very often, simply a tremendous amount that's *interesting* in each day's paper. It's a real bargain, a vast amount of information for the price. But how do you manage to pursue true interests which appear in newspaper articles without having an inordinate amount, merely, rather, an excessive amount, of your working day gnawed away by reading the paper. What interest does one ruthlessly cut off on a particular day? How balance the need to move on with spotting an item of extreme interest? Probably easiest, certainly most pleasant, to just keep on reading. But, then, at day's end the sense of not having done enough is accentuated.And what about other ephemera? There are so many publications, and so many have intriguing material which can easily seduce and absorb one, if temptation is permitted even the slightest flicker.

"Yes, it seems like the problem of how much time to spend with something like the daily paper is a particular specimen of the general problem of sensing time racing along while one is not accomplishing nearly enough, as it expires. The grains trickle relentlessly from the hour glass—but what have I done? What should I have done? What must I do? How fast, exactly, are the grains dropping? How much time is left to do what I want (can?) do? What is that? What, precisely, do I want to do? Communicate more widely. But is that realistically possible? Not if I don't start. But how much do I have to say? Perhaps not very much.I must synthesize. But of how much cogent synthesis am I capable? How much equipment, how formidable an armamentarium, for synthesis do I possess?

"And, in addition to the paper, there's all that crap that comes in the mail. The flagrant junk stuff just gets immediately chucked away. But if you even skim the literature that accompanies all the fund appeals for good causes it takes time. And, also, after you've read the affecting appeals themselves, about all the admirable work which could be accomplished if only adequately supported, you have to write out your checks. You can't really resist if you've read the appeals. Literally, starving childen in Africa, dis-figured young adults in South America, tsunami victims in ... They're all worthy. But then, there comes to mind the oft—mentioned assertion that with too many charities most of your contribution goes toward financing further fund-raising activites with only a relatively small portion applied to the mission, itself. But as a friend of mine of the past, Howard, (he still lives in New York,) used to say: if you don't contribute a dollar then you've not even done ten to twenty cents worth of good. If that's the way the system works, that's the way it works. You're not off the hook by indicting its imperfections. I recall reading, sometime, somewhere, that a French philosopher, or some such wag, once said: 'The fact that you can't do everything is no reason for doing nothing.' Surely someone should have said that. T.R., Teddy Roosevelt, had it as 'Do what you can, with what you have, where you are.'

By the way, I wonder what's happened to Howard. We'd been pretty good friends, but contact waned when Anna and I moved to Chicago.

"Anyway, with all this sundry reading, (biographies and novels, too, occasionally,) bedtime creeps around moderately quickly. Not to mention I spend some time some evenings writing in this journal. Another of its purposes. And it helps; I get a better hold on things. It steadies me."

Martin was irritated at his obligation to visit Chrales Grey in the hospital. Truth to tell, Charles,(as he always insisted he be called, "Chuck," or "Chas" would never do,) was one of his colleagues he liked least. Which was saying quite a bit—as there weren't more than a scant few to whom "like," even stretching it expansively, could be applied.

But when Martin had been in the hospital himself, almost a year ago, for his prostate surgery, (the damn thing had grown so large it was blocking his kidneys, causing him to awake in the middle of one night with excruciating lower back pain,) quite a few of the faculty had visited. Among them were even some with whom he most, and most often, disagreed. On everything from the most trivial law school administration detail to the advisability of economic sanctions against South Africa in behalf of accelerating the demise of apartheid. And some of them had gone so far as to bring gifts, books or magazines and offered to do chores, errands, etc.

Grey had not been one of them. In fact, he hadn't even sent Martin a card or note. Not to mention that he hadn't even inquired as to how Martin was faring after Martin returned to the office. The first time they'd met, after Martin's re—appearance Grey acted like Martin had never been absent, as though nothing even slightly out of the ordinary had happened to Martin.

But all of this didn't really matter, was somewhat beside the point. Martin had surely never been excessively kind or generous to some of those who came to his hospital bed. Of course, complete accuracy demands recognition that a few, at least,weren't being especially attentive or friendly, but, rather, just wanted to conduct an on—site inspection of the damage he'd incurred.

In any event, the surgeon who'd operated on Grey had called one of the Assistant Deans at the law school and told her that Grey would have to spend a number of post—operative days in the hospital, and that he just seemed like one of the loneliest patients he'd come across in many years of observing those recovering from back surgery. He suggested that the Dean get some people to come up and keep Professor Grey a little company. Assistant Dean Smith had dutifully, one of the strengths of assistant deans is dutifulness, circulated an all-faculty and staff memo suggesting that Professor Grey would be grateful for bedside visitors. And so the octopus of obligation had, once again, ensnared Martin.

While on the bus heading toward the hospital, Martin further fueled his irritation by musing on what things, exactly, made him dislike Grey. For starters Charles was as about as conservative as law professors got in 1989.He was sixty—two and solidly in the mold of the prior pedagogical generation. Like the one that had taught Martin at Harvard Law School. His specialty was corporate finance and he seemed to reflect just about every one of the "values" you'd expect a CEO at a Fortune 500 company to trumpet. He thought the biggest problem facing the United States was the (im)balance of payments. Highly right wing fiscally, grudging about *any* government expenditures for social or need based programs, he was much more concerned with the interest rate for the 30 year T—Bond than with anything to do with how ordinary, hard—working folks might be making it, or not, day to day. He wasn't down only on the "welfare cheats," but on anyone who might be given a benefit which could cause his own tax bill to increase by even a scintilla. For Charles the ultimate measuring rod for any administration came down to how much the Gross Domestic Product had increased on its watch.

Martin particularly disliked him for how Grey "related" to people. He'd probably not had much practice Martin supposed. He hadn't married until his mid—fifties and was already divorced not more than a year later. He lived alone and except for the year of marital bliss, Martin remembered her as a sweet—looking, dignified woman who was a hospital administrator, had done so since his college years. In light of the very speedy marital dissolution Martin wondered whether Charles hadn't lived alone, so to speak, during a good deal of the brief marriage as well. He utterly condescended to the largely minority staff at the law school, was continually querulous about the inefficiency of just about everyone on it, including some who, by popular acclamation were highly efficient, and very, very rarely, almost never, had even a shred of a personal word for any "underling." They were, simply, support staff to him, lowly cogs whose sole function was to assist Charles Grey. He didn't have to do anything of any sort for them. And he most decidedly didn't. A modest season's greeting gift, for example—*completely* out of the question.

A few years ago, Martin had had to go to lunch with Grey to discuss something related to a faculty committee on which they were both serving. Grey had suggested the Art Institute cafeteria, just a few blocks from the law school. Martin had practically visibly winced at how completely brusquely Grey had treated the African—American women who were the servers. When he told the sandwich—maker what he wanted on his Swiss cheese on light rye, (he'd mentioned to Martin that he always ordered that when he came to the Art Institute,) he barely audibly mumbled "Please," and only because it was a pure linguistic reflex that he'd been taught long ago in post—Bellum Baltimore. But "thank you" when she actually handed him the specified sandwich went beyond even his superficial courtesy quotient. And when the elderly black man who cleaned off the tables had accidentally brushed his hand against Grey's arm when wiping down the table that Grey and Martin were about to sit at, and had offered "Oh, I'm sorry, sir," in penance,

Grey hadn't responded with any reassuring or consoling remark but, instead, had given the seventyish fellow an annoyed stare. Grey was the type of man who believed that every "violation" of a "rule" ought to be penalized by the prescribed sanction—howsoever small the peccadillo and whatever the reason, justification or possible excuse for the odious transgression.

Martin was concentrating so hard on the aspects of Grey's personality which annoyed him, that vast corpus, , that he'd already walked the two and a half blocks from the bus stop and was in the hospital lobby, before realizing that he hadn't brought anything for the patient.

Fortunately there was a gift shop right at the lobby level. Martin quickly decided, he certainly wasn't going to agonize over the "perfect" gift for Charles Grey, on the latest thriller—espionage best seller. The sight of it in the shop struck Martin immediately because Grey had once exulted about how much he enjoyed books about spying and spy novels. At the time, and now again, the thought flitted that spying probably represented the kind of derring—do and gutsiness which Grey, himself, would never have the mettle to engage in but was something he wished he dared to do.

When Martin came in to the hospital room Grey was in an arm chair at the window directly across from the door. He seemed thinner than when Martin had last seen him and was slumping a bit as he looked out . Martin stood in the doorway for a few seconds before Grey realized that someone was there. As he turned his head in Martin's direction he pushed down on the chair arms to make himself more erect and after a look of momentary surprise had travelled across his regular, good-looking features, he boomed, in the heartiest voice he could muster, "Why Marty, Marty, nice to see you. So good of you to come."

Martin walked towards Grey, holding out the book he'd just purchased.

"Glad I could make it; it's nice to be here, Charles. They can't be treating you too badly because you look pretty good."

Martin thought he'd try a sprinkle of humor, despite his having always felt that one of Grey's most flagrant deficiencies was a decided lack of a sense of humor.

"I can't say that it's the absolute best, I've ever seen you look, you understand" Martin offered, with a grin, "but considering, not at all bad. In other words pretty good shape, for the shape you're in."

Grey's expression remained vigilantly alert.No concessions to even the glimmer of a smile.

"I feel well. I can't complain. Actually, I'm feeling pretty near tip— top. And it's great to have the surgery behind me."

As Martin walked toward the other chair, to which Grey had gestured him, he found himself already thinking about how much longer he would have to stay before it would be appropriate to leave. When he'd decided to come he'd solaced the prospect by assuring himself that he didn't have to stay for more than twenty minutes.

Martin hadn't even fully sat down when Grey, nervously, as though to avoid even a single moment devoid of chatter, asked about the re— modeling of the room in the law school used for mock trial competitions and clinical trial practice courses. Once on the terrain of business and gossip they were able to deplete ten—fifteen minutes. Some colleagues they mutually disliked, so skewering these was a way of conversing without strain developing between the two of them.

But Martin noticed that surgery had certainly not cured Grey of his extremely irritating habit of breaking immediately into what Martin, or anyone else, might be saying , whether or not Martin was even close to completing his thought, just as soon as a Charlesian reaction or comment of his own occurred to Grey. Occasionally, Martin would get so irked at these brusque interpolations, unexpected from one so superficially proper and polite, that he wouldn't yield, as he usually did, when Grey began inserting his comments or fulminating. Instead he'd start speaking more rapidly and loudly himself , trying to actually drown Grey out, so that Grey would have to stop and be the one to listen. Sometimes it worked. But if it did it made Martin feel childish. Surrender or petulance, his two options.

Since a segment of Martin's mind remained outside the conversation, as though to maintain its sanity and, also, to observe just what imbroglio the rest of his mind was involved in, he found himself amused at how Grey had accepted the espionage thriller gift. He'd glanced at the book jacket cover, almost furtively, as recognition of the title and subject had flickered in his eyes. He looked up quickly when Martin gave it to him and hastily said, "Oh yes. Looks good. You shouldn't have gone to the trouble—but I know I'll enjoy it."

As the robotic prattle about subjects that neither of them really cared much about wore on Martin gauged how much time since he'd arrived had elapsed. He had a fairly infallible awareness of what time it was, to ten—fifteen minutes accuracy, even after it had been hours and hours since he'd actually looked at a clock or his watch. So, even without being able to finesse a nanosecond glance at his wristwatch, Martin was virtually certain that more than twenty minutes , probably almost half-an-hour, in fact, had gone since he'd shaken Grey's damp and spare hand.

"Well Charles, I've picked your brain about this stuff long enough. I must be getting tiresome. I should get out of here and let you get some rest."

"Oh, no, Marty. Don't worry about me. I'm feeling very well. No, not a bit tired actually. But I'm sure you have better things to do, on a Sunday afternoon, than sit here in an antiseptic smelling hospital room listening to an old man ramble on."

Martin mused that the effort to elicit pity, perhaps self—pity, did not wear very well on the too often insensitive Grey.

"Well, anyway, I'd better be shoving off. Can I help you back to bed before I go?"

"Oh, no. No need to. I 'm fine right here. It's nice to be able to sit up like this. I'm enjoying it and feeling well. Might read a bit of the book, in fact, after you go. Then, in a little while, the nurse'll be along …"

"O.K., then, Charles. Keep up the good work and I'll bet that I'll be seeing you in the corridors and old familiar places in not much more than a week. In the meantime, if there's anything I can do … You know, an errand … or just anything at all …"

"Do you really mean that Marty?"

Martin, flustered by the question, tried to be as smooth as possible in concealing it. At least he hoped he'd pulled that off.

"What do you mean do I mean it? Sure I mean it." He hoped his voice didn't sound too limp.

"Well a lot of people just say that, you know, perfunctorily, but they don't really want to do anything. They just use it as a form. But if you really did mean it there is something I could use."

Martin had trepidation about hearing what it was, but he tried mightily not to show that Grey had, indeed, caught him out offering to do what he didn't want to do at all.

"No, no problem. No problem at all, Charles. What can I do for you. What is it?"

"Well there's actually something on my desk at the office that I'm ready to do some work on. Eh, since I'm feeling so strong already ... If you could bring it to me , I think I could be a bit productive, even while I still have to be here ..."

Martin realized that if he said what he was genuinely thinking, what he most likely would have advised a true friend—why in hell would you want to bother yourself with work, (especially given the high triviality of most of it,)when you're in a post—surgical hospital stay; why don't you just take it easy, relax, read what you want to read, until you're ready to resume the tedium of normal routines, surely surgery gets you that much of a pass—Grey would only further (and self—righteously) feel that he'd demonstrated the emptiness of Martin's offer, that Martin didn't want to do him any favors at all.

After hesitating, Martin finally said, "Well, why don't you just tell me what it is and I'll definitely pick it up. Although it goes without saying, Charles, that I take a very dim view of, and can by no means approve of, this workaholic attitude."

Grey didn't respond in any way to this comment—Martin's concession to himself to say what he would have said to someone with whom he was much closer. Actually to anyone in the normal range.

"I'm not asking you, you understand, to bring it back today, or anything like that. No, it wouldn't have to be today, or even tomorrow. Just any time, when convenient, in the next few days."

"Right, Charles, that's no problem. Just tell me what it is, describe to my abysmal sense of direction where it is in your office, and I'll get it back to you here in the next day or two."

"Oh, that's great, Marty, that's great."

After Martin left he thought about heading right for the office, fetching what Grey wanted and bringing it right back to him. Might as well dispatch another chore as soon as possible. But as Martin walked down Michigan Avenue, on the beautiful, sunlit Fall afternoon, the air virtually crackling and full of possibilities, the way it was when you were seventeen and it was October, World Series time, and magnificent ascents were ahead of you, he knew that he just couldn't, immediately, take another round of Grey's ersatz cheerfulness, stiff upper lipism and unremitting stuffiness. If he were to bring back the file this afternoon, Martin ruminated, he wouldn't be free to just leave and be off. He'd have to sit down and fill up another twenty plus minutes with that insufferably pseudo—upbeat chit-chat a propos of absolutely nothing, nada, zero. The tenaciously rigid formality of Grey's manner, the unyielding demeanor that seemed his very quintessence demanded it. Martin just couldn't face it without the respite of a day or two. His face was perhaps about relaxing from the tension that it always felt when he spoke to Charles Grey for more than a very few minutes. He hoped that the vise on his facial muscles didn't bloom into a full—fledged headache. He wanted to imbibe the remaining effervescence of the afternoon in peace. He would walk until he felt very tired. Surprisingly soon he did.

Martin usually was asleep very soon after putting out the bedside light. Getting to sleep, as with many of his contemporaries, wasn't the problem. But too often he'd awake after only two or three hours, hit the bathroom to urinate and then find he could not re—descend into that pitch black warmth. A classical sign of depression he'd been told. His mind would start whirring, his problems marching, one after the other, in seriatim lock—step, unceasingly .

But tonight he didn't feel himself falling asleep as easily as customarily. Although enervated from the brisk walking on Michigan Avenue the tension,(and the anxiety, he suspected—when would *he* again have to be hospitalized—and for what?) engendered by the visit to Grey still gripped him. Intermittently he summoned to mind Jenny Hauser. He even considered employing her as a subject of masturbation. But mostly he kept re—playing the visit to Grey and dwelling on the fact that he would soon have to repeat it, in order to bring him what he'd requested.

He also mused upon the time he'd filled in for the priest on the faculty, Father Michael Briere, S.J. A few years ago the Jesuit had thrown his back out, severely, and had been ordered to lie flat on it for two weeks. It meant missing five or six of his Contracts classes. It's a tremendous burden to make up two weeks, at least, of courses—

especially when the whole semester lasts only about three months. Since Martin also always taught a Contracts section he'd offered to teach the classes Briere would not be able to meet. The cleric had accepted gracefully, with effusive thanks. He'd made it a point to repeatedly assure Martin, at the time Martin was actually teaching the classes, during phone calls by Martin to find out how Briere was feeling and to brief him on exactly what Martin had covered, and, also, after he'd returned to work, that he hoped there'd come a time when he could "do the slightest something" in repayment for this huge favor.

All that, however, hadn't stopped the priest, only weeks later, from speaking, at a faculty meeting, in passionate, rather bitter, opposition to a proposal made by Martin to adopt special efforts to ensure the hiring of an African—American professor. Briere had virtually ranted. But Martin "understood." The man didn't have to change his ideas, basic ideology perhaps, just because Martin had done him a considerable favor.

What Martin hadn't understood at all was the incident several months later. He had agreed to speak, for fifteen—twenty minutes, on a Saturday morning, to a group of collegians, possible applicants for admission. It was an advertising session for the school—display of wares in the hope of selling prospective customers. After he'd committed, but before he had mentioned the date to Anna, she made a doctor's appointment for the same Saturday morning. She expected him to drive and accompany her because she was very nervous about the visit. (It turned out she had every reason.) Martin had re-assured her and said that she needn't re—schedule to the M.D.'s next free Saturday slot, which could have been weeks off. He'd simply explain the circumstances to Briere who definitely owed him one.

But Briere had staggered him. After Martin had explained, the priest, blithely, nonchalantly as imaginable, had said the words which Martin knew he'd never forget. "You know I'd love to help you out Martin, but Saturday is the only day I have to myself and if I had to come down here in the A.M … well it just destroys the whole thing for me … I'm extravagantly sorry, my friend, I really am. Just be sure to let me know when there's some other way I can help you. Only too glad to do it."

Martin hadn't been an innocent, callow young man when this had happened. He knew people weren't pure—even the good ones. If one didn't catch on just by having a certain number of years pass, then certainly you got to comprehend that particular truth, unequivocally, after practicing law for several years with a large New York firm, as Martin had. Nevertheless, Martin had been sharply flabbergasted by Briere's glib turn down. He'd actually felt a little something more drain from him. It seemed particularly ironic that it should have been a cleric who was responsible for sapping one more drop of that precious fluid—faith in human nature.

"October 1

"I'm glad that I've started keeping this occasional journal, because maybe putting this down will help me grapple with it better than just continually turning it over in my mind. Anyway, I hope it will. So here goes.

"The day after I visited Charles in the hospital I resolved to get the chore over with—pick up what Grey wanted, from his office, and deliver it to him. At which time I was certain I'd be told by him how much he was enjoying the book I'd brought him and how much he was looking forward to getting back into it. I went to the Dean's administrative assistant , formerly the person would have been a 'secretary,', to get the keys to Grey's office. But she told me that Professor Rudley had just picked up the key because he had to get something from there. She thought that if I ran right up Rudley would still be there and I'd be able to go right in and get what I needed. Rudley was there all right. He'd visited Grey after me on Sunday afternoon and told me that Grey had asked him to get a different file from the office and bring it to the hospital.

"Naturally, the point is that even if Grey had only remembered the second file after he'd already asked me to bring him the first, he could have told Rudley that I'd be looking for that first one and could have suggested that Tom and I coordinate our efforts so that one of us picked up both files. That way only one of us would had to return for another hospital visit.

"Of course, there's no rule against visiting anyone in the hospital twice, especially when a patient is there for an extended period, but from what Rudley said it didn't seem that that was what either of us was planning. The most Grey seemed to inspire, if that's the word, is duty—a very long haul from authentic friendship.

"It's just possible that when Grey asked Tom to get the second file he'd forgotten that he'd asked me to bring one too, but neither Rudley nor myself thought that very likely in view of the ultra precise tabs Grey kept on all his banal doings. (Also, if that had been the case, he should have asked Rudley to bring the one he'/d assigned to me since that was still presumably his first choice.) No, Tom and I agreed that Grey, simply, was manipulating another hospital visit out of each of us. We hypothesized that he might be sensitive to "appearances" regarding how many, or, more accurately, few, visitors he had. And while neither of us was very pleased at this prospect, each intimated more than a bit of pique to the other, we decided that he and I would each trek back with the file he'd been assigned. And that neither would mention a word to Grey about encountering the other in Grey's office. Let the man have his little triumph, if that, indeed, was what it was.

"I just can't sort out my true reactions to this. On the more humane hand it was certainly pathetic that Grey had to resort to such ploys to get people to visit him in the hospital. Contrarily, he was characteristically a quite selfish and manipulative person and this episode seemed to be a quintessential exemplification of such traits. Whatever time and inconvenience which might be involved to Rudley and myself seemed not to matter at all to him. He just didn't care how burdensone it was, not that it was *that* onerous, to either of us to come back a second time. He only focused on getting what he wanted—however trivial. Trivial to others, however, one supposes. Apparently not to him.

"He wallowed, if, indeed, he didn't revel, in trivialities. Someone would definitely tend to respond to the patheticism, soften with compassion, were these moves of Grey not so god—damned, right on the mark, typical of him. No question—he was a manipulative and selfish man and the fact that he was now ill, and probably miserable, didn't mean that his manipulative and selfish maneuvers were 'caused' by his plight and not authentically reflective of his basic character, composition, genetic code, whatever you want to call it.

"But the Italian writer, Ignazio Silone, described a scene he witnessed as a small boy when a political dissident who'd been apprehended was being led off to the jeers of a watching crowd. When Silone asked his father for an explanation his father noted the politics involved but then said, in criticism of the taunting crowd and in urging compassion: 'He may be innocent and, in any case, he is unhappy.'

"However, while 'why' Grey acted as he did might be an 'interesting' philosophical question, what the bottom—line hell difference does it really make why Grey acted inconsiderately to Rudley and myself. Whatever Grey's condition and/or motivation, the way he acted was sufficiently streaked with insensitivity to others, maybe even malice, so that I certainly don't like him any better than I previously did. Probably, truthfully, I like him even less. Which makes me wonder whether I should like myself (even?) less. Shouldn't I do better, be more tolerant? But where does tolerance ooze into senseless, i.e. non—sensical, moral indulgence? Why do I have to know? Why can't I just assume that tolerance is legitimate?"

CHAPTER THREE

SLOUCHED AT HIS DESK, in his medium-sized office, but with a small window, Martin attempted to concentrate on the recent issue of the "Yale Law Journal" he'd been valiantly trying to plow through. It had an article by one of the leading Contracts scholars in the country and Martin keenly felt he *should* read it. Supposedly one must "keep up." He had managed to get through more than a third of it. Solid, very, and impeccable in scholarly details, analogies, legal reasoning etc., etc., but oh so very drab. Martin kept on seeing the perfect arc of the swing of Snider, No. 4, and the poetically graceful way that the Duke of Flatbush ran down towering drives in centerfield, instead of anticipating and analyzing the next argument of the article.

Last night he'd watched his video, purchased just a week ago, of the 1952 World Series between his beloved Brooklyn Dodgers and their hated New York Yankee rivals. He'd been musing on it ever since. Even when he had gotten up in the middle of the night, for the usual trip to the bathroom, it had immediately clicked into his mind and he started imaging scenarios which could have changed the ultimate outcome and given his passionate loves, the Dodgers, victory. The Dodgers really were his true loves! Once they'd moved the franchise to L.A., when he was eighteen, he had no longer cared about them—he'd grown as cold as an intense lover sneeringly spurned.

Snider had homered twice in the sixth game, when the Dodgers were leading the Series three games to two, but each time with no men on base and the Dodgers had lost, allowing the Yankees to even the Series. And the next day the pin—striped ogres of the Bronx always, almost, so damn smugly successful, had beaten the Dodgers 4—2 to, yet again, win the Series and monumentally frustrate the emotions of three million Brooklynites. Oh that seventh game!! And oh that seventh inning of that seventh game!! The Dodgers were trailing 4-2, but in the bottom of the seventh, Ebbets Field trembling in pandemonium, the Brooks loaded the bases with only one out. And Snider and Robinson coming up. The beautiful to watch Duke of Flatbush and Robbie, No. 42, the number which had become known world—wide. Jack Roosevelt Robinson the most courageous man there could ever be, who'd made baseball, finally, the *national* pastime. The first Black man to play in the Major Leagues. He'd absorbed incalculable racial abuse, not to mention simply pure rank hatred, from opponents and even from some of his own teammates, when Branch Rickey, the religious, moralistic Dodger General Manager, who remembered that a Black teammate on his college team was told he couldn't register in a certain hotel, had brought him up to the Majors, five years before, in "The Great Experiment." Robinson had prevailed above it all, to become Rookie of the Year in 1947 and the Most Valuable Player in the National league in 1949.

What an example of beating adversity for an eight—year old!! No. 42 remained one of hero—worshipping Martin's supreme heroes. Even now, forty years later, it was rare that a week went by without Martin thinking of him, one way or another. Robinson had followed baseball with so much social service, so much great civil rights work, before his death at only 53 in 1972. He would often repeat to himself what the great man had written in his autobiography, I NEVER HAD IT MADE: "I have devoted my life to service. I don't like to be in debt and I feel that I owe. Some of my friends have told me that I've repaid the debt a thousand fold. But I still feel that I owe." And he'd repeat to himself, even more times perhaps, antoher sentence there, Robinson's motto: "A life is not important except in its impact on other lives." How No. 42 had lived that credo!! How Martin wished he could! There was a man who burned to change the world—and surely had.

But Snider had popped up to the third baseman. And Robinson, the indomitable Jackie, had, this one time, also failed—he, too, had popped up—yet had almost succeeded. He had connected very solidly, but had hit the ball virtually straight up. But toweringly. The wind caught it and was buffeting the ball around erratically. Tough to follow. The Yankee infielders seemed mesmerized, they all hesitated, as it gyrated. With two outs all the runners were going. So, had it dropped, all three of them, two for sure, would have scored. And, suddenly, it looked like it was going to drop!! Only at the very last shred of a second, Billy Martin, the Yankees scrappy second baseman, raced in and grabbed it— at his very shoe tops. It wrenched Martin every time he reviewed—and he did in his mind's eye often re—play the scenario—this pulse accelerating sequence .Fate just hadn't wanted to relax and relent.

Mercifully, the Dodgers had beaten the hated Yankees in another seven game Series a few years later, in 1955. They became the first team to win a Series after losing the first two games. The borough's millions KVELLED, as the Yiddish has it, with utterly unrestrained delight. The Los Angeles Dodgers went on to win several World Series, but to Martin they didn't count. The only gold standard one was on Otober 4, 1955 at 3:55 in the afternoon, when the young Dodger announcer Vin Scully, whose mom was listening nervously, in between many walks of the dog to calm her nerves, finally intoned: "Ladies and gentlemen, the Brooklyn Dodgers are the champions of the world." Scully had later admitted that had he tried to elaborate emotion would have overtaken him.

Martin saw Snider's seamless swing propel an arching homer over the forty foot high right field screen, onto Bedford Avenue, and Robinson sprinting with irrefutable determination on the basepaths. How lusterless ,in comparison, was Contracts!! How about just –How lusterless Contracts!!

"October 5

"The question is: how does one person accomplish anything? How do I accomplish anything? What do I mean 'anything'? I mean something *worth* doing. What do I mean '*worth*'?

"I suppose that a lot of people would say I accomplish something worth—while every time I solidly prepare for a class and then teach it. Presumably I've taught seventy—five individuals SOMEthing. And they've learned—they now have new knowledge. Some thing. They've grown in mastery, power,or, at least, technical ability.

Unfortunately, that's not what I mean. I, simply, don't particularly value the type of thing I've taught, e.g. how to analyze and argue about, (from both sides,) Contracts disputes, problems and situations. And I'm exceedingly dubious of the use to which, I greatly fear, they're going to put this "knowledge." No, what I most deeply mean is something that helps to make things better where betterment is sorely needed. Improvement— that's what's wanted. "Make the world better" is a highly simplistic, yet intensely accurate, way of expressing it. Heal some hurts, ease some pain, open up life for someone who's,so far, had the door brutally shut in her face. The world isn't really in need of an additional lawyer— "liar"/"lawyer"— and surely not a wholesale lot of them.

"When I say 'accomplish something' I mean on more than a fragmentary basis. I do volunteer to tutor at an inner city high school and also for an organization that helps teenagers, who had to drop out of high school, to get their equivalency diplomas. Admittedly, this helps, to some degree, a few individuals. But I'd like to be involved with something that has a broader impact,something a little more widely reaching, if not also dramatically lasting.

"I guess I'm really talking about changing things in general, social structures. E.g. reallocating wealth, transferring from rich to poor in ways that move toward eliminating poverty and utter deprivation. But that's politics. And, always, the political avenues in late twentieth century America are promenades to futility. Politics on the grand scale, that of the nineteenth century theorists, involving transformation of society's fundamental configurations, can't happen in the mean— spirited corridors frequented by contemporary, petty, sleaze infected pols primarily focused (primary focused?) on which special interest's bidding they have to do to secure their next significant campaign contribution. Revolution clearly is impossible. And equally impossible, in such a sordid environment, seems revolutionary change by "working through the system." The system always retracts in self—protection and constricts us all to exhausted conformity.

"I don't know why when I'm writing in this journal I so often feel impelled to pronounce Pensees. (Pace Pascal.) But I do. Sometimes stirring words can seem to drive politics—or, at least seem, in the past, to have driven them. 'Some men see things as they are and ask 'Why?' I dream things that never were and ask 'Why not?' GBS, George Bernard Shaw, that old Fabian Socialist, if I'm not misquoting. 'And if others have seen it as I have seen it it may be called a vision rather than a dream.' From that magnificent nineteenth century polymath, artist, craftsman, poet, preserver of landmark buildings, furniture maker, social critic, William Morris. ("I have often thought, how would I feel if I were born poor against the system.") What further ensigns does an idealist need in his backpack to continue to fight on? Unless it's Theodor Herzl's 'If you will it is already more than a dream.' My most moving moment when we visited Israel, other than, perhaps, landing at Ben Gurion Airport in Tel Aviv, was encountering, on Mount Herzl, Herzl's burial site, (in 1897 he had declared 'In fifty years there will be a Jewish state;' he was optimistic by one year,) a massive block of black marble with absolutely nothing on it except, in brilliant gold lettering, HERZL.

"Words can evoke the images and feelings which most cheer us. As Shakespeare knew, they can 'summon to the sessions of sweet thought … ' Walking down a wide, tree-lined avenue, mid—autumn, sparkling sunlight showering perfect 65 degree warmth, just after 4:00 P.M., a peerless afternoon, a savory dinner , then a satisfying evening of reading, listening to music, or just chatting with someone you love, awaiting … We are delighted, happy, content with life. At least momentarily insulated from its otherwise almost ubiquitous perilous shoals.

"I may want to speak to you, (I do!!) to reach you in such an evocative way. So that I can, perhaps, evoke many different types of feelings and emotions. But I may not have a 'voice,' i.e. (writing) style which can achieve this successfully. My heart may sing and throb sympathetically with you, yet my voice may be without winning lilt. 'Between the idea and the reality falls the shadow.' T.S. Eliot. Between the idea and the creation … Effective "art"ifice is needed.

"We also learn and are inspired, by the words, as well as the examples, of our teachers. Some have the formal title, but others enlighten and enrich us even though they are not, as such, teachers. Henry Adams, long ago, insisted, 'A teacher affects eternity; he can never tell where his influence stops.' High, and so true, praise. How often you remember just a single idea ,one sentence, a single phrase, a mere brief admonition from a true teacher. The Assistant Principal of the elementary school I attended once gave a school—wide speech, all the classes were congregated in the auditorium, in which he urged: 'Make your better best and your best better.'"Or was it, 'Make your best better and your better best'? No matter, the lesson of constant striving for improvement imperishably registered. I remembered it, didn't I? As Churtchill said in a talk he gave, during World War II, to the boys at Harrow School: 'You must never, ever, ever, ever, ever, ever, ever give up!'

'We never forget the nobility of effective teachers, the grace and dignity with which they conduct themselves. They represented a dissenting approach to life. One transcending the conventional and prevalent white hot materialist mentality which Wordsworth brilliantly inveighed against: ' The world is too much with us, late and soon/ Getting and spending we lay waste our powers.' These teachers demonstrated the countervailing power of inherent decency, compassion, gentleness, questing idealism, wisdom and staying aware of the constant precariousness of human existence.

"I sharply remember a college Philosophy professor who was approached, after class, by a friend of mine who wanted to ask a question about something that had been mentioned during the class. The professor said that he couldn't speak with him right then because he was already late for a meeting. My pal accepted being 'blown off,' as today's students would say, as the prerogative of a distinguished and busy senior professor harried by a neophyte student. But that very same evening the professor phoned my friend, (having gone to the trouble of getting his number from the registrar of the university,) apologized, again, for, in fact, having had to rush to a committee meeting and then proceeded to discuss, at some length, the issue which had provoked my friend's curiosity. What force such 'education' has! How powerfully such an example of so conscientious a teacher, who utmostly respected, a sincere, inquiring student, who genuinely wanted to learn, spoke to this impressionable youngster. In so many ways!

"But how is one to tell the truths one knows? It must be by simply stating them, straightforwardly, more or less, by weaving them into an artistic creation which displays, rather than shouts, them.The forthright statement may be flat at best, tendentious at worst and, in any event, not absorbing. Maybe even off—putting. An artistic presentation is … Well, more artistic. More likely to initially compel an auditor's or reader's attention. But what if the teacher can't conceive an appropriate/effective artifice to serve the purpose? Then he's left with only the truth. One he's ineffectual in disseminating. A truth known only to him, so to speak. Is a clumsy artistic attempt better than no truth dissemination at all? How clumsy? Too clumsy will also result in no dissemination at all. And no dissemination at all will amount to no dissemination at all.

"On the other hand, is there *any* truth not already told, in some artistic form or another? Nevertheless, reiteration helps truth prevail. Some, probably many, truths make their way excruciatingly slowly. Their wisdom must be taught again and again, to generation after generation … So, truth, even if hackneyed seeming, should always be articulated, by some means at least.

"Words can resurrect vignettes from our past which taught us significantly and deeply. But is our word portrait compellingly suggestive to others, so that they too learn? Are the verbal pictures we can paint meaningful, in an educational way, to others? Will they draw the same (any) lesson which we did from what we describe? That's our intent in describing. But what if they find, if not nothing, something else in the words used.; i.e. a different lesson? Then we would have 'reached' them, but not as desired. We'll have stimulated but not, necessarily, taught. Yet stimulation also leaves tracks, inscribes impacts.

"Whatever the answers, the possibilities, the contingencies—I want to tell one true story, enfolding one truth. I think I'll write a short story about it. When I was about nine, already a *fervent* Brooklyn Dodger fan, I was listening, (on the radio, then!!) to a game in the presence of my middle—aged aunt. At a crucial moment in the close, hard—fought game, very important to the fortunes that season of my beloved team, The Dodgers' brilliantly fielding third baseman, Billy Cox, No. 3, inexplicably dropped the easiest of pop—flys. If he had caught it, as he would have 999 times out of a thousand, the Dodgers would have escaped the inning, and a very perilous situation, unscathed. Out of sheer pre—adolescent frustration and abject disappointment I excoriated him with whatever expletives there were in my child's vocabulary. After my bitter vituperation had sputtered into almost inaudible mumbling, without my aunt having at all reacted, she, finally, looked me straight in the eye and quietly said, "Has he ever done anything to help the team at an important moment?" Oh, had he!!! Oh, did I learn something!!! Who wouldn't from such a story! Even if it is something one already 'knows.' Or should know—but not yet, at nine.

"Words are very important in re—teaching and re—learning. Learning is solidified, becomes confident, by re—inforcement, i.e. re—learning. Confirmation of what we know allows us to continue knowing. Perhaps to know even better. John Dewey contended 'The function of education is to prepare us for more education.' The transmission of knowledge to another is persuasion. Words are the lubricant of persuasion.

"There's no great obscurity, I've come to believe, about *the* cardinal virtue. It's, simply, 'There but for the grace … ' In a word, compassion. We who do not suffer, who suffer least, must share that gift by alleviating the sufferings of others, as much as possible. This is fundamental, absolutely irreducible. If someone doesn't embrace this sentiment, (but not sentimentality,) we have to try to foster it. We'll fail with some, probably more than a few, perhaps many. Some people will never feel that way.They'll persist in narcissistic focus only on their own well being. They're just built that way. Nevertheless, this is the faith that animates our deepest roots. We're accorded no dispensation to flag. As the Torah says, 'The task is long, the day is short. Begin.' Beethoven's Ninth resounds to 'All men are brothers,' as Schiller's poem proclaimed. The world is a community. There is a 'commun'—ness in it, rather than a disparate aggregation of lonely, solitary, sequestered atoms colliding, as each desperately searches out its own orbit of maximum gratification. If some, even a great number, after education, guidance and instruction can't appreciate there but for the grace of God they go too—so be it. But no need to accede to their 'right' to rest on that philosophy. We're completely confident that our credo is essential for a better world and we'll strive and fight, forever, to implement it. We weep for the afflicted and won't ever, ever, ever, ever, ever, as per Churchill, rest until all those unafflicted are heartsick at the afflictions of others.

"Those who see themselves as basically good, as good people, as fighting the good fight, like to see good triumph. Goodness triumphant inspires. But they're acutely aware that that's, by no means, necessarily the destiny of goodness. The universe seems impersonal, insensate to goodness, just as so often to evil and, therefore, frequently impervious to the most strenuous of efforts to make good, righteousness happen. Notwithstanding, those dedicated to goodness must persist. Continue without any assurance of success or reward, whatever. That is the mission. Despair, fatigue, discouragement and resignation the enemies. To fight the good fight means to be as beneficent as is within our control. And, pace Churchill, to never give up. To persist in loyalty to goodness, for goodness's sake—and loyalty's too. For goodness sake, onward!

"To back down from the flamboyantly high—falutin' to the particular, the so—called bottom line is that I feel blocked. Impotent. (A word that loads on an additional concern.) I want to create a meaningful, worthy difference but am, essentially, without salient ideas how to do it. It seems that I'm intensely, but futilely, grabbing for the unreachable. I don't think it's immodest if I observe that I seem to want to do what may be beyond anyone's power. The world is too big for us, late, soon and definitely now.

"But that's not actually 'it.' It's not that only transformation of the universe will satisfy me: I just want to do something that I, at least, think is an important contribution. I can't save anyone's life by brilliant, innoavtive surgery, but I would like to make some valuable improvement in currently unfortunate, despondent lives. I've tried to volunteer at various social service organizations. Sometimes they've had trouble finding anything at all for me to do, other times they've been interested in me only in so far as I might be able to raise money or contribute heavily myself and in yet other instances they've assigned me a make—work, or entirely menial task which got me to sensing that I was merely being indulged.

"But I must keep at it. I have to keep trying, keep coming at it. I'll keep going. What is it that Beckett wrote in 'Waiting For Godot'—'I must go on. I can't go on. I'll go on,' wasn't it? But I'm not optimistic. Very far from it.I feel useless or pretty much so. I surely do.

"However one tries to prod and goad oneself it is despairing. I know that it's late now. Past my usual bedtime, as they say. And I'm pretty physically tired. But the overwhelming fatigue that sweeps me is much more pervasive and malign."

To get an item on the agenda of the monthly faculty meeting a faculty member had to submit the topic, to the Dean's secretary at least a week prior to the meeting date. Martin had submitted "Commitment To Hire Minority Faculty" over a week ago and, now, the meeting just a few days away, he found himself thinking about it. He'd brought up the same issue a year or two ago, but without success. His proposal was simple: since there was only one Black professor out of the thirty—eight full time faculty, this law school, in the very core of Chicago, which had one of the largest Black and Hispanic populations in the country, should make it its no—nonsense business to hire at least one other *qualified* Black or Hispanic faculty member. Only if no *qualified* minority candidate could be found should non—minority candidates be considered for openings.

Martin genuinely thought this idea unobjectionable, except, perhaps, amongst the die—hard 'merit'ocrats, since he'd taken care to specify that a minority person was not to he hired simply for the sake of hiring a minority, but only if he or she were a qualified teacher. But things had turned out much more controversially than he'd anticipated. First of all, quite a few professors resented being told that they'd been remiss: that they hadn't already done right by minorities. Then there was what Martin thought of as the backlash to affirmative action group. These colleagues felt that, in a general way, "they" had received enough "breaks" over the years and that no special efforts or "set—asides" for minorities were necessary or appropriate any longer. Finally there were the purists who just, always, wanted to hire the "best" candidate, each and every time, whoever it might be, no—holds barred, on merit as the supreme be-all and end-all standard. Yet, despite this considerable critical mass of opposition, there were many good—willed faculty members, especially among the younger professors, who thought Martin's suggestion eminently fair and reasonable. Consequently, his resolution had ultimately lost, but by a close vote. Something like 19—17 was what he recalled.

Martin was surveying this past history, in his mind, in preparation for the debate at the coming meeting, on his way from the elevator and down the corridor that led to his office. But before he could make it safely into his own office and close the door against the world, i.e. students and even faculty who regarded an open door as an incontrovertible sign that the occupant was just craving to "schmooze," for at least a half—hour, he had to sidle past the open door of Nathan Ornstein's office. He did succeed in clearing the door, but not the range of Ornstein's rich, gravelly voice, which called, "Martin, oh Martin," just as Martin was fumbling for his office key. He stopped groping for it and trudged the three steps back to Ornstein's office.

"How goes it Nat? What's up" Or, at our age, should I ask 'Is anything up?'"

Ornstein, a burly type, almost surely a good twenty—thirty pounds over where his physician would have recommended the scale stop, about five years older than Martin, had only a meager sense of humor at best. But Martin refused to let that stop him from bantering in the same way he did with most people. Unrelieved seriousness, especially amidst banalities, was so tedious. Anyway, what style could possibly work with someone who taught Real Estate Transactions and Complex Real Estate Transactions one semester and Secured Real Estate Transactions and Real Property in the other. Even though they were"neighbors," across the corridor, Martin and Ornstein didn't say too much to each other, beyond "How're things?" unless there happened to be a particular piece of school or professional business on which one needed to deal with the other.

Apparently Ornstein had some such business now. Predictably he had not the slightest reaction to Martin's allusion to the sexual problems of middle—aged, getting older men, nor did he try to volley back Martin's banter in any way.

"I was wondering if I could have a word with you. That is, if it's convenient. I just saw you passing ..."

Martin wondered how the aggressive real estate man would take it if he said no, not a convenient time at all. But he nudged temptation aside.

"Sure, what can I do for you?" Martin said,(restraining himself from "What can I do you for?") almost brightly, as he leaned against the door jamb.

"Well, I was just looking over the agenda for next Thursday's faculty meeting and I saw your item ..."

"Never say die, I say."

"Well, yeah, that's usually a good philosophy. But in this case it's also sort of my point."

"Then we agree?"Martin grinned.

"No, no, Martin. Look, forgetting the merits, we just had a go—round on this a year or two ago. I don't even remember how I voted. But it was definitely fully discussed and the faculty made a very considered and conscientious judgment. Shouldn't we live with that for a while?"

Funny, Martin thought, how Ornstein couldn't remember how he'd voted when Martin distinctly recalled that "Nat," as faculty closer to him called him, had been one of the most vigorously outspoken opponents of Martin's proposal. Some of what had come out of the man's mouth could have been bottled as one-hundred and ten proof vitriol. In fact, right after that meeting, one of Martin's colleagues had opined, lawyers were always opining, that he felt that much of Ornstein's attitude stemmed from sheer bigotry. Martin could now add detesting such rank dissembling to Ornstein's demerits on the human being check list.

"Shouldn't live with injustice. And, by the way, I can refresh your recollection on how you voted, if you'd like." Martin did love to puncture lawyerly disingenuousness whenever he could.

"Well, it was a closed ballot, so I don't know how you could know how I voted," Ornstein counter—punched.

"I guess I just have an imperishable hunch. I could fill you in on my reasoning if you want."

"In any event," Ornstein's voice was rising a bit, "I don't think this is a matter of justice or injustice—just another of those mundane policy issues."

"Well, one man's mundane is another man's Tuesday," Martin smart—alecked. He was starting to feel like an amalgam of silly and ornery.

"I couldn't help overhearing the debate as I was going past." In the corridor, behind Martin, Mary Hanks, Assistant Professor, had materialized. She was blond, elegantly slim and with features just barely imperfect enough to give her character, save her from being a Catherine Deneuve double. Only in her second year on the faculty she had practiced law with a largish New York firm before this job. She taught corporations and other business oriented courses and, typical of most junior faculty striving for tenure, she didn't say much—especially to senior faculty members. But, she could be personally reticent as well as mum politically. Sometimes, when Martin passed her in the halls, or the street, she'd react warmly to his greeting or even initiate the "Hi" routine herself. Yet, at other times, and they could be very soon after a "warm" occasion, she wouldn't respond to his smile or nod and acted as though she hadn't even seen him. Despite the fact that Martin was pretty sure that this was just idiosyncratic," eccentric" behavior it somehow made him feel, especially when he was depressed, even more insignificant than he already did. But he'd heard from more than one colleague that they'd been treated similarly by her. In any event, she seemed to want to talk now.

"And since I couldn't help overhearing, I thought I might as well put my two cents in. Although in these inflationary times maybe it'll be worth a bit more. Also, frankly, I have a few minutes to kill."

She smiled, less than radiantly, but still quite beautifully. Martin had always thought her, through the veil of her strangeness, even more than quite beautiful, in a remote objet d'art sort of way. Martin smiled a little himself, in his quite crooked, unbeautiful way. Ornstein just stared at her, as though sure he wouldn't like what she'd say, but resigned, anxious to get it over with. Notwithstanding the courses she taught, Hanks was faculty pegged as unmistakably over to the left on the political spectrum.

"I mean we've got such a comparatively large faculty and just one minority. Shouldn't we, just out of elementary social responsibility, hire some more?"

Her voice remained pleasant in timbre, but there was a clipped quality to her speech which reflected the directness of her thoughts and feelings.

"But Professor Hanks," Ornstein started intoning, just short of putting his student-to-teacher-voice into full gear, "we weren't even talking substance, just procedure, you know."

"I guess that because I teach so much procedure I like to talk substance," Hanks rejoindered.

"Do you not like teaching your courses?" Ornstein said archly, but quickly continued, sighingly "Well, anyway, and perhaps you, er ... overheard, my point to Martin, Professor Steen here, was that we amply discussed this issue and came to a decision on it only recently. Why do it again?"

"Because, hopefully, the decision would be made correctly this time," Hanks shot out, even before Martin could.

He contented himself with nodding vigorously and the single word, "Exactly."

Ornstein jerked his head up sharply. "Look, it's two against one, so we definitely can't talk substance. But …"

Martin couldn't resist interjecting, "But, Norm, how do you know you're the one if you don't even remember how you voted last time?" and then looking over at Mary. He felt a little shabby doing it but was, nevertheless, glad that she chuckled at his gibe.

Ornstein's irritation was growing palpable. He jerked his head again and, gesturing at the papers spread on his desk, continued, "But, regardless … I don't want to be inhospitable … but I do have to finish up some things."

Martin waved in understanding as he stepped away from Ornstein's door and he and Mary Hanks headed down the corridor toward their offices. Once he'd ambled the few steps back to his own office he looked towards her, ready to take leave with one of the myriad platitudes used for such purposes; viz., "See you soon," or "Take care." But she stopped at his office door herself and seemed to want to talk.

"I don't think you've killed off every one of those minutes you had to get rid of. Want to shoot the breeze for a bit more?" Martin offered, holding the door open for her.

She took a step toward the door but, then, reluctantly stopped. "I really would like to—we should strategize on how to win this minority thing—but, truly, I should get back to my office. I have two classes to teach tomorrow and I'm not really prepared for either."

Martin was inclined to say: look do you want to bullshit for a few minutes or not; if you put off getting to work this long it can certainly wait a few more minutes; either you do or you don't; don't make it a federal case of indecisiveness.

Of course he said no such thing(s.) He did know, for sure, that he wanted her to stay because he felt like chatting with a simpatico soul who, by the way, happened to be damn easy to look at. He hoped that what he thought were his discreet glances didn't have the mien of leers to others— not to mention Mary, herself. In fact, he'd found himself getting an erection, not that frequent an occurrence any longer, when she'd come into his mind, or he'd spot her passing. Especially, *pace* Women's Lib, when she wore high heels. She had long, strong, very appealingly curved legs that were definite erection material to a leg and ankle fetishist such as himself. But maybe she'd prefer to start reading text books a few minutes earlier instead of talking to him. It could also be that she did want to talk with him but didn't want to "impose." Maybe she felt that he was too busy to want to gab with someone as young as herself.

But all Martin did say was, "I understand; when duty calls it calls. Maybe we could talk about it some other time; soonish."

Her eyes seemed to light. "I'd like that. I really would."

After Martin had gone into his office and closed the door he permitted a feeling of well being by convincing himself that she'd really meant it. Sometime, indeed, he might just risking asking her to lunch, whatever …

Chapter Four

Martin, as he turned from his left side to his right, started momentarily. He'd been dreaming about how Mary Hanks's long, honey—blonde hair had lain casually on the neck and shoulders area of her simple, crisp white blouse. He thought, before he'd gotten completely comfortable, his right arm under the pillow on the side of the Queen—sized bed on which Anna had slept, that if he didn't ask Mary to have dinner with him soon he wouldn't be able to ever do it. The faculty meeting at which his affirmative action proposal was to be discussed was only days away. Maybe he should get up right now and write a note to himself so that he wouldn't forget. Writing things down was, now, the only sure way of remembering what should be done . But before he could summon the requisite resolve he was seeing the calves of Mary Hanks's legs and sleeping soundly through the rest of the night. One of the very few times that had happened in the last few years.

"October 18

"This is completely ridiculous! What am I, a kid afraid to ask a girl out! I'm a forty—eight year old man who was married for over twenty years. Ask her out, or don't. But, for God's sake, don't agonize over it. Interminably! I remember when I was in college riding the subway up to Columbia and kept seeing this Barnard girl. She'd get on at the 34th Street stop, where the Long Island Railroad, servicing all those post World War II suburbs, connected up with the IRT Seventh Avenue line which sinewed through the more urban neighborhoods from Brooklyn, where I got on, to Columbia's Morningside Heights area, and on to upper Manhattan. She was cute, attractive in a blond—cherubic sort of way, rather than strikingly beautiful or anything like that. I kept furtively looking at her and, finally, we'd seen each other so often, been in the same subway car so many times, walked up the stairs from the' 116th Street/Columbia University' station platform so often that, very naturally, we just started smiling at each other and, eventually, just casually talking to one another. Yes,I even spoke to her!! I don't know from where I summoned such fortitude but after only five or six chatting encounters, I asked her for her phone number. And, can you believe it, she wrote it down on a corner of a sheet of paper in one her notebooks, ripped that corner off and awarded the jagged edged scrap of paper, bearing the precious information , to me.

"Then commenced the purgatory of my agonizing and indecision. Had she *really* wanted me to have her number, so that I could formally call her for a date, or had she, *really* just been compelled to hand it over because I'd asked .I mean since we were acquaintances, who spoke to each other on an every—other-day face-to-face basis, she couldn't just very well say 'No,' could she? But she could most assuredly say 'NO!!' resoundingly, in fact, if I asked her to go out and she didn't want to; if she thought of me only as someone with whom she bantered a few words, now and then, as someone would to just about any person you kept on running into at the same place, the same time of day, every few days.

"This kind of she loves me—she loves me not back and forth self—tormenting rumination was material for days and days, stretching into weeks, of resolves to call, broken resolves and intense misgivings. My recollection is that it consumed almost a month of self—debating indecision.

"During those weeks of unceasing second—third-fourth guessing I stopped seeing her on the subway. A new semester had started, her schedule had probably changed. Even I didn't strike out for the seductive self—deprecating territory of surmising that she'd decided on some alternative means of transportation just to avoid me. At least I don't specifically remember doing that.

"When I finally marshaled all my guts and did call, after not having run into her for a few weeks, it was a bit awkward, it felt very awkward, to identify myself to her memory. Maybe a comment on her memory and associated mental powers, I don't know, but that's the way it was. After some mutual stumbling she finally allowed as how she did remember our subway encounters and told me that she'd acquired a boy friend since we last met. (I don't think this is what the phrase 'quick worker' we threw around then referred to.)As a matter of fact, on her new schedule, she'd met him on the subway. I kept the 'etcs.' brief.Devastating to my nineteen year old, Caspar J. Milquetoast sensibilities.

"Well, is that where I'm still at?! Either ask her, or don't. Just don't be Hamlet!"

After his Wednesday class, officially over at 3:50, but which usually carried on for a few more minutes, —once Martin realized he'd passed the finish line, that he could stop whenever he wanted, he didn't mind going on for a bit— Martin gathered his books and notes and headed to his office. As usual, after returning from this course, Martin felt so drained he immediately sat down and just stared off into space. These performances in class, and somewhat theatrical performances they certainly were, seemed only seemed to get harder, not easier, as time went by. A teacher's experience gave more assurance and command, but the years that had also piled up sapped energy, vitality and, most of all, enthusiasm. Martin was so intent on instant relief from the ennui induced weariness that he hadn't bothered to put away his materials on the shelves in his office where he customarily kept them. Rather, he'd dropped immediately into his swivel chair, letting his book and notes fall right on to the desk in front of him.

Now, as he slumped aimlessly, feeling it a herculean effort to look straight ahead, he realized that while he'd taken his text and two manila folders full of notes to class, there was just one folder of notes lying beside the book on the desk. Martin instantly realized that he'd done what he typically did once or twice a semester—swept up, at the end of

ﾟ

class, only some of the notes he'd brought in. This could happen when he was especially anxious to escape , to not remain as prey for too many pointless student questions. Questions asked not so much because they really needed answering but mostly because a professor was in easy range and could conveniently be peppered with them.

As always when this mishap occurred, Martin was now intent on hurrying back to the just departed classroom and retrieving the missing notes before a student, lingering over re—assembling his own books and notes, made off with such a treasure trove. Some students, probably, to be fair, even many, Martin thought, would bring the notes to his office right away. But some, Martin was very, very sure, would definitely not. The latter types would hope no one would notice their making off with the professor's notes and would make as much selfish use of them as their fertile minds could conceive. So far, nothing untoward like that had happened the times Martin had left the notes. But this fact did nothing whatsoever to allay his current anxieties.

As Martin hurried through the halls he was slowed somewhat by the need to return the "Hello, professor"s wafted at him by two or three passing students. A great many students were most pleasant that way. They'd usually greet Martin affably, with some degree of warmth actually. Even most of those who didn't like his teaching style, or the "rigorous" demands he made, were courteous.

By the time that Martin reached the backdoors to the classroom he sensed that not more than ten minutes or so had elapsed since he'd left the room and he had pretty bright expectations of finding, once again, that his notes had not fallen into the wrong hands. A quick peek through the little eye—level window in the door reassured him. There indeed seemed to be a manila folder, with yellow foolscap papers sticking out of it, on the instructor's table at the front of the room. Martin's anxiety ebbed and he opened the door calmly and quietly.

That's when he was stunned! Just to the right of the door two figures were undulating against the back wall. A tall male student and a compact female one. Martin recognized the young man as a student in his Contracts course. But he couldn't observe much of the young woman in the very brief glimpse he allowed himself before he very quickly, as silently as possible, closed the door and walked rapidly away from the room. He'd taken in dark hair, plaid skirt and brown shoes with low heels, but the woman was basically hidden from view by the male's body. Both students were fully clothed, but there could be no doubt that they were moving their bodies exactly as a couple abandoned to sexual intercourse would have been gyrating.

Well, thought Martin, as he trudged back to his office, live and learn, as the adage says. He'd never experienced that one before. These students do, in fact, always have a new thing or two to teach you. They must take more seriously, than Martin had believed them capable, that other adage—that a good teacher is taught by his students. Martin had almost reached his office and was trying to figure how much more copulating time he should allow for, before he went back for his notes, when he suddenly realized that he couldn't be sure, not at all sure, that the female of the heedless duo was not Jenny Hauser. Hadn't she been wearing a plaid skirt today?

"October _____

"The release of night is blissful. At night you're *entitled* to relax. Not necessarily from hard work, or concern about all you've been through during the day. But, at least, from the prod of conscience that you should be working hard or doing something productive. At night you'd slow down and recoup your resources even if you'd been extremely energetic and goal achieving in daylight. The tendency would be to not concentrate on accomplishing much, or doing anything significant. So, in the evening, when I'm not really 'doing' anything, not getting anything 'done,' I don't have to be as tormented by guilt as during normal working hours when I'm just watching the time running emptily into itself. Or when I'm flailing away at a lot of fatuous details about which I don't really care and for which I have no respect.

"Words continually seduce those who love them. They tempt wherever and whenever they appear. They lead us to places we might not otherwise have ventured. We love to read one word after another, especially if they are put together attractively. By such charms we're inveigled into reading about things we didn't know we were interested in. Interest engorges as words draw us into their harem. On a given day I'm confident I'm going to restrict my "Times" reading to a few 'pre—selected' articles which caught my glancing eye. But, so often, when I start reading political analysis, or reviews of certain concerts or books, suddenly, completely spontaneously, a caption or headline about something entirely different beckons. While I expected to be concentrating on some speculative forays regarding Democratic vs. Republican political machinations, and/or a review of an Alfred Brendel all—Beethoven recital, seamlessly I find myself deeply involved in a story about a newly published account of Englishman Robert Scott's early twentieth century gallant, foolhardy, imperishable expedition to the South Pole. I 'must' read certain newspaper reports when I see them, whether, originally, I wished or intended to, or not. Admittedly, part of the pull may be substantive: I feel that I should know about certain things as a good citizen or well—rounded person. But the medium of the message, well crafted words themselves, can also, many times, mesmerize and, ultimately, as I said, seduce one.

"And seduction often leads to proselytization. Frequently an article I'm reading reminds me of a friend or acquaintance who'd be interested in it, or to whom I can make a point by transmitting the article pertinently underlined. But how time consuming it can all become. On some days the seduction leads to irritation that so many ramifications have ensued. But there's really little choice. The words are not just insidious. They're also imperious and unrelenting in their demands.

"We also, we lovers of words, occasionally demand that we be courted by words. We search them out if they're not immediately enticing us. There was the booklover who told of once being somewhere where there was no obvious reading matter at hand. She became so desperate for the balm of words that she found herself reading a Toyota maintenance manual. She *had* to have some words. Her lust is insatiable. No sooner are some, several, many volumes ingested, digested then she must have more. She is a nymphobibliomaniac. I, myself, am a word satyr. The specific form of the illness assumes different guises in different patients, but there are so many who are so ill and needy for reading and writing, for words. Pour les mots, las parabalas, etc., etc. But how we value and enjoy, exult in, our medicine.

But, as words are seductive, they can also be peremptorily insistent. Sometimes when we don't really want to deal with them they compel us to do so. Some words just catch our eye and we decide that we just have to continue reading the article, memo, document, whatever they begin. It may be due to the comeliness of the words themselves as they bewitch us or because of the subject they import to us. In any event, we feel we're obliged, mandated to read more. So words enslave us both as perfume and as predators.

"Thus night is balm to my unsatisfied itch to achieve something worthwhile, worthy. During day I'm constantly assaulted by awareness that I'm just mechanically pushing along, not accomplishing anything I'm really proud of. Night tranquilizes these throes. It entitles quiescence, aimless moving no closer to anything. I.e. not moving.

"Just writing words confers a sense of productivity. We've done something, made something, literally produced something when we capsulate a thought or idea in a sentence, phrase, even a notable fragment. Insofar as a person needs a sense of achieving goals, problem solving, creation, to feel as though he's fully living, writing words, even arranging them orally for effective speech, helps to fulfill us. A well written paragraph is a product we designed, crafted and ultimately produced in final, polished form. In the lexicon of that titan of English empiricism, John Locke, we've mixed our labor into the final text and so it becomes ours. We own it. And now it can be utilized to achieve objectives, integrated into more extensive projects, written or otherwise, or, just displayed, perhaps, for its intrinsic attractiveness.

"Words are also comforters. Merely returning to ones which have given pleasure in the past, such as a favorite poem, novel, essay provides a sense of calm, control, well being. Even just thinking about returning to such words can engender contentment.

"Morning stabs a shock of responsibility which I usually can't meet. Most days involve only mechanical obligation, there's nothing provoking the kind of inspiration from which I can draw self—respect. I don't feel that most of what I do really needs to be done, or, even more depressing, should be done. I do it simply because it's there—and I surely don't have much else to do. So I count on night to rescue me from all the misgivings and self—flagellation. It permits me to rest from myself, even before giving my body physical respite. Night is friend and haven."

CHAPTER FIVE

THE MONTHLY FACULTY MEETINGS were held in a large classroom. The almost forty full—time faculty members, (or as many who came,) distributed themselves randomly, amongst the almost one hundred student seats, while the Dean stood on the platform at the front of the room. He conducted the meetings as closely, or loosely, in accordance with Robert's Rules of Parliamentary Order, as he was inclined, or as various professors, with various purposes, ulterior and otherwise, would allow.

Meetings opened with ten to fifteen minutes of announcements and such. Then the agenda items, characteristically three or four, circulated to faculty about a week prior to the meeting, were taken up in the order listed. Discussion on each item, at least from Martin's point of view, went on for, conservatively, fifteen or twenty minutes beyond totally exhaustive airing. Just when it seemed that everything that could possibly be said had already been said, and more than once, someone, yet again, repeated something that had been voiced multiple times. Then someone responded with an observation, also fulsomely heard by that time. For this meeting the last of the four agenda items was "Efforts To Hire Minority Faculty Members."

Martin did his best to, basically, be oblivious to discussion of the first three issues which took more than an hour and a half. But he wasn't always successful. Such momentous conundrums as whether Torts should be given in the first semester and Criminal Law in the second, or vice—versa, or whether two or three credits of academic credit should be accorded for being on the law review, were vigorously debated and declaimed about. In addition to the boring and essentially trivial nature of such "issues," it always seemed as though they'd just been discussed with equal fervor, by those passionate about them, only a few meetings back. Not more than a year or two, at the very most.

When discussion on the next-to-last agenda item had reached utter completeness and depletion the Dean, Franklin Weymouth, a straight—ahead vest and three buttons suit type, fifty seven, nodded at Martin and said:

"Professor Steen placed the final item on the agenda. Marty ..."

He started describing the simplicity of the proposal, but he couldn't get more than a sentence or two into what he hoped would be his exceedingly brief presentation. When Martin felt strongly about something he tended toward emotionality, perhaps just too worked up. Therefore, he liked to keep things succinct, to avoid getting ineffectively, too chaotically, carried away.

But suddenly Norman Ornstein cannonaded: "Why do we have to discuss this at all? It's a waste of time, isn't it? We dealt with the very same issue only a year or so ago."

After some seconds of complete silence Martin sighed deeply and was on the point of responding when Bill O'Connor, a thirty—fivish Associate Professor, with a headful of tight red curls, expostulated, "If that were the criterion we'd never have any meetings. Every item on every agenda, at least as long as I've been here, would be ruled out."

This incited some titters and guffaws but Weymouth held up his hand, as though warning traffic to stop, and stolidly commented:

"The item's on the agenda. As far as I know, and I'm still learning of course, but we don't have any rule about items being excluded from agendas because previously discussed; recently or otherwise."

He nodded to Martin to continue, as Ornstein vigorously shook his head, side to side, muttering in exasperation.

"As I was saying ... This resolution is very simple. It only commits us to employing all conscientious efforts to hire a qualified faculty member. Its thrust is that we will hire a *qualified* minority person for the next opening and not fail to do so just because there's purportedly a superior or better qualified non—minority candidate. That's really about it. Our faculty is almost forty strong, but with only one minority on it. We should do better—at least as well as so many other institutions which take affirmative action to ensure that their staffs have minority representation in some reasonable proportion. Well, as I say, that's about it. Simple and straight—forward and fair and decent also. With no deterioration of the competence criterion. A good thing to do. The right thing to do."

Pin—drop silence for a few moments, then a bit of stirring. Finally, gradually, several hands went up.

The Dean gave the nod to Sarah Ellison, a forty plus Associate Professor who would never become a full professor because she never published anything—not even an Op—Ed, not to mention scholarly articles. She was a not very attractive, quite unhappy divorcee who had been teaching at the school for going on fifteen years. Her academic background was weak, by contemporary standards, in terms of college and law school attended. But she was close friends with a female V.P. high up in the university hierarchy and that was her life—line to her teaching position. Unfortunately, she wasn't much better at teaching than at research and publishing. Her dry, stolid, decidedly un—dramatic style wasn't very popular with the students who had to take her first year Property course, nor with those who thought they needed, for future career plans, her seminar in Family Law Problems. (Otherwise known as Philanderers, Sluts and Orphans.) But she was entirely loyal to the university administration, always at the ready to represent and push its concerns and interests. In fact, some law faculty were convinced that she was a spy, who reported to her Vice—President pal who said just what at every faculty meeting. More than once or twice a professor had run into her in an elevator, headed directly up to the executive suites, immdediately after a faculty meeting had ended. However, one of her strengths was that she spoke in a very well modulated, reasonable sounding voice.

"Our first obligation as a respectable law school has to be to the students we're training for the profession. We shouldn't hire anyone just because they're Black, Hispanic, Asian or a woman, whatever. We shouldn't set aside a place for such a specific purpose. Our responsibility, our very raison d'etre, is to furnish sound instruction for aspiring members of the Bar, not to make or implement social policy ..."

Martin, getting so impatient and irritated that he didn't even bother trying to get the Dean to call on him, broke right in:

"But Sarah, don't forget that my proposal is that we hire a *qualified* minority. By definition, that's someone who's, at least, very solidly competent. We, simply, don't pass over someone like that just because there's someone else who's not a minority whose credentials are the slightest bit better. That's the point of the resolution. The minority candidate doesn't have to be the absolute top—best, Alpha, Supreme Court caliber applicant to get the job. But she or he certainly has to be well qualified; someone who clearly, unequivocally, I don't know how to put it any more strongly, would be a very fine addition to this faculty."

He didn't say what he was, uncharitably, thinking. And what he bet some others were as well: the person would have to be someone with a lot better formal qualifications and a lot more to offer as a scholar and teacher than you, Sarah.

Weymouth nodded at Roderick Payson, a senior full professor, about five years older than Martin. He taught Business Planning and tax courses in an unflairful but good enough manner and came out with a distinctly modest article, every few years, on an acutely esoteric aspect of a recent tax or corporate law "development." He had a real gift for top-o-the mornin' oratory, however, impressively resonant voice rolling out from his tall, beefy body. He frequently served in a moderator or emcee capacity at university wide ceremonies or functions. He began by clearing his throat—very resonantly.

"I fully understand that my good friend and colleague, Martin, is not proposing that we hire any minority candidate who presents him or herself for a job here just for the sake of hiring a person of minority background. I clearly take his point that we seek only a *qualified* minority; one who could competently, or better, do the job that we are all about . Yet he does also acknowledge that acquiescence to his suggestion might well put us in a position where we would be obligated to hire someone much *less quailfied* than other candidates it might be our good fortune to have seeking to become members of this fine faculty. In other words, we might, under the strictures of Martin's resolution, have to settle not just for second, third or, even, fourth best, but, all too possibly, something like sixth or seventh best. While fully mindful of our serious social responsibilities to contribute to a just and decent society I don't know that we've yet reached the embarrassment of riches stages of the Harvards and Yales, the Stanfords, so that we can afford to appoint anyone but the very, the very best person we can get. This is still a growing law school. Not only physically, but by that I mean growing toward realization of its full potential and achievement. Make no mistake, we are indeed dynamically growing but, by no means, yet there. I don't know that we should compromise our opportunities to attain that full intellectual and institutional growth by constraining ourselves to an abstract, self—imposed obligation to appoint someone who is considerably less gifted in our earnest estimation, and we all have different gifts, than a number of other young men and women whom we could enthusiastically, no reservations whatsoever, invite to join this evolving and striving faculty. So, Martin, my deeply respected colleague," (Payson did favor and defer to Ivy League graduates,) "while basically in full sympathy with the unquestionably laudable objectives of your carefully thought out resolution, I'm just not at all sure that this faculty is yet in a position where we can afford to jeopardize aims crucial to our own development and growth. I'm sure that Martin understands that, in many ways, I couldn't be more in accord with him. But I'm afraid that I'm not yet entirely comfortable in pursuing those laudatory interests at the risk of imperiling our more direct, concrete responsibilities right here, in these very rooms, to be just the very best law school we can make ourselves, by unremitting concern, scrupulous care—taking and truckloads of very hard work."

As he concluded, Payson looked around at various colleagues in various parts of the room, as though to absorb their plaudits for his so sensible, logical, cogent objections, points and apercus, so adroitly and mellifluously voiced.

The Dean, after looking around a bit himself to canvas how Payson's remarks had registered , pointed to Anthony Padilla, a second year Assistant Professor, who taught Criminal Law and a seminar in Civil Rights Law. It was always difficult for junior faculty to speak at meetings where sensitive, emotion riling and emotion roiling subjects were debated. Whatever they said had to offend some, very probably a considerable number, of their colleagues. And who could predict how such offending comments would be factored into future decisions, on tenure and promotion for the speaker, by those who hadn't appreciated the comments. In such situations hardly any of the untenured professors dared to speak up, not to mention out. They also sat there intensely hoping that if it came to a vote it would be by closed ballot.

Even in situations where there was no pressure Anthony Padilla tended to speak haltingly, choppily, rather than fluently. But he felt strongly about certain things and had a good measure of energetic commitment.

"I don't know … maybe it's just too clear to me … I mean I don't see it as so involved, so … I mean perplexing an issue. At least *some* of what a law school should be about is *justice*, right? Wouldn't it be just to help along a just social policy? Minorities are entitled to be represented proportionately, aren't they? We've got only one on our faculty now. That's not doing our part … We should do more … Well, I guess that's about it … The way I see it …"

Elaine Ryan, only a few years out of Stanford or Harvard, (Martin couldn't remember all the dazzling details of all the dazzling resumes,) and "interested," as young academics put it, in the business and tax "areas," (she taught one course in Corporations and one in Personal Income Tax,) slowly raised her hand. Weymouth boomed out: "Professor Ryan."

Professor Ryan wore horn rimmed glasses, a no—nonsense, very short hair—do, was married to an already highly successful young investment banker and in also just about every other respect exuded a highly crisp, business like demeanor.

"I see it very simply, too. But I'm afraid it's the other way around from Tony. Where quality and competence are key, indeed crucial, merit must prevail. Being a good law school professor, as I'm finding out, requires an enormous amount of skill, bed rock ability and sheer intellectual dexterity. We shouldn't compromise, not a bit, on such characteristics in selecting colleagues. As for minority representation, minorities should be *truly* represented, according to their merits. Of course no member of an ethnic group should be deprived of something he or she deserves because of racial prejudice, or anything pernicious like that. But minorities shouldn't be given preferences, either, simply because they're minorities. If that happens then minorities who authentically earn something by ability are suspected of having gotten there through a back door, by a free, or at least preferential, ride. If minorities get what they get by truly earning their advances then they, and everyone else as well, will feel much better about their representation in the professions."

Professor Ryan stopped talking just as crisply as she'd articulated her thoughts and sentiments.

Dean Weymouth quickly added, "I must say that much of what Professor Ryan said makes good sense to me."

Martin thought he knew some of what might be going on there. When Weymouth had come aboard, several years ago, he'd had somewhat of a reputation as a male—chauvinist, anti—woman sort in his previous Deanship. But he'd found out, shortly after he got here, that that was his reputation and since then he had diligently worked at disabusing the suspicious and disapproving from continuing to think such thoughts. Now he saw an opportunity to further hone that aim by showing his appreciation of Ellen Ryan's remarks while simultaneously bolstering the opposition to Martin's proposal. Weymouth had been against it when Martin had introduced it before and Martin had been sure that he would still be opposed. After all, the university's trustees, who ultimately evaluated and passed on a Dean's performance, were, by and large not keen adherents of affirmative action. Most were from an older generation and had older fashioned ideas.

Norman Ornstein's hand shot up again and Weymouth quickly called on him.

"Yeah, since we are going through all this again, on the so—called merits, I see it pretty simply the same way. You know, we're subject to the Constitution too. The university must crack down quite a bit of federal money. The Constitution says to treat people equally as people—on the merits. Think about it: it's as bad to discriminate for as to discriminate against, because discriminating for someone means that, you're, assuredly, discriminating against someone else. Let abilities and merits, not extraneous factors, rule. If we have a job we shouldn't set it aside for any one group or type of person. It should go to the absolutely best person for the job—that's how we all got our jobs—the hell with the rest of it."

There was a smug, triumphant quality to Ornstein's voice as he resoundingly concluded. And, as soon as he had stopped, two or three people did clap briefly. Weymouth discouraged the applause with a downward gesture of his right hand and recognized Mary Hanks who had propelled her right hand ceilingward a few seconds after Ornstein had muted his trumpet.

"The only thing wrong with what Professor Ornstein says," Mary began, in a not too audible, somewhat husky voice, "is that the Supreme Court hasn't interpreted the Constitution in the same way he has. Set asides to implement affirmative action goals have been upheld for a long while, and frequently, too, by the Court."

She seemed to have finished, since she was silent for several more seconds, and Weymouth was already scanning the room for other potential speakers. But she suddenly added, in a voice seemingly on the cusp of cracking, " But perhaps Professor Ornstein understands the Constitution better than the Supreme Court does. I'm sure he believes he does. But I trust the rest of us don't think so."

Even though this remark won its own meager smattering of applause, Martin, although he admired her courage, thought it probably would have been better had she stopped before explicitly attacking tubby Norman. Just pointing out his error, his misunderstanding of the law as it had actually developed, his ignorance, willful or otherwise, of "the living constitution," as it were, might have been more effective as well as more judicious, more "lawyerlike." But, then again, she may just have found Ornstein irresistible to hate. Martin certainly understood that.

There were one or two more comments on each side. Basically, of course, repetitious of those that had already been made, repeatedly. Then, even in this voluble group, the impulse to be heard, to dazzle others with self—regarded brilliant and sparkingly articulated observations seemed to fizzle out. Weymouth asked if they were ready to vote and this incited twenty more minutes of debate on whether a closed ballot was necessary. Closed finally won in, an ironically fitting, vote on the vote. In the end Martin's motion lost 21—15. Close enough to be respectable, but not so photo finish as to be bitterly frustrating. And final enough to be weightily depressing.

After the meeting broke, Martin, dispirited as he was, went to the offices of some of those who'd spoken up for the proposal to thank them for their support. When he knocked on Mary Hanks's door, (was he knocking on the others just an excuse to knock on hers?) there was no response. Maybe she'd made a quick-get-away or, perhaps, she just didn't want to be disturbed.

Martin went home, ate a barely palatable t.v. dinner—any t.v. dinner was barely edible, but "cooking" was even less palatable—and then allowed himself to descend into full-fledged depression. He thought of calling Mary Hanks but just couldn't rouse the determination and energy to actually do it.

***

"Words and other gestures among people can bring them together, if not unite them completely. By exchanging words, and through them emotions, beliefs, perceptions, etc., etc., people can connect in varying degrees of intensity and intimacy. In forging friendship they can also strike a more common attitude to the universe. This can be an order of battle of sorts, one by which to approach transforming the is, the here and now, into the what should be, the finest possibilities we can conceive. Inter—personal connections and support, the fortitude they muster, are the fuel of never dying idealism.

"What else but the coiled, compact, condensed power of words used poetically instigated Shelley to apostrophize poets as 'the unacknowledged legislators of the world.' What seductive suggestiveness and inspiration in Stephen Spender's single line, 'I think continually of those who were truly great,' or in Wordsworth's 'The world is too much with us late and soon/Getting and spending we lay waster our powers.' Or in Emily Dickinson's 'If I can keep one heart from breaking I shall not have lived in vain.' They are agendas for living. They effuse the courage, resolve, the strength to face, yet one more time, implacable hostility, cunning cynicism, moroseness. The world's unyielding harshness , the numerous adversities it concocts for the collective, as well as for just about every individual.

We go forth and forth, ('I go forth for the millionth time ..." Joyce concluded 'A Portrait Of The Artist As A Young Man,') and forth, whether we succeed or not. We cherish the victories, agonize over the losses and know, determinedly, that with Spender, Wordsworth and Dickinson behind us we shall never give up. (With Churchill, called to mind by the last words of the preceding sentence, too, for that matter.) I just looked up Joyce's exact words. He must have been enkindled with just such reinforcement when he wrote 'Welcome o Life! I go to encounter for the millionth time the reality of experience and to forge in the smithy of my soul the uncreated conscience of my race.'"

CHAPTER SIX

NOT ONLY WAS MUSIC solacing when Martin himself mangled it at the keyboard; the real thing was even better. Recordings of course, although Martin still didn't have a CD player. (Too 'new—fangled' after only five or six years. But he did own what had to be a high percentage of all the long—playing classical discs ever produced.) But there was, also, Orchestra Hall. One of the most attractive things about living in Chicago. Home of the Chicago Symphony which liked to tout itself as the world's finest. Martin didn't believe that for the sheerest instant—nor did the rest of the world, in the face of those minor ensembles, The Vienna Philharmonic, The Amsterdan Congertgubouw, the Berlin Philharmonic—not to mention the homegrown New York Philharmonic and the Cleveland Orchestra. But the CSO was certainly very, very good and, in any event, good enough.

Martin liked to buy tickets for the Friday afternoon concerts which began at 1:30. That way he had something to look forward to after his Friday morning Contracts class. Perhaps lunch in one of Marshall Field's seven differently themed restaurants, one for each floor of the department store. That's if he didn't brown bag it.

Then great music—sometimes at least. Maybe even Rudolf Serkin or Maurizio Pollini doing Beethoven's "Emperor" Concerto or Itzhak Perlman making his violin flawlessly intone the majesty of the Elgar

Concerto. Martin, of course, preferred the eighty—five year old Serkin, one of his all—time favorites, to the only fiftyish Pollini, but it was necessary to acknowledge that the old guard was passing. Serkin, (who now had a son, Peter, himself a world class pianist,) expressed more of the poetry of the music than the technically super—proficient Pollini. But perhaps the Italian would mature into profounder insights. Similarly, Martin would have preferred to hear the now almost seventy—five year old Yehudi Menuhin play the Elgar. He had, after all, played it as a sixteen year old prodigy with Elgar himself conducting, stunning the composer not merely with his technical dexterity, but also with the depth of his interpretative powers. (Martin cherished that recording as one of the prizes of his collection.) But the forty—fivish Perlman came to Chicago quite often, Menuhin only once every five years or so. Each time, therefore potentially the last.

What Martin didn't like about the Friday afternoon concerts was that, basically, they were (old) ladies' days. He wasn't an ageist. After all he was at the stage where he couldn't afford to be any more. But so much of the audience seemed to be there only because they were "supposed" to be. After shopping extensively in Marshall Fields and meeting their friends for lunch they brought the capacious, stuffed full shopping bags to Orchestra Hall where they planted them at their seats in such a way as to make the aisles to many rows of seats virtually impassable. Especially the narrow, not nearly enough leg room ones way up in the Gallery where Martin sat for economic reasons. They also seemed much more interested in continuing their lunch conversations, often about which friend had which ailment, than in listening attentively to the stupendous sounds produced by the Chicago Symphony. This seemed especially true if the orchestra was playing anything composed by anyone born after Brahms was. ("There's nothing I can hum; hardly any tunes at all.")

As Martin settled into his seat, after squeezing by three separate bulging shopping bags, he wasn't overly excited anticipating the all Brahms program, Perlman soloist in the Violin Concerto, Daniel Barenboim conducting. First of all, he just didn't admire Barenboim's work much—even the Chicago Symphony deserved better. Secondly, yet another Brahms Violin Concerto and yet another Brahms Second

Symphony. Great as such music was it could no longer be fresh for Martin. Hardly anything was.

Nevertheless, he dutifully began reading the program notes, including the well-known resume of Perlman's meteoric rise from polio—racked child, he still could walk only with formidable looking crutches, to international super—star who had played with virtually every, if not, indeed, *every* leading orchestra in just about every nook, cranny and crevice of the world. When he came on stage, since he had to manipulate the crutches, he couldn't carry his violin and bow. Only after he'd negotiated to his chair, just at the left of the conductor's podium, would the concertmaster hand Perlman his Stradivarius which the concertmaster had brought out with his own violin. Because of how heroically, grandly successfully, Perlman had triumphed over his handicap, Martin always felt guilty at not appreciating the accomplished fiddling more than he actually did. The man's playing was perfect—but not probing or penetrating. That's what Martin had concluded after hearing Perlman in several live concerts and he'd been only marginally assuaged in the guilt trip he'd taken when after a performance, at London's venerable Royal Albert Hall, on the very first trip Martin and Anna had taken to Europe, a "Times" critic had referred to the "glassy perfection" but superficial quality of the Israeli violinist's performance of the Elgar Violin Concerto. Martin hadn't been sure whether "glassy" was a typographical error for "glossy" but decided that either word sharply and justly critiqued the scarcity of involving musical substance in the virtuoso's rendition.

However, once the orchestra had swept into the ravishing melodies of the concerto and Perlman's violin had begun soaring both as partner with, and over, those massed streams of sonorous eloquence Martin began to be pulled in, to virtually wallow in the rich, luscious sounds. But not completely. Every now and then he'd emerge from the floating reveries to look around. To see if the house were full; just how many people were sleeping or obviously bored; how many had been beguiled into absorption by the irresistible flow of great music. As he peered down from his mid-way up seat on the gallery's left side he estimated that no more than ten to fifteen percent of the audience was male and that at least seventy—five percent of the women were more than sixty years old.

But, Martin became abruptly aware, by no means all. Off to his left, in the second row of the gallery, there was a young woman, with, even allowing for the over one hundred feet which separated them, one of the most beautiful faces he'd ever seen. Because of the angle at which he was staring he had only a three—quarter view. But he was totally confident that the other twenty—five percent would live up to this incandescent impression, notwithstanding that one could be disappointed by full view in these situations. The music was now completely background. Martin kept gazing at that perfect face.

Suddenly there came to mind the title of a Francoise Sagan novel, one she'd written somewhat after she'd first arched to celebrity in France, and subsequently the rest of the world, with her first book, BONJOUR TRISTESSE. The title which had leapt into the lap of Martin's consciousness was AIMEZ—VOUS BRAHMS? Well, apparently, this goddess did like Brahms. That's what Martin now longed to say to her. With a little variation. Variation was part of music too: as in theme and variations. Yes, he wanted to say something like "Do you like Brahms too?" With the "too" not meaning "as I do," but, rather, "as well as being as beautiful as you are?" In other words, "You look as magnificent as you do *and* you like Brahms,i.e. classical music, as well?"

Martin became aware that the concerto was in its final, head—long, rousing *allegro giocoso* movement, the last stages of it to boot. He had stopped caring whether Perlman was digging meaningfully beneath the surface. Continuing to enjoy her flawless face which, nevertheless, shone with definite aspects of character, he'd become completely pre—occupied with how the rest of her would look, when she stood up, during intermission. But—it was really *if* she stood up. Many concertgoers, of course, remained in their seats during intermission. Not everyone took as many precautionary trips to the bathroom as Martin in an effort to ensure never having to step over anybody during the third movement of a symphony. She was wearing a blindingly white blouse with a palish blue courdury skirt. Both thrillingly set off the medium length, but still abundant, chestnut hair. He could make out also that the blouse was configured very appealingly by her upper body.

The applause was more than warm. Perlman always got more positive reaction than anyone else who played at the same level. For the braces, as it were. Perlman and Barenboim were taking their bows, an episode in concerts which Martin usually enjoyed watching. But now he just kept on thinking how he'd really like to say to her, "And you like Brahms, too?" And why not. Maybe he should. After the concert was over. At the least she'd be flabbergasted by the line. No one would have tried that one on her before. Shock effect.

Some were now rising as they continued applauding.(Perlman usually got at least a half—standing ovation.) She was clapping energetically and now she, too, got up continuing to vigorously applaud with broad motions. She was just a bit short, not quite statuesque range, but Martin definitely liked what he saw. The skirt was tight enough, without being impudent, to lend allure. There was absolutely no doubt about it: she was what was known in Martin's distant adolescence as "A real piece of ass." At this point Martin preferred terminology along the lines of "a beautiful young woman."

The applause was petering out and some who'd stood started shuffling toward the aisles. Others who'd stayed seated rose now for the same purpose. But some who had stood were settling back into their seats, part of the group which would not file out during intermission. She was amongst them and started flipping through her program again.

So, Martin wouldn't have the opportunity to approach her during intermission unless he were to meander directly up to her seat. He didn't and headed out for his customary expedition to the Men's Room. That task executed he didn't have the courage to stroll down the aisle to get to a vantage point in front of her seat which would allow a "casual" better look at her. So he just went back to his seat.

She'd found something in the program to be engrossed in. A good sign—perhaps she appreciated written material as much as she did Brahms. From this perch he could find no flaw, whatsoever, in that ravishing profile. A true, elegant beauty. With, incidentally, plenty of sex appeal.

Barenboim came out in his businesslike, "Lady, where do you want your Brahms?" affect, discharged a perfunctory bow or two and struck up the Brahms Second Symphony. Soon Martin was again enveloped in the plush textures, the rich swatches of melody. Yet not completely. Just as he was being carried afar he'd remember to glance over to his left at her wonderful youthful beauty. It was when he thought of it in exactly that way that he began to realize just how ridiculously he was on the verge of acting. She was very beautiful *and* very young. She was still in her early or mid—twenties. He a mere wisp from the feared fifty mark .How did he expect her to relate to him. He was her father, not her boyfriend—not to mention a prospective lover.

He continued glancing furtively but now his heart sank, rather than leapt, at how astonishing her appearance was. Sure it was possible; fifty year olds did, sometimes, marry twenty—five year olds, or have affairs with them. Older women and young men, too, now. But it certainly wasn't very likely. He'd probably just be sharply validating that old bromide; no fool like an old fool.

Anyhow, who knew how'd she respond, or not, if he actually spoke to her. Maybe she had no interest in music, whatsoever, was just there because someone, her boss for example, had a ticket he couldn't use. Yes, maybe he would have evoked a completely empty look, one oblivious to his wit, if he'd propounded the "Do you like Brahms, too,?" question. Now the strains of the Second Symphony seemed all lugubrious and bereft of vaulting joy. And that couldn't be accounted for solely by Barenboim's lackluster conducting. She would, at least, have been wonderful to kiss.

At home that evening, Martin thought he'd re—affirm the wonders of the Brahms Second, in his mind's ear, by listening to the 1950s recording by the New York Philharmonic, led by the great Bruno Walter, a magnificent all—around humanist as well as a superb conductor. As those fervently romantic, yet also elegantly perceptive sounds, that Walter induced the orchestra to articulate, surged him away to peace, Martin's right eye gave way to an occasional twitch as he realized that, in some way, he had to solve his woman problem—more precisely his lack of one.

"Words also give pleasure when used to tell about valued, cherished memories. Words as the medium conveying recollection are pleasure deposits. They produce the pleasure of expressing the memory and, therefore, pleasure is taken in the words as the instruments of pleasure production. Pleasure linked to pleasure.

"There's also pleasure in simply remembering, re—hashing, whatever you want to call it, words whose reproduction in mind, speech or writing is pleasant, soothing, inspiring, consoling, stimulating. For example, I love and often think of the words with which Stephen Spender began the poem for which he'll probably always be best remembered, (and for which he'll probably always be remembered;)viz., 'I think continually of those who were truly great.' I think continually of those brilliant words. I think a great deal as well of, and find inspiration in, Thoreau's confident pronunciamento, ' He who advances confidently in the direction of his dreams and endeavors to live the life he has imagined will meet with a success unexpected in common hours.'

"Words so bountiful with pleasure don't have to be great literary ones. I derive incomparable satisfaction, as a rabid fan, of the BROOKLYN, (as opposed to Los Angeles,) Dodgers, now thirty plus years gone from Brooklyn, when I recall the only time the Brooklyn Dodgers ever won the World Series. On October 4, 1955, the then young Dodger announcer, Vin Scully, (still at it today in Los Angeles) after the last out had been registered said, only, 'Ladies and gentlemen, the Brooklyn Dodgers are the champions of the world.' Despite the many years Dodger fans had lived through utter frustration and exasperation waiting for that apex moment, Scully confined his exultation to that single declarative sentence.He did, he later revealed, because he would have lost emotional control, so great was his relief and joy, had he embellished or expanded. He'll never forget those words, (as I confirmed in a bit of correspondence I had with Scully just a few years ago,) I'll never forget them, nor will many more thousands, if not millions more, who heard them come over the air on that beautiful Fall day. Reviewing words that have meant so much to us, from time to time, is immeasurably pleasure providing. Not memory alone gives us the gift. Also the memory of particular, inspiriting words.

"Generally we control and use words. But sometimes they seize and capture us. We think or hear a word whose very sound or definition tickles or caresses us pleasurably to the point where we forage for an opportunity to use the word.We develop such a strong yen to express it that we manufacture the need to deploy it. We find a way to nudge the conversation so we can utilize the words in a sentence that, then, fits into the context. Or we shove our writing in a direction which seems to require the word for effective articulation of thought. Just as it is with people, so it is with words: if we love them they have power over us; we must respond if they beckon.

"Sometimes a word captures us simply by its sound. Its meaning is almost, or actually, irrelevant to the pleasure that pronouncing and hearing it give. Edgar Allan Poe's 'Tinntabulation' is a sound one wants to experience for itself. Perhaps this phenomenon is especially prevalent in 'beautiful' languages like French. 'Bien entendu' sounds so comely, just for itself, irrespective of its meaning of 'Of course.' Speaking French one might contrive to respond to a statement with 'bien entendu,' or to interpolate it into your own statements or assertions just for the sheer sake of its sound. Someone can be enraptured by words in many ways, dans beaucoup des modes. See James Joyce's FINNEGAN'S WAKE. See it—but just try to understand it—as opposed to hearing it.

"Perhaps it's the combination of beautiful sounds and beautiful words that accounts for the powerful appeal opera has for some people. But I think that that's not exactly accurate because it seems the words really are 'pure' sounds, additional to the musical sounds, generating beauty. It's the sound of the word as a musical sound, rather than as a mere conversational word, which really produces the surpassing effect. The words are a musical accompaniment to the principal music; i.e. the music music. But, even so, the words may produce more beauty in the 'customary' sense of the beauty they engender even when not allied with music. Surely not true of all the words in an opera. But it could certainly be true of some.

"There are so many combinations of words which it is so satisfying to roll in our mind's mouth, as well as our physical mouth, and savor. Leonard Bernstein entitled one of his compositions 'Chichester Psalms.' A lovely configuration of words, sounds.

"Sometimes words are moving both because of their tones, pure sound, and their overtones, meanings, connotations. Or, vice—versa. We love to wade and bathe in both the sound the word makes and the meanings, the associations, it conjures up. Words are a tremendously fecund and also an inexhaustible mine of pleasure and gratification. As long as we have words enchantment is possible.

"Words also pleasure by tactile sensation. It's often enjoyable for partisans of words, those with affection for sheer words, to form words manually with a pen or pencil. Satisfaction from the physical act of writing. Even people with 'bad' penmanship can truly enjoying forming, spelling words with a writing implement. The effect can be heightened with particular 'favorite' words or with ones especially apposite in the context .Even typing words at a computer keyboard, or a rapidly becoming old—fashioned typewriter, can give the same kind of happy experience. (But not, it seems, as much as the actual manual forming of words does. Maybe because in typing there are many more errors, as by striking the wrong key, than occurs by hand.) In the same vein is the shaping by mouth and the projection through speech of (especially) certain words.

"Words are tools of pleasure and can be utilized, assembled, arranged in various permutations and combinations to an edifying result. Incontrovertible proof is the fact that sometimes we will say a phrase or write a name just to 'hear the sound of it," or 'see it on the page.' People will write a whole list or series of an identical name or phrase. By such means words convey vicarious happiness. We live or re—live experiences and events by resorting to and summoning words. In one of his sonnets Shakespeare wrote, 'When to the sessions of sweet thought/ I summon up rembrance of things past.'And a translator rendered Proust's multi—volumed masterpiece as REMEMBRANCE OF THINGS PAST.

"Of course words are, conventionally, instruments of vicarious pleasure when we read or hear them and they transport us to a place we should really like (prefer) to be. In such an instance an individual has been 'lucky' in being affected in a way she (very likely) hadn't anticipated. She's been pleasurably taken by surprise. But when we purposefully wield the powerful words the vicarious phenomenon is much more intentional, more to our specific purposes. We anticipate how preferable it might be to be elsewhere, doing something else, being with someone not presently here and we designedly seek to evoke the desired state by playing with words. Words are toys which we use to brighten life when its luster has momentarily dimmed."

CHAPTER SEVEN

"October____

"SOMETIMES I REALLY WONDER about myself; just how *abnormal* am I? I don't necessarily mean abnormal in a pejorative sense. Although we could play with that possibility. I mean I wonder just how different I am from so many other people in the kinds of things that I carry around with me. Baggage that I can't let go of, stop thinking about. I think they call it repetitive thoughts in psych jargon now.

"There's one that's about thirty years oldalready. I've never forgotten it and it comes to mind at least a few times a year, maybe more—every year. At sixteen, in my senior year of high school, neither I nor my two best friends, my constant companions in the all summer day long stickball games, on the sweltering Brooklyn street, behind the six storey apartment building in which we lived, had ever been out on a 'date' with a real live female. We thought about girls a lot and masturbated over them almost as much—when we weren't studying for tests in school, on which we invariably scored 'A's or '98',' or something like that. Or when we weren't playing some sport or worrying over whether the Brooklyn Dodgers would hold on to their league—leading perch,(just like us at the top of our class,) and go on to win the pennant. But none of the three of us had ever actually asked a girl to go out. Something like picking her up at her house, holding her by the elbow crossing a street, paying her admission to a movie, etc., etc.

"Of course it was the 'etc., etc.,' in which we were most interested; but not much hope of that since we weren't even competent enough to achieve these simple scene setting preliminaries. What we were really interested in was apostrophized in the response given by one of our fellow stickball players, a college man, two years older than us, who made it known that he had a very plentiful, active social life, when someone would ask whether he'd enjoyed himself on his date the previous night. He'd casually say, 'Yeah, she was a nice girl, I had a nice time, it was O.K.' Then he'd grimace his features into something like our callow conception of what a tough or 'hard' guy looked like and, after a noticeable pause, would growl, "Yeah, I wanted to fuck her.'

"In any event, the mothers of we three social misfits talked it over and vigorously concluded that something had to be done to get us into social proximity with females our own age. The solution which this summit conference quickly produced was dancing lessons. That was to be the ticket to our shedding our severe cases of disabling shyness and induce the self—confidence to talk to girls and, hopefully, eventually, even adequate resolve to ask them for official dates. Each of us was signed up for a series of five introductory lessons, on Saturday mornings, (so as not to interfere with our homework and studying for tests on which we could excel ,) at Dale Dance Studios, Flatbush and Church Avenues. (Brooklyn, with probably the largest Jewish population of any city in the world was, nevertheless, known as the borough of churches.) We three musketeers trooped in together, naturally, in numbers there is a little strength, to find about ten more not too post—pubescent teen—agers. An almost even distribution between males and females. All were to be instructed by Miss Brown, herself not too many years older, with a slim figure which, nevertheless, had many wonderful curves, turns, contours.

"But this undeniable pleasure also carried problems. For, while it certainly wasn't hard to accept her instructing us in how to negotiate our feet through such incorrigible seeming challenges as the cha—cha, (then all the rage,) and other esoteric art forms, tango, rhumba, samba, and even though she minimally succeeded in getting us to bumble through them so that the dance we were purportedly 'doing' appeared recognizable, her pedagogy required that she dance, at least for a few moments during each lesson, with every member of the class. For we males this entailed 'holding her close' and 'leading' her, although, of course, she constantly instructed us, sotto voce, in every movement of our feet. I surely didn't mind holding that trim waist, bearing that sweet smelling curvaceousness, topped off by that fresh, girl—next—door, very pretty, twentyish face, 'close,' yet the very enjoyment of the experience bred great anxiety about participating in it. To be blunt, (or pointed,) while I really wanted to hold her closer and closer, just walking up to her, arms outstretched, prepared to dance, produced quite a ferocious sixteen year old's hard-on. Clearly, I didn't want her to know that that sort of thing was going on. Actually I *did* want to feel it rubbing intensely against her, while we 'danced,' but that wasn't possible, was it, without her being aware that her thighs, pelvis, etc. were being so assaulted. I never had the courage to broach this problem, (bring it up, so to speak— pun definitely intended,) with my co-dancer pals, but I was deeply suspicious that they were experiencing the very same dilemma. And that they, like me, most probably thought about it quite a lot, in bed, at night, in the hazy minutes before sleep. If they did not, indeed, at that very time, do something about it, i.e.handle it, (another pun! I'm full of them tonight.)

"But it's not this problem of erotic stimulation from Miss Brown which I recall several times a year, for thirty plus years now. No, the chronic problem derives from an incident that occurred at the final, (blissfully,) lesson of the course. Miss Brown felt (hoped?) that by then she'd taught each student enough so that for closing time each kid should dance with an opposite sex partner while she evaluated her work. This was a fearsome enough prospect in theory, not to mention that not one of the six or seven high schools girls in the class was anywhere remotely near as intriguing, interesting or provocative as Miss Brown. In fact, with Miss Brown around, they hadn't even come in for sufficiently intense scrutinization to be meticulously and exhaustively assessed, by we guys, in the ordinary way. I.e. the assignment of grades ranging from 10, highest, to 1, lowest, in such discrete and sophisticated categories as 'face,' 'tits,' 'ass,' 'legs,' etc., etc. We were *really* sophisticated, weren't we!

"In any event, Miss Brown paired me with a perfectly pleasant, basically non—descript girl who was just as shy as me and perhaps even more tense. Our teacher settled at the piano and ordered us to have a go at the cha—cha. I was rampantly self—conscious at having to hold my fellow student, who might, theoretically at least, be considered some sort of sex object, *in front of other people.* Peers no less. I could barely touch her. And since she very much seemed of the same limitlessly diffident mien,she barely brushed my right shoulder with her left hand. But the pressure was predominantly on me because I had to keep my right hand and arm precariously near her waist. We literally stepped all over each other in the thirty seconds that Miss Brown's rudimentary pianism insisted we maintain the pretense of executing the cha—cha.

"When the tremendous release of the piano's silence finally came we instantly dropped our arms, unable to look at each other. Of course we hadn't really looked at each other while 'dancing,' either. But she had the courage and poise to try to direct her eyes in the general direction of mine and mumble a clearly audible, 'I'm sorry.' I, wanting desperately to assure her that I was just as regretful for being as clumsy and maladroit as I'd been, said 'Me, too,' as quickly and energetically as my anxiety—riven energy level would permit. I congratulated my self for not having been too tongue—tied to have made the effort to save her feelings as much as she, so sweetly and graciously, had tried to save mine.

"But then I began thinking. And, as mentioned, haven't stopped thinking about this for years and years now. What if she interpreted my 'Me too,' as 'Yeah, I'm sorry too, for how *you* danced ,' or, 'I'm sorry, also, that I had to dance with *you.*' If she was so frantically insecure as to have had to mumble an apology to such a complete klutz as myself then she surely could have been so insecure as to have easily mis—interpreted my words unfavorably to herself. The insecure seek out slights assiduously.

"Maybe it's just the lawyer in me that's even aware of the *possibility* of this alternative, subtly denigatory connotation of my benignly meant words. I still put mental body English into hoping that by my inflections and by my expression she truly understood that I was trying to solace her rather than be vicious. But it's merely a hope. I remain bitterly chagrined by the words I uttered every time I imagine that that shy, gentle young girl, without a shred of personal confidence, might have used them to lacerate herself into even more anxiety and vulnerability. Why hadn't I just said something like 'It was all my fault," or, 'What are you sorry for, I stepped all over your feet.' Probably because it was too many words, since it was hard enough to respond in any way, especially with all the other kids, including my two friends, standing and watching. But, therefore, I may have inflicted pain when I had intended, and tried hard, only to offer balm.

"'Dancing' and 'dances' are rife with searing emotions for teen—agers. Intimations of life's sharp disappointments and bountiful angst. I once read the recollection of Allard Lowenstein, a courageous anti—Vietnam War Congressman before he was assassinated, attending his first dance, when he was fifteen. More disturbing to him than his own profound fright and extravagant awkwardness was his noticing the girls who stood alone for the entire evening without once, not even a single time, any boy coming over to say so much as a word to them. Just his recounting of the experience made me cry. Lowenstein said it made him into a Socialist. We must fight for those who cannot fight for themselves and, on their behalf, never give up. 'We shall not flag or falter. We shall go on to the end … ' In Sean O'Casey's play, "No Red Roses For Me," one of the characters says, 'I go to fight for dark places.'"

"October___, '88

"Another incident I continually think about, more and more, actually, as I proceed toward elderliness and the inevitable, goes back almost as far—but not quite. For this one I was already in college, so it had to be at least two or three years later than the dancing lesson episode.

"It involves a cousin by marriage, Sam M., husband of my dad's niece, Sadye, the tremendously overweight daughter of my dad's sister, Raisa. My father was in his fifties when he married my mother, (his third wife, the first two had died,) and very much toward his late fifties when I was born. So, by the time I was conscious of him Sam was already in his late forties and by the time this, for me, particular for imperishable incident occurred he was in his late fifties.

"Sam, an orphan, was brought up by his paternal grandfather in New Haven and being a precocious, but also impecunious, youngster went to the local college-Yale. The family stories put him very much at the top of his class, maybe even valedictorian, (this part has fled my memory,) and he very much wanted to go to medical school. But money was an acute problem and he had more or less resigned himself to the frustration of this dream. But one day, shortly before graduation, Sam, (in the bossom of the extended family he was 'Shmuel,' Yiddish for Samuel,) was browsing the student bulletin boards and suddenly saw his name: Yale Medical School awarded one full tuition scholarship to a Yale College senior and he'd been selected. Not at all shabby for a Jew, in the 1920s, at Yale, not then known for excessive tolerance or hospitality to Jewish students. Sam's exultation was boundless and he raced all the way home, on foot, to tell his grandfather.

"I'm not through with this story, but it just reminded me about the experience of a man, today an eminent rabbi, who, as the son of poor immigrant parents living in Baltimore in the late 1930s, applied for a scholarship at Johns Hopkins, when Nazism's vicious ascendancy was becoming undeniably apparent. Part of the process was an interview with a faculty member. As his interviewer the boy drew a professor with an obviously Germanic, not to mention Prussian ,name. While nothing devastating happened during the interview the young aspirant was certain he'd not succeeded. But only several days later a letter came from the university informing him that he'd indeed been awarded a scholarship. Still flabbergasted he immediately called the professor's secretary for an appointment so he could thank the professor. At their meeting he ran on and on with effusions of thanks while the professor said hardly a word. The boy tried repeating his profuse thanks but got essentially the same very muted reactions from the scholar. He saw that it was time to go. As he rose and started his good—byes the older man suddenly said, 'Some day, young man, I'm confident that you'll be sitting in my chair. When you do remember that you always help the poorest and the least; the poorest and the least, that's whom you help.'

"To return to Sam, naturally he did as brilliantly at medical school as he had at Yale College. He was urged to go into research. But he felt he owed, he wanted to serve, directly and immediately. He needed, but didn't have, the necessary funds to establish a practice. His grandfather and my dad's brother—in—law, Irving, who'd made a not so small fortune in small real estate transactions, arranged a match: Sam would marry Sadye, the daughter of Irving and Raisa , the distinctly unprepossessing heiress.

"Sam moved with his new, loveless bride to Brooklyn and opened a practice. He became a God. It sometimes seemed like everyone in the borough knew of him and, surely, everyone who actually did know him loved him. People felt they 'got better' simply by hearing him urge them, in Yiddish, 'Yashah Koyach,' take strength. I vividly recall that when my parents took me to him, for childhood stuff, we waited literally for hours and hours in his bulging- with- patients office. But if you were too sick to come to him he came to you. After the endless office hours he made his house calls, driving himself through clogged urban traffic and finding seemingly non—existent parking spaces.

"The house calls were myriad, and all over the borough. Stories got to family members about his coming into households where there was not only sickness but where he sensed want, perhaps poverty. He'd call his wife and tell her to find out the nearest grocery store and to phone in an order to be delivered to the needy household, charged to Dr. Moscowitz. He never told anyone about these incidents, but she did. Apparently he never forgot where he came from—a not inconsiderable talent. Then or now.

"Not that he couldn't afford it. Since his practice was frenetically busy it was also highly remunerative. He became a wealthy man. But he gave a lot of it away. He was very active in the Brooklyn Jewish Center and made large donations. He'd tell people he couldn't wait to retire so he could spend a lot of his time in its substantial library of Judaica. He remained , as he'd been at Yale, a man of the book. At heart an intellectual and scholar. He also made considerable contributions to the United Jewish Appeal and was an ardent Zionist.

"In the Spring of 1947 I was in bed with some childhood disease or other and he made one of his housecalls. I can still see him in our small apartment's one bedroom, where I still slept, (my move to the sofa bed in the living room was still a year or two off,) exulting triumphantly that the United Nations General Assembly had just voted to partition Palestine into a Jewish state and an Arab state. The Jewish people, almost recently exterminated by Hitler's Holocaust, were again, after two thousand years, to have a homeland! He was quite a bit overweight, with a very round cherubic face and a large head of full gray curls. He was the most beaming, ecstatic earthly angel anyone would ever see.

"His energy was as immense as his enthusiasms. He was a full, eager participant in the doings and activities of the Steen Family Circle, founded, at the time, by my dad, his three sisters and his remaining brother . I remember that Sam even served as president one year. The meetings were at a different aunt's or cousin's homes each month. Some of the cousins who'd been successful had emigrated to New Jersey and a family with cars would drive those without them to the meetings in these Jersey homes. Sam Moscowitz, after a day bulging with hospital rounds, office visits and housecalls would pick up me and my parents, his wife and daughter also in the car, and drive us for a solid hour, even a bit more, depending on traffic, to a Jersey suburb while chattering animatedly, all the way, about a variety of stimulating topics. His interests and concerns were as wide as his joie de vivre.

"Then he'd proceed to conviviality with just about every person at the meeting. But sometimes he'd get a call advising that one of his patients was going into labor. He'd drive by himself all the way back to Brooklyn, deliver the infant, get in his car again and drive back to Jersey for the last half an hour of socializing and, yet again, climb back into the car and drive his family and mine back to Brooklyn, arriving home sometime after midnight. I haven't the slightest shred of doubt that he was in the hospital, making his rounds, by, at the very latest, 6:00 the next morning.

"One time my mother got tremendous,fearsome swelling of a leg, (poison sumac was the culprit,) in the middle of the night. She called him and when she and my dad got to his office around 3:00 A.M. (he lived on the second storey of a two storey house, the office was on the ground floor,) he was at his desk, the desk lamp the only light on, with several medical journals spread out before him. He was so absorbed he was hardly aware they'd entered through the door he'd told them would be ajar. These were the days, (before group practices or partnerships,) of the sole general practitioner, taking care of the entire family, and I suspect the man slept three hours a night. On a good night, as they say.

"But he was irrepressible. When he made a house call to our six storey building, rather than wait for the elevator, with black bag in hand, and despite his girth, he bounded up the stairs to our third floor apartment. The irrepressibility was part of all his enthusiasms and his ceaseless quest for knowledge. All the world, everything significant going on, was his ken. It was Sam who told me that a black baseball player would become one of Brooklyn's beloved Dodgers before any of us had even heard of Jack Roosevelt Robinson who, of course, became the most beloved Dodger of all time. In fact, the most beloved athlete there can ever be.

"It was Samuel ("Shmuel") Moscowitz who knew that that astute and complex practical visionary, Branch Rickey, Dodger General Manager, had, in 1945,signed Robinson and that he'd had a brilliant rookie year in organized, (i.e. white man's) baseball in 1946 with the Dodgers' top farm team, the Montreal Royals. Most Brooklynites first became conscious of the great Jackie on opening day, April 15th, of the '47 season. It'd been announced only several days before that he'd be brought up to the big team, the Dodgers themselves. Sam Moscowitz was glowingly pleased that *our* Dodgers, the long underdogs, the often losers, but always loved, would be giving the black man, the long persecuted, the forever underdog, the rarely loved, his chance. Jackie Robinson then vindicated not only an entire race, communicated not only with the entire world, but he made Sam Moskowitz, M.D., Yale '24, Yale Medical School '28 an infinitely proud, an extremely exuberant man. Justice could be brought to the world!

"The pace, or perhaps too many piled very high pastrami sandwiches at Ben and Hy's Delicatessen, just a few blocks from the Ebbets Field, home of Robinson's Dodgers, probably some such combination, broke Sam Moskowitz. In his mid to late '50s, when I was in my late teens, and doing very well at Columbia, with his solid encouragement and vociferous satisfaction, he had to have surgery for stomach cancer. I wasn't told directly but picked it up from overheard, whispered conversations amongst various Steen family members. I didn't really comprehend what was going on. The surgery was pronounced a success, at least by him, and I remember him at one of the family circle meetings expressing thanks for having been brought back from the brink and crying at Jane Frohmann's singing of "When You Walk Through A Storm," when it wafted through from a radio left on to provide background music. I was sharply shaken that the omniscient, the omnipotent Sam Moskowitz, who seemingly cured people by his very personal incandescence, was weeping, that he could have something to weep about.

"Not too long afterward there was a second surgery. Not much was said about it. I assumed it was just another hurdle he'd easily vault.

"A few weeks later, at another family circle meeting, he asked me to come with him into a small unoccupied room. When we sat down he asked about what courses I was then taking, whether I was enjoying them and so forth. But soon, although it wasn't one of the things I'd mentioned, he started talking about 'Hamlet.' He quickly got to Polonius's speech where the old man advises, 'And this above all, to thine own self be true, and then it follows, as the night the day, that thou cans't not be false to any man.' At Yale in the '20s he'd learned it straight—the distilled wisdom gleaned by a mature man from the experience of a lifetime. The quintessence of how to negotiate the many shoals and perils of living. It was very sound advice, the best, as Sam saw it.

"Of course it comes from a longer speech containing other pithy nuggets such as 'Neither a borrower nor a lender be,' but the beatific Shmuel quoted only the 'To thine own self be true' portion. What was he really trying to say, as a dying man, from his own experience? Marry for love, not money? If you really want to do something like research then, somehow, do it and don't rationalize doing something else instead? Or was he actually re—affirming his commitment to the vast amount of service he'd rendered and, implicitly, urging me to a similarly worthy life?

"I don't think that I consciously felt that he was mentally meandering as death approached. Yet, on some level, I realized it was a valedictory of sorts. A valedictory from a valedictorian class man. I sensed that he was trying to tell me *something*. But I was already too smart. I resisted him instead of accepting and supporting. I had imbibed, in no less an authoritative place than a high school English class, the 'modern' interpretation of Polonius's speech: the fatuous platitudes of a doddering old man, simplistic, exorbitantly impractical pieties. I, above all, knew better than to take the superficially wise words at their face value. They were conventional clap—trap, fit only for the ingenuous, the totally uninitiated to believe about the harsh, merciless, compromise inducing real world. I was a bit annoyed at Shmuel for trying to palm off these threadbare nostrums on my oh so sophisticated teen—age self. I had transcended this nonsense. In this matter, at least, I knew more and better, was more up to date than Samuel T. Moskowitz B.A. Yale '24, M.D. Yale Medical School '28.

"So, in our last meaningful encounter, I, with what must to him have seemed flagrant callousness, repudiated the gem, whatever its essential connotation, that a wise, gentle and good man, touching the last earthly places, had tried to confer on me. I remember just wanting him to stop talking, so I could leave the room in which we were cloistered, and get back to where everyone else was, the party.

"Unlike the Dale Dance Studios incident, I don't recall instantly feeling guilty and unworthy about my brusqueness. The guilt didn't really start seeping into me until six months, maybe a year, later. By that time Shmuel had died. But before he did, my mother, secretary to the Administrator of Brooklyn Women's Hospital, saw, one afternoon, from her office window, Sam Moskowitz walk up to the entrance of the hospital where he had, literally, delivered thousands, if not tens of thousands, of infants. He shuffled more than he walked, already too ill to practice, and was almost always at home in the time remaining. He stopped and looked up at the hospital building, and just gazed at it for several, very long, minutes. Then he turned, head down, and, very ploddingly, made his way back to his car.

"When he died I went with my parents to his funeral on a Sunday afternoon. But I didn't go out to the gravesite for his burial. I was eighteen, solidly headed for Phi Beta Kappa, (he would have loved that,) and had a crucial exam in British Constitutional History the next morning. I had to study, far bigger fish to fry.

"It wasn't too long after the funeral that I began skewering myself over how insensitively I'd acted towards Sam Moskowitz and his final words of advice. His legacy to me. Since then I've obsessed on my arrogance, youthful arrogance to be sure, but arrogance, nonetheless, untold times. Maybe the sagacious and humane Shmuel understood and forgave my air of superiority, my obtuseness, my swaggering obnoxiousness. However, maybe, despite his maturity and wisdom he was, at the very least, disappointed. And hurt, too, although by then beyond being hurt.

November_____,

"Recently, I awoke with an ineffable sadness for Barry Gottlieb. When I was a Brooklyn teen—ager he lived in the same apartment house, but was a few years older. He seemed like a typical adolescent male until he changed. As best as I can remember he, pretty suddenly, had become almost grotesquely overweight, huge gut, and very aberrant in his behavior. He seemed 'hyped—up,' boasted of romantic conquests which all the teens to whom he congratulated himself knew had never occurred. Generally he seemed very disoriented. As my mom would have said, maybe she did, 'He was not the same person.' His parents started looking very concerned .

"I no longer recall whether this was pre or post 'change,' but do remember watching him playing in a stickball game with guys more his own age than I was and them jeering him unmercifully, sharply deriding him for his athletic inadequacies. Was this a component of what disintegrated him or was he already ill and struggling when it happened? I can't remember clearly, but I think it was in the early stages of when he began to fail. And neither can I bring back what eventually happened to him, but suddenly we didn't see him around the house or neighborhood any more. Had he been institutionalized? Sent to relatives for a 'rest'? Where was he?

"I don't know, but I do know that he must have been immeasurably sad and broken to have emptily boasted to us as he transparently did. I can only think of him as a decent enough individual whose life must have been shattered forever.

"What could mere words have done for him? How can they help to repair such tragedy? A seemingly normal person felled into incapacity, in youth. Maybe my anxieties are exaggerated and Barry recovered to lead a relatively normal life. But I don't think so. I feel so, so sad for him. In fact, I'm crying right now. The weakness of words to accomplish; yet their power to express.

"The issues for users of words is how to express values. And, before that, what values to project. It's very difficult to represent a cherished value so that it exerts maximal impact on an audience of listeners, readers, etc. But that's merely a matter of esthetic judgment and skillfulness. Which values merit expressive endorsement is an eternally raging debate.

"Many conscientious intellectuals are completely confident that values are so totally subjective that arguing about them is ultimately useless and unprofitable. I.e. that there is absolutely no 'logically' conclusive way to prove the validity or invalidity of an asserted value; e.g. compassion is a noble human quality. Now such assertions about the complete subjectivity of value judgments could be disputed—but it's unnecessary for the word user to take that on. I'm sufficiently secure about the soundness of my values, many others are as well, and my task is to promote them by persuasive words so that others come to value the valuable, as I see it. The work is to find the mode of expression that will win adherents to your values. That's the initial step toward their being effectively adopted in human experience.

And the word user must decide which words are most suitable to convey intended meaning practically, not abstractly. The capacities and dispositions of the relevant audience have to be guaged. The most esthetically elegant means of expression may not be the most effective way to get across what she most wants to say to most of those she hopes to reach. Even an 'educated' audience in 1988 may require different words, than a similarly educated one in 1968 would have, for maximum effect. Not to mention affect.

"Is the writer 'responsible' for readers' changing sensibilities so that he must accordingly modify what would otherwise be his style, or should he write as he himself, (and, presumably, some others too,) would want to read and hope that his audience is moved toward becoming more 'educated,'" and, eventually, more attuned to what he's actually put down. This general problem has various aspects: how widely does the word user want his words appreciated; how narrowly can he accept 'communication;' should the serious writer disregard quantity of readers reached or reachable and, as a 'moral' matter, write the best he, himself, thinks he can, heedless of extent of receptivity? The user of words must weigh and balance quite a few imponderables, in addition to dealing with the quicksilver of words themselves.

"It also seems that, perforce, the serious word user is a moral agent.

Words can agitate, indoctrinate, move, even, sometimes, transform the world. So she who deploys them has a responsibility.

"A word user can believe that if she can only utilize her instruments to make others see it as she sees it that then there'll be more unity of belief and attitude and the world will improve. I sense that many musicians think of their instruments in a similar way. If they can move listeners with their music as they feel it and are moved by it then people will be 'improved' in the most profound sense. They will be more at peace, calmer, need to perpetrate rapacity and brutality less, need to strike out and injure others less, need to viciously compete less. 'Music soothes the savage beast' is also a credo. Gustav Mahler's Second Symphony is sub-titled 'The Resurrection,' and many superb musicians must feel the redemptive, cathartic, cleansing, healing power of the music. Music is a wondrous, magnificent art. A balm to life.

"Words, of course, play their part in History too. They're the instruments by which History is rendered. So words become exceedingly potent teachers since History is a grand sermonizer. It often provides lessons taken as a guide to present and future conduct. As Santayana observed, 'Those who do not learn from History are condemned to repeat it.' While History is, objectively, the facts as they are, what in fact occurred, it is also words, written after the occurrence of the facts themselves, which relate the past to us. As soon as words are intermediaries between brute facts and the accreting knowledge and learning of someone who wasn't there interpretation has occurred. Words tell history by portraying and interpreting it. Since they tell it in one, or several, ways, rather than another, or others, they, inevitably, 'slant' it. The nature of the incline is a moral choice. So words which report history are, as they are so often in other respects, moral agents. We 'learn' as the teaching words tilt us.

"There's one more incident, which I still carry around, that I'd like to expunge—by writing about it here. Not that that will do it. But maybe help—a little. It involves my dad. Max was born in Kovno, Russia in 1884, and came to this country- (this 'goldeneh medineh,' in Yiddish, this golden land,) the strains of whose national anthem, within his hearing, any time, any place, invariably evoked his quickly rising to his feet as he placed his hand over heart-at the turn of the twentieth century. One of his proudest accomplishments was writing a song. Notwithstanding he'd learned his English at night school, on the lower East side of New York City, after working all day in the garment industry, he wrote lyrics for a song for Theodore Roosevelt's 1904 presidential campaign and as a very young man, still brimming with vitality and hope, he sent it off to the President. Max often referred to the gracious handwritten letter, personally signed by T.R., that he'd received in return. That sort of thing still happened then. And how Max must have enjoyed it, way beyond my understanding then, when, just about fifty years later, his son won an essay contest in his junior high school on Roosevelt , received a medallion with the likeness of the twenty-sixth president and was invited to a ceremony with youngsters, from all over New York City, who had also penned winning essays.

"Since Max was in his mid-fifties when I was born we never had a 'normal' father—son relationship. The atypical age gap always made him 'stand out' as my father and I generally felt the awkwardness. For example, when I was about seven our little family went on a vacation to a resort in the (in)famous Catskill Mountains, about two hours outside of New York City. My dad and I played catch with a pink rubber ball, one of the very popular, at least amongst we Brooklyn boys, 'spaldeens,' (from the manufacturer's name, Spalding,) on the expansive lawn in front of the resort's main building containing numerous guest rooms and the main dining room. But the grass was wet and I threw one inaccurately to Max so that he had to start and lunge for it quickly. On the slick grass his legs went out from under him and he fell clumsily, like the more than sixty year old man he was, and painfully. Later in the day, when I was just hanging around with other kids my own age, one of the guests, a woman who must have been in her late thirties—early forties strolled over to me and asked whether the man I'd been playing catch with was my father. When I said he was she asked 'How old is he?' I answered, truthfully, that I didn't know. She then suggested I ask my dad and report back to her. When I did innocently approach my parents a few minutes later and asked about Max's age they both became exercised to the point where I understood she'd put an illegitimate question to me. Finally, my mother told me to tell the inquiring woman that if she wanted to know she could ask my parents herself.

"Although my dad was almost sixty years older than I was and, for one reason or another, couldn't do too many things that other fathers did with their sons, he, nevertheless, managed to teach me things. Like the time when I was eleven and the three of us had eaten in a cafeteria in Brooklyn. After we'd finished my mom went to the ladies' room while Max and I waited for her at the table, the dirty dishes scattered on it. The cafeteria employee whose job was clearing was maneuvering a wheeled cart, on which he piled dirty dishes according to size, from table to table. He seemed in his forties and had a withered arm which couldn't do much. But he was doing well enough with his other arm. He was working his way toward our table but first had to stop at one where a very well dressed man was waiting for the table to be cleared so that he could comfortably spread out his own food laden plates. When the white jacket, baker hatted, withered arm employee got there Mr. Imperious and Immaculately Groomed started castigating him for not clearing fast enough. The employee neither looked at his critic nor said anything. He just kept clearing as fast as he could. When he'd finished he rolled the cart to our table and started on our dirty plates. Max, jerking his head in the direction of the petty tyrant, said to the clearer, 'Can't he see?' The employee looked up at my dad, smiled shyly, yet with some warmth, and then continued about his business of clearing. Always help the neediest and the least, the eternal wallflowers at life's dance.

"By the time I began college my dad had turned seventy. Yet he still took the subway to his job, punching the time clock by 8 A.M., as a cutter for the childrens' clothing manufacturer he'd labored at for over thirty years. Monday through Friday, and for many of those years, half a day on Saturday. But, finally, there must have come a time when, although still willing, probably even still somewhat eager, he could no longer do the job. The growing number of mistakes more than negated his long experience and savvy. He was told that he was 'laid—off.'

'He'd been laid off before, not an atypical occurrence over the many years, but on those occasions business, genuinely, "was slow.' There just wasn't enough work to make it economically prudent to keep the plant open. Characteristically, he'd call on the Friday afternoon of a week during which he'd been unemployed to be told whether to report into work the following Monday morning. Usually these fallow periods would be relatively brief, two or three weeks, a month at most. But this time was different. On Friday afternoon, week after week after week, he'd call his supervisor at 'the place,' as he and we referred to the plant, only to be told that there wasn't enough work, 'things were still very slow,' so that he shouldn't come in the following Monday.

"After this routine had gone on for several months he called his union representative. My memory wavers into haziness here, but I seem to recall his telling us that he didn't get very straight or satisfactory answers. I don't know whether he intimated to my mother and me, or I just figured out for myself, that the union rep seemed to be in some sort of complicity with the employer to ease Max out. He made his Friday afternoon call several more times but, finally, just stopped. Nor do I remember whether he had finally been conclusively told that he was through or had eventually girded himself sufficiently to, at last, accept the 'message' which they'd been unmistakably sending him.

"Trying to remain unbowed, he went around in the neighborhood, from sole proprietor store to sole proprietor store, soliciting, practically begging I've no doubt, for part time work. He'd never been without a job, except for the few odd days here and there, since he'd come to this country at fifteen, and he wasn't about to start being permanently unemployed in his seventies, if he could help it. But he couldn't.

"Defeated in his quest for work, he didn't have much choice but to sit at home most of the day, nodding into cat naps on the couch, trying to read books he wasn't really interested in, waiting for my mom to come home from her job. One evening she was at her second job, as a cashier at the bingo game run by the hospital whose administrator she was secretary for, and I had plans to go out with some of my new found college friends. Suddenly Max said to me, 'Please don't go out." I asked why not. 'I'm just afraid to be alone,' he answered. Although I had enough endemic compassion to call my pals and say that I couldn't make it, I bristled with annoyance and irritation at my father. I sharply told him that since he wasn't 'sick' or anything like that I really didn't understand what he meant or just what the hell he was talking about. His only response was: 'I hope that in your life you'll never have such a feeling.' (I'm getting there.) Anyway, while I might have experienced guilt at the grudging way I did the right thing, (I don't choose to reflect on the contemporary possibility that Max might have been being 'manipulative,') I did, at least, manage to do it.

"Although only about seventeen when it happened, I did sense that the way my dad had been 'retired' from his job was not the way it should have happened. I was outraged at the rank injustice.It may have been my equivalent of the Allard Lowenstein —wallflowers at the dance experience. It ripened me for the democratic socialism I would eventually come to fully embrace, as a passionate political commitment, during a college course with a young, brilliant, dynamic professor. The way my dad had been relegated to the scrap heap of the no longer useful was not the way to treat the weak, the depleted, the very vulnerable. Society, collectively, had to provide a more compassionate, more humane solution and environment.

"Max continued to fail which caused me to grow more and more embarrassed by him. Yet he tried manfully, nobly, to maintain interest in my beloved Brooklyn Dodgers. As an immigrant he'd never really gotten deeply absorbed or involved with the great American pastime. Of course, like just about every other Brooklyn resident, he was very aware of the Dodgers and 'rooted' for them. But his interest hadn't been more than glancingly casual until, as a seven year old, tutored by a baseball loving uncle and swept along by friends, I became enraptured with the perils, pitfalls, pratfalls and fortunes of 'Dem,' i.e. our, 'Bums.' Although most of the times I paid my sixty cents to sit in the bleachers at Ebbets Field it was with friends, occasionally I would go just with my dad. (One time he and I even prevailed on my mother to come too. It was 'Ladies Night'—women admitted free.)

"The incident I keep thinking about so much, I don't think I'll ever stop, happened on a briiliantly bright Saturday afternoon. An early version of an 'Old Timers Day' scenario took place before the actual game and that former Dodger great, pitcher, Dazzy Vance, was in uniform and threw a few. My dad, then in his late sixties, voiced, more than once, how impressed he was that Vance, then in his early sixties, could still do something like that. But, as I've already written, Max hadn't really known much about baseball technically and now that he was getting pretty old and increasingly confused he didn't really follow the details of what was going on in the game itself very well at all. While once I'd become a rabid fan he always wanted the Dodgers to win for my sake he certainly didn't know the 'fine' points, such as who was hitting for what average, who led the league in RBIs, or who the starting pitcher's for tomorrow's game would likely be. Actually, as I look back, I believe he may have even thought that the very brief pre—game Old Timers action, an inning or two at most, was, in some sense part of the regular Dodger game we'd come to see.

"Once the game had begun his failing eyesight straining against the blinding glare of the midday sun resulted in his understanding extremely little of what was happening on the field. Quite a few times during the afternoon, after crack of bat against ball and the subsequent roar of the crowd he turned to me and asked 'What happened?' This started making me very uneasy because right behind us there were three or four guys, in their twenties, who, I could tell, from their chatter and observations, were very intense, knowledgeable fans. They knew the batting average of every player on the field and all the relevant tactics and stratagems at the appropriate times. In order to deflect, diminish whatever attention they might focus on us, because of Max's frequent and insistent questions, I tried to make my answers to him as succinct, and subdued as possible. I also was pretty sure that any more extensive explanations would make him none the wiser, so to speak. Finally, after I'd been mumbling my replies in as *sotto* a *voce* as possible, throughout most of the game, in the seventh or eighth inning, in a tight moment, the Dodgers executed a spectacular Reese-to Robinson-to Hodges 'bang—bang,' (as the great Dodger announcer, Red Barber, would have put it,) double play to get out of a very threatening jam and hold on to their precarious one run lead. After the home crowd's tremendous and ecstatic roar had subsided, Max, yet again, turned to me, and, with more than a tinge of defensiveness in his voice, asked 'What happened?' Before I could deal with this as unobtrusively as possible the 'senior' guy in the covey of experts behind us leaned forward and with great exasperation and annoyance, verging on derision, shouted directly into my dad's ear: 'Double—play; six-to four-to three;' (shortstop to second baseman to first baseman.) Max looked at him, as though in thanks, and nodded vigorously, although I'm quite sure he had not the slightest idea of what 'six-to four-to three' meant.

"While I knew that the young and sassy Mr. Know-it—all had done something very wrong, cruel really, by butting in with his extravagant irritation toward the confused old man, I was, nevertheless, acutely embarrassed that it was *my* father whom I was with and whom I was somehow responsible for, who had occasioned the expert's wrath. At that time my own self—esteem was so low that anyone, everyone, was entitled to be full of ire at anything I might have done, anything I might be or anything I might be connected with. I should have been stronger,even if only internally— I didn't have to say anything. But because I wasn't I haven't been able to forget that I was ashamed of my father when he was trying to be loving to, and young for, me. Yeah, I know now that people can say I was only a child really and shouldn't be so hard on myself, but I can't forget that instead of loving my dad in return I was annoyed at him and wished that, for that moment, he didn't exist.

"So, whatever the rationalizations, explanations, justifications for my traitorous emotions, I've never been able to stop believing that Max, ("Mordecai,") who sailed steerage from Russia to begin a new century and a new life, as a teen—ager in this country, who was respectfully dubbed 'the rabbi's son' by a gang of Irish youths whose efforts to maul him he'd beaten off by swinging out with a plank which happened to be lying in the street, who married three times and fathered three children, the last of them, when he was in his mid-fifties, me, who, until the very end of his life, revered the beautiful Socialist agitator and street corner speaker, Rose Pastor Stokes, and who, in his fashion, continued to believe in the ideal of Communism because, as he said, 'What Communism really means is justice,' and who, although we were a lower class household which should have gotten the 'New York Daily News' or the 'New York Journal American,' always brought home the prestigious "New York Times," who bought me a two—wheeler bicycle with the forty dollars it took him endless months to save up from the daily pittance my mother doled out to him as lunch money, and who didn't die before he told anyone and everyone that he could get hold of, including the attendants in the nursing home, that his son went to Harvard Law School, deserved better of that son. Forgive me daddy."

CHAPTER EIGHT

MARTIN WAS SITTING IN his office trying to concentrate on his notes for the next day's Contracts class. It was always so ponderously boring to go over notes he'd studied so many times before. It had been almost twenty years since he'd started teaching Contracts. When it came time to prepare for a class Martin had to practically literally,, as well as drag out the relevant notes, drag himself into position to stare at them.Once he began, however, it wasn't *that* bad since there was some satisfaction in re-acquainting himself with how the questions he'd formulated to ask the class, in his first two or three years of teaching, were still effective in evoking the points which needed to be gotten across. (Or, at least, they should have been effective in eliciting such points—some students seemed impervious to any means of instruction howsoever brilliantly presented by whatever pedagogic genius.)

He began mulling over a problem which often bothered him when he pored over his class notes; viz., were these particular pages so yellowed, wrinkled and dog—earred that they should be copied over on fresh pages of foolscap? Just because he, essentially, was using twenty year old notes it didn't mean that the students should be signaled unmistakable evidence of the fact. Anna had admonished him about this years back, already. The mental states of the students counted also. If their morale about a teacher got low, the teacher's morale could also be lowered. Assuming there was room for it to go lower than it already was in Martin's case.

Engrossed as he was in these expandingly complex thoughts about trivialities, Martin almost welcomed the rap at his office door. Characteristically he didn't appreciate such knocks since the vast majority of times they came from students all too eager to have a professor's views on, even involvement in, *their* trivial problems. Usually whatever Martin was doing was considerably more interesting and important than what they were serving up.

After he shouted "Come in," (it was a point of honor with Martin never to pretend that he wasn't there when he was, a stratagem seemingly employed by quite a few other faculty members,) Jenny Hauser opened the door.

She had on a crisp white blouse, tight enough to indicate the alluringly shaped full breasts, a tight, but not too tight, crimson—toned skirt which revealed enticingly shaped legs supported by black pumps with a trifle less than medium heels. Business—like enough attire, yet … Martin couldn't help re—affirming mentally that she was just so fine to look at. There was even freshness and a daub of innocence in the rather open, alert-eyed face, features close to perfect.

"Professor, could I talk to you for a few minutes? Or am I disturbing you? I could come back some other time."

"No, no problem; this is alright. In fact, why don't you fully get your money's worth and have a seat, too."

As he gestured toward one of the two vacant chairs opposite his desk, with what, he hoped seemed, some degree of graciousness, Martin, surprisingly, found himself putting a bit of charge into trying to sound energetic and vital for her. When she sat down she crossed her legs, with a graceful swoop, in a way that did nothing to decrease Martin's desire to show to good advantage to her.

The smile she gave him could certainly be described as sweet. Martin, making an effort to project cheerfulness asked, "What can I do for you?"

With male students he often transmuted this opener into "What can I do you for?" or even "What can I do to you?" in order to dispel any undue student solemnity. But he tried hard to remember to never begin that way with females. Especially highly attractive ones. He thought it particularly essential to avoid such flippant terminology in this case. It was all too easy for him to lapse into musing upon wanting to do things *to* Jenny Hauser.

"I was just wondering about something we were discussing in class last time."

"And what particular thing would that be.? We discuss so many things in every class. Not the least of them, nor the least often discussed, being the very meaning of life itself."

But she didn't giggle the way she was supposed to. In fact, she appeared somewhat puzzled. Well, Martin thought, certainly didn't score with that one. Perhaps another, at the right moment, would be more successful.

"It's just that stuff about contracting to sell the same thing to two people … I, like, didn't understand the conclusion we came to … , if we did …"

She smiled the virtually irresistible smile as Martin registered some mental surprise. And, at his stage of experience, surprise at what students didn't understand was quite rare. How, he quickly ruminated, could she not know or understand, the conclusion, as she had put it. He had brought the point out and illustrated it three or four times during the classroom discussion, in an effort to ensure, that for one of those very rare times, just about everyone in the class "got" it. Apparently not *everyone*. Martin recognized that the point started out seeming counter—intuitive to your normal, common-sensical individual. But, usually, after his deft analytical chiseling and hammering it emerged as pretty clear to the class at large. So how could she …

Martin resolved to concentrate on the smile—and the legs, also, which she now re—crossed.

"Well, Ms. Hauser, what exactly is it about the conclusion, or anything else for that matter, that you don't understand?" Martin believed in prodding the student to refine her thinking enough to be able to articulate her exact problem as precisely as possible. At least make them focus in as best they could, instead of sitting there lethargically, throwing out a random word and grunt with the expectation that the teacher will then lecture profusely to them, down to the smallest detail, for minutes at a time, summing up, the student hoped, as much as possible of the entire course.

"Well, I mean, if there's only one pen … how can you possibly sell it to two people … I mean only one can get it, right?"

Martin intensely disliked repeating the same point over and over again in class, so he surely despised repeating it some more outside of class. But he always girded himself to try to do so, as clearly as possible, when students confessed their confusion, too often seeming like complete ineptitude, in his office. Could he do less for the radiant Jenny. She of the dazzling smile and superbly curved legs.

It began to occur to Martin that there was a question as to whether Ms. Hauser was actually trying to have Martin feel the smile as incandescent, see the legs, and other anatomical areas, as very desirable indeed. Could it just possibly be that the delectably endowed Jenny was really interested in him more than in Contracts; that, even, she'd faked her confusion so that she could wear her tight blouse to spectacular effect and cross and re—cross those so inviting legs in those very provocative heels.

"Well, does it help if we say that I can *contract* to sell the same pen to two people even if only one can *physically* wind up with the pen itself"?

"But then the other one has … like nothing and you haven't sold the pen to more than one person," she offered with an insouciant, almost charming amalgam of triumph and puzzlement.

"But Ms. Hauser, if I made a contract with the second person to sell her the pen then doesn't she have a contract entitling her to buy the pen? And what does a contracting party have under a contract? That is, supposing the contract is not executed, by the other party, as its terms provide?"

"What does the person have under the contract … ? Well, you just said that she doesn't have the pen …"

"But, Ms. Hauser, what is it, then, that she does have? What does a non—breaching party to a contract, which has been breached by the other party to the contract, have?" What is she entitled to?

"Have? Like I … ?

"Look, Ms. Hauser, suppose I just contracted to sell the pen only to one person, namely you, but then reneged on turning it over? What could you do?"

"I could sue you!"

Martin mused that "sue" was always a word that tripped to student lips with great celerity. That was the business they were there to learn.

"That's right, Ms. Hauser. And in suing me you'd be trying to exercise your 'what' under our contract? You'd be suing to enforce your 'what' under the contract? You'd be suing to enforce your … Just fill in the blank, Jenny—I mean Ms. Hauser."

"Oh, professor, it's o.k. if you call me Jenny," she giggled, but, then, quickly, said "I have rights."

Another thing seemingly every student knew, with passion verging on hysterical absolute certainty, that he had plenty of.

"Exactly, Ms. Hauser; you could enforce your rights under the contract. So, just because a contract is formed doesn't mean that everything it specifies and provides for will actually physically happen. But if one of the parties is responsible for causing things the contract provides should happen to not happen then the other party can do something about that. Specifically, the other party can enforce her rights, just as you've pointed out. In other words, the party who doesn't do what he promised to do can't, necessarily, be made to actually do it, but he can be made to suffer consequences for reneging on the contract, on what he'd contracted to do. On, that is, his promise. So, if I sell the pen, or more precisely, contract to sell the pen to two people, while only one of them can get delivery of that actual one pen from me, the other can enforce her rights against me and I have to … I have to 'what," Ms. Hauser?

"Like … pay?"

Martin had pretty confidently counted on being able to make her say that other magical word.

"That's exactly right. If the breaching party has caused damage by making the other party spend more for such a pen than she would have spent under the contract, then the breaching party has to pay for the damage, the difference. So, while the innocent party doesn't wind up with the specific pen he bargained and contracted for, he gets put in a position equal to the one he'd have been in if the contract had been executed—a pen of the type provided for in the contract, for the exact price provided for by the contract. That's because if when the breaching party doesn't deliver the pen, the other party, the non—breacher, has to spend more for the pen he has to go out and buy elsewhere, the substitute pen, so to speak, he's entitled to recover, from the breaching party, the amount over the contract price, if any, which he had to pay for the substitute. So there you are— he gets the type of pen for which he contracted at the price he agreed to pay for it. That's why it's called 'Expectation damages.' Ultimately he gets what he expected as a result of entering into the contract.

Jenny Hauser had her puzzled look again but, finally, strained a smile.

"But ... not the exact pen that you said you'd sell to him ..."

A little more of this, Martin thought, and he might actually emit a scream of frustration rather than merely feel that one was imminent. Although he strove against it his voice began to take on an edge.

"But Ms. Hauser, does he really care about that exact pen, when there are a million others just like it in the world? A Bic is a Bic is a Bic, as long as he winds up with the kind of pen he wanted and agreed to buy, at the price he'd agreed to pay for it, no?"

"Well, no ... I guess not ... but he, like, still doesn't have that exact pen ... So you didn't sell the same exact pen to two people ... But I'll think about it. I'll work on it ... I sort of see what you mean ..."

Perhaps, Martin fleetingly mused, he should be delighted, pedagogically, that she hadn't ended up thinking that she'd convinced him of the impregnable cogency of her original position.

"Anyway, professor, I was wondering if I could ask you some other things ..."

Martin, blissfully, welcomed the change of subject. In fact, he became more alert, hoping that she might bring something up, having absolutely nothing whatsoever to do with law, that could conceivably be mildly interesting to him. Was he starting to have hopes that, to complement her suggestive self, she'd say something to him which could be interpreted, even if it took a lot of stretching, as suggestive too. He put effort into making sure that he kept his eyes on the general area of her eyes and face, that they didn't wander to areas it might be more arousing to gaze at intensively.

"Oh, sure, go ahead, Ms. Hauser."

"Thank you. I know that it's like early to be thinking along these lines, like, you know, about what I'm going to do with my legal education and all that. But, you know, we kids actually do like think a lot about what jobs we're going to wind up with … I mean whether we're going to get what we want … Not that we really, at this point, like even know what it is exactly that we, you know, do want."

Martin thought he should probably be grateful for the relatively few "likes" and "you knows" which peppered her rambling. Others did worse.

"Well, Ms. Hauser, I'm not really that well versed about, or connected into, the job market around here, but I'm happy to talk to you about it in general terms, tell you whatever I do know that might be helpful."

"I guess I was just wondering what sort of job I might get, you know actually wind up with. Like what kinds of things are really available, what's actually out there … I suppose I've already heard enough to know that some of that depends on how you do, you know, like where you finish in the class …"

"I'm afraid that there's no doubt that that's reality. Unfortunately, I suppose, some types of jobs just aren't accessible to a student around here unless she's done very, very well academically."

"I guess you're talking like about the, you know, big firms?"

"Yes, that's one area where grades seem to weigh very heavily. "

"And 'very well' means that you have to be, like, one of the top four or five people in your class?"

"I don't know that things are pinched quite as narrowly as that. But, surely, from a school like this it means you, at least, have to be in the top ten percent of the class. Preferably, probably, the top five per cent."

"A school like this? …"

"Well, as you, of course, know, there are different tiers of school in the universe of law schools."

"But this is a good law school, isn't it?"

When asked this type of question Martin was always tempted to really let go with his true feelings. To say something like: actually there are only ten to fifteen truly high quality law schools in the almost two hundred in the country. The rest really aren't very good—even the very best of that residue are mediocre. But even Martin had ripened into his late forties knowing that this was unnecessary; impolitic certainly and needlessly deflating and derogatory too. He'd gotten to the point where he could temper his aggressive impulses, possibly self—hating ones was more accurate, in these situations and he exerted pressure on himself now to do just that. Since, at this kind of juncture, he tried to save the feelings of students who were basically anonymous to him why wouldn't he take care with those of the comely Ms. Hauser? Wasn't he really interested in possible future contact, (an interesting word in the context,) with Ms. Jenny Hauser? If so he certainly wouldn't want to gratuitously offend her for the inconsequential sake of letting off a little steam which came, essentially, from his *own* dissatisfaction at teaching at a less than premier school.

"Yes, Ms. Hauser, this is a decent law school in the sense that you can get a good legal education here." Martin authentically believed this. Many of the faculty were highly competent lawyers and teachers from whom a conscientious, diligent student could get solid training in that much heralded mystique of "thinking like a lawyer." So he didn't feel he was dissembling in handing out such re—assurances.

"However, Ms. Hauser, as with many other things in life, unfortunately, there's a status hierarchy amongst law schools. There're the so-called 'Ivy League schools,' like Yale, Harvard, Stanford, Columbia, Michigan and so on and so forth, and those pretty close to them like Virginia, University of Chicago, UCLA, etcetera. In major cities, like New York, Chicago, Los Angeles, Boston, San Francisco, what have you, the prestigious firms, the ones with several hundred attorneys, whose business is composed primarily of heavy duty corporate accounts, your IBMs, your General Motors, your T.V. networks, these firms pretty much confine their hiring to graduates of these types of top tier law schools. More precisely to graduates of such law schools who're in the top quarter or third of the class. If they do even so much as consider someone from a law school outside this Olympus it pretty well has to be someone at the very top of the class. Now, as these ever growing giant firms have more and more need for sheer horsepower they need to widen the pool of associates. So, they might reach a little lower down than the very top of the class as far as interviewing people from what they think of as the distinctly second—rate, end quote, schools. But only the slightest bit further down, not far from the very top at all. That's why I mentioned the top five per cent of the class before as a minimum realistic zone for any student at this school who has any aspirations to join a firm like that.

"Naturally, I hope I do that well. But I guess everybody does. So it turns out that ninety—five per cent are disappointed, doesn't it?"

When a student said that sort of thing Martin always wondered whether she was seeking succour from professorial authority; whether the student wanted him to say something like he thought she had a good chance, maybe even a very good chance, to wind up in the top five per cent—she seemed to be doing nicely in class discussion, seemed to have a good solid grasp on the work ... , etc ... etc. However, except for the rare, exceedingly rare, instances in which Martin could actually effuse such encouragement, he was tempted to ask the presumptuously esteem seeking student what college he'd attended, what courses he'd taken there, what grades she'd received in them, what her score on the Law School Admission Test had been and, then, point out the type of profile likely just outlined didn't suggest a top five percent finish as the surest bet in the world. But here, too, he usually restrained his more irritable, aggressive impulses.

"That sounds pretty much like a general description of much of life."

"What?" she exclaimed, genuine confusion assailing her fine features.

"You know," he began, the phrase momentarily unnerving him;- was he beginning to talk like her? "I mean that ninety—five percent of people are, ultimately, disappointed by life. They don't get quite what they expected. In the same way that ninety—five percent of your fellow students, as you just pointed out, are going to be disappointed at not winding up in the top five percent of the class."

"Oh, yeah, I see." She actually brightened, as a child who has finally caught on does . "But I guess I was hoping that if I did all my work and did alright I could get a good job. Like with a firm which would pay the going rate. I guess everyone wants the top dollar that the very big, the prestigious firms pay. But if you can't get that, at least something not too far out of line from it."

"So, I'm understanding from what you're saying that what you're interested in doing with your legal education is related to the job you can actually get which has the most dollar signs attached to it. I mean you're really not interested, at least not yet, and remember you are, after all, only in the first half of your first year of law school, so who knows what you might end up wanting to do, but right now it's not the type of legal work that interests you so much as how much you could make at various jobs."

"I'm not sure what you mean. But what you said is right. I mean is there anything wrong with wanting as high a paying job as you can possibly get? It's, like, after you pay so much for your legal education and take out all those loans and stuff, 'ya know, you want to start getting some of it back as soon as you can."

"No, I have no trouble understanding that, and I'm not minimizing it, either. But you know you have to try to arrange things so that you have some chance to enjoy what you're doing also. You want to like your work, have at least some enthusiasm for it, want to go to it in the morning and not just watch your bankbook grow."

"Well, it is sort of fun to see the bankbook balance go up. Not that that would happen for a long time with most of us—certainly not for me, anyway. I mean most of us kids are so heavily in debt, just paying for law school and everything, that it's got to be like a while, I mean, before you could even think of starting to bank it. But the fun is in the money too, isn't it? I mean, like, that's why everyone does everything, or most things anyway, isn't it? That's our system, right? You want to have the good things, you want to get them for yourself. So you're willing to study hard so you can get to be somebody. And then you're willing to work very hard so that you can cash in, earn the things that everyone wants. Like, I mean, the foreign sports car, or the boat that you can take out on the week—ends. Or whatever it is that turns you on, And like you want a family and everything. Even though, right now, I don't even have a boyfriend, I mean a steady, like, 'ya know, or anything like that. I'm too busy here. And then, after that, you want the best for your family and kids. So that all takes money, too. So you have to get it somehow."

She had it all planned and figured out, without the slightest shred of unconventionality intruding, didn't she, Martin mused. But, after all, he was the teacher; he should try, shouldn't he.

"But Ms. Hauser, and I'm probably most likely repeating myself, but don't you have to remember that most of your time, or a great deal of it, anyway, is spent at your job? The concrete, material rewards that the job allows you to acquire- the fact is that it's those you actually spend relatively little time with. Very little in fact. How many hours will you be on the boat, or whatever, compared with how many hours you'll spend at the office? High powered lawyers, and even not such high powered ones, always seem to have something in their briefcase and the briefcase always seems to be with them. Nights, week—ends and so forth. Do you ride the trains or buses? How many times do you see someone who you're pretty sure is a lawyer—you know from the way they strike you and the way they're dressed and such—with the open attaché case, poring over a lap full of documents and papers?"

Why was he getting so worked up, as though pleading a case? His own case? His own case with her? "So, as I say, doubtless repeating myself again, if you don't like the work you're doing, at least somewhat, and the way it is out there that's what you're doing most of the time, things can get pretty grim. You could find yourself pretty damn unhappy, actually."

Her features, so attractive that they could stir Martin to the verge of aching, yearning, didn't change much. Her eyes remained steady.

"I don't know, professor … I really don't know …" She shrugged a delicate, insouciant, feminine twitch of her shoulders. "I've never heard what you're saying …"

That provoked Martin to think no you don't know much, and you haven't heard much, and you don't know much other than what you've heard. But he didn't let such thoughts become spoken ones. He withheld once again. If he voiced them even someone so unsubtle as Jenny Hauser might realize that she was being criticized, condescended to even, and he definitely didn't want to have her feel that way.

"I mean, professor, that someone should like, you know , just concentrate on all the good things, you know, like the ones I mentioned, and enjoy them … and like accept the hard work as what you have to go through to get them. What you have to go through to get what everyone wants and what everyone would go through to get, if they could …"

Should Martin tell her that James Keir Hardie, the Scottish miner who was one of the founders and early luminaries of the British Labour Party, had once said something like, "Work is man's fulfillment, not his negation." And that William Morris, that born to great wealth English polymath—artist, designer, poet, social critic, philosopher—was very much of the same mind. But somehow, Martin further thought, this did not seem like a fruitful or meaningful thing to do. She was already starting to shift in her seat, reaching for her books and hand bag.

"O.K., Ms. Hauser, I hope you find what you want in a career. It's very early for you yet and it takes time to focus in on exactly what it is that you really think is worthwhile going after. Who knows, something which you perceive as very desirable today may look a lot less attractive in a year or so. And, by the same token, something you've never even given a thought to, so far, may suddenly seem like a path you'd very much like to take. You know there're things one can do with a solid legal education besides working for a very large corporate law firm. We could discuss things like legal aid, or public defender, or poverty law work, or government service, or, even, teaching for some examples. But I'm sure you're very busy and have to get going soon, and I have to finish up some things …" He slid some papers together on his desk. "So maybe you'll want to do a little more thinking, get a little more law school experience under your belt, take a look at what different areas of the law can offer … And, maybe, you'd want to chat with me again. I'd always be glad to hash through these things with you …"

Still in her chair, she'd completely gathered up her text books and note books and had bag in hand. The books were in a neat stack against her chest, so Martin was no longer able to enjoy the distraction of that delightful sight.

"Yeah … I could do like some thinking," she allowed in a low and unconvincing voice. "Then maybe, 'ya know, I could ask you some more questions and stuff", she trailed off. "Well, thanks a lot for your time, Professor Steen."

When she went out of his office Martin appreciated the rear view as much as he had the frontal one.

"Nov. 3

"I think I might actually enjoy writing in this journal, tonight; instead of it just being a shield against despair. Jenny Hauser is fun to look at, a really nice figure, for sure, to go with those very, very attractive features. So, maybe, she'll be fun to write (fantasize?) about.

"That's the good part. But, then, there's the non—physical part. Is she just young, or is she singularly unimaginative and very, very dim? How the hell am I supposed to know, anymore!! I'm verging on being two and a half times her age. Maybe she's just twenty—one years old, not dumb.

"And why did she come to my office? To really talk and ask questions, about Contracts and careers, or because she's a little interested in me other than as one of her teachers? She did drop in that line about not having a steady boyfriend, didn't she? Was that just something which came out as a natural, innocuous conversational phrase, or was it calculatingly directed to me as a piece of encouraging information?

"She did ask a question about Contracts and where else would she go to do that but to her Contracts professor. Unfortunately, she was incredibly thick about the whole thing. First of all, I explained the god damn point very clearly, insistently so, several times in class and, then, I thought I'd made it unmistakably limpid in my office. But she just couldn't get it!! No matter what I said it just didn't penetrate, (last word a Freudian slip?) That's a little much even for a first year student. She's definitely not a natural at legal analysis. But who cares—in a wider perspective I might consider that a compliment to her. I, myself, certainly, no longer have any great affection or respect for *legal* analysis. But, frankly, it's not just that she's not talented at coming up with analytical insights or distinctions on her own—she just couldn't catch on to a rather straightforward explanation put right in front of her, repeatedly. Let's face it, I'd just have to conclude that, simply, putting it bluntly, she's not very smart, bright, too sharp, whatever phraseology you want to use.

"And so damn conventionally Yuppified, too! As far as plans for the future or objectives in life she can't seem to think past paradise according to the t.v. She's definitely purchased a lifetime, non—cancellable pass to the Bourgeois Amusement Park. But, again, couldn't this just be 'innocent' youthfulness? She could change, mature, couldn't she?

"Oh come on!! I'd love to really believe that— in behalf of her beauty—but I've got to stop kidding myself. How much capacity for change could there be in someone who said some of the things that she said? What is she going to do—suddenly become a radical Socialist! She might mature a bit, hopefully anyway, but I don't think there's ,much room for revision of her basic likes, dislikes, attitudes, values, beliefs, etc. But what right do I have to be sure? Maybe she would change under appropriate influences. (Is 'under' another Freudian slip?) Maybe she's really very teachable. That's where I come in, right?

"In any event , why do I have to go into all that? She sure looks wonderful to hold. As that pal I used to play stickball with, back in Brooklyn, was so fond of saying, 'I'd like to fuck her!' Why can't we just have something on that basis: a dalliance—is that what it's still called?

"But, first of all, how do I know she'd be amenable? Not to mention the ethical problem of 'dallying,' if that's the term, with a woman who's currently a student. Not a problem since the grading system is anonymous; the professor is just grading a number, not a name? Of course it's still a problem! How much extra tutoring would she wind up getting? Maybe she'd ask for a hint at what an exam question might look like, in bed—or, god knows, in what other context. But even pushing aside all these not inconsiderable ethical considerations, how do I know she'd be willing? In fact, I'm very far from knowing anything of the sort. I could wait for more encouraging evidence, but maybe she thinks that she's done all the signalling and 'winking' that she prudently can. And, naturally, a gal has some pride too. So we could be endlessly waiting for each other.

"On the other hand, think how crushing it would be if I 'made a move' and she wasn't receptive . 'No, that's not what I meant, not what I meant at all.' Isn't that a line from T.S. Eliot's 'The Love Song of J. Alfred Prufrock'? (Some poem for an undergraduate, even a Harvard one, to have written, eh!!) I know essentially nothing about her. What if there were an unsuccessful gesture, a rebuffed overture, on my part? Would she keep her mouth shut and just let the rejection stay impaled in my heart? Or would all her class mates, as well as certain select faculty members, in other words just about everybody in the god—damn school, know that Professor Steen had lusted futilely, maladroitly, after Jenny Hauser? (Which would I mind more—that they knew that I'd lusted or that my lust went unfulfilled?) And what if I lusted to satisfaction? A young woman might be even more inclined to share that news, including perhaps full reports on the most graphic details of the expressive, (imaginative?) forms my lust took.

"But let's forget about all the practical details. What about the nature of the 'relationship' with her- if there were one? What does she have to offer beyond the physical? At the least, she's very young. Accepting that that's the main reason for her seeming inability to converse at all stimulatingly, her glaring lack of sophistication, and so forth, the brute fact is she certainly didn't give any hint that she's a fount of fascinating trivial gab, or anything else, in our little encounter in my office. Besides bed and meals what would we do together? Try to get her to understand Contracts, Property, Torts on the most rudimentary basis? Go to rock concerts? I very strongly suspect that Brahms is a name with which she's not familiar.

"And that kind of relationship, even if it turned out great physically, (by no means a sure thing—do I still remember what to do and how to do it?—does she have any idea that older guys aren't young guys?) might it not, ultimately, deepen depression rather than generate unalloyed joy? But why discount the thrill of the physical so much? It's quite a lot of joy to make love satisfyingly, maybe even exultantly, ecstatically. Love? That's just a figure of speech. Why not good sex for what it's worth? Tingling nerve endings aren't bad you know.

"But, if, from the very start, you know that's all it can be, that it hasn't even the slightest possibility to become an otherwise stimulating or enriching experience, then, when the inevitable disenchantment seeps in and corrodes it all, it's piercingly depressing. It's not that all of a sudden something has gone wrong. There always was something fundamentally wrong and you knew it was just a matter of time until the underlying problem would take its toll. A bit like ignoring a red warning light on the dashboard of your car; you know it's only a sheer matter of time until the problem it's signalling will erupt into being full blown and probably make the car undrivable.

"She sure is fuckable, as we adolescents used to love to say. But it turns out that's not enough for we considerably post—adolescents. That's life, as they say. She's undeniably ignited my interest but frustration seems to inevitably lie at road's end. Maybe I can damp down the depressing aspects of this scenario by telling myself that I'm just keeping things on hold. Maybe Ms. Hauser will show further interest—maybe she'll drop by again. And maybe with more contact she'll display more and more interesting aspects than she's had a chance, or been inclined, to show so far. One can hope can't one? One better keep on hoping, shouldn't one?

"Nevertheless, there'd still be all the practical problems of an amorous relationship with a student …

"Words seem to become frail and spastic when they can't articulate precisely. When they can say something like 'The book lying on the cushion of the chair which is in that corner has a grey binding' they are confident and potent in conveying just about anything, and everything, their user wants. But when they're deployed to make assertions like 'The tax legislation Congress enacted last year is unjust because … ' they become much less trenchant, more halting and, finally, inconclusive. In those ways in which words can speak with exactitude they can, in fact, be made exact by careful tailoring and polishing. It just takes determination to get them to be more precise. However, in more speculative realms, for example aesthetics or ethics, where agreement or consensus is much harder to come by, the words used, no matter how elegant, deft, gracious or cogent fail to clinch. While just about everyone might agree that the slateof the blackboard is black, there'd likely be much sharper difference s of opinion on whether it is desirable to discipline children more frequently and intensely rather than less so. 'Discipline,' 'intensely,' 'more,' and 'less' are all rather weak, willowy reeds in constructing an airtight argument ion such an issue. Such words wobble and stumble as they try to get their user from here to there. In such situations we feel that words are not completely within our control, not reliably responsive to the touch of our needs and purposes. In short, they can't achieve *exactly* what we want. Nevertheless, that's not to say that we won't continue to use them to try to do what they can't. They remain instruments, imperfect as they may be, in moving us toward our goal(s.) And it's also not to say that even though a particular point or proposition remains generally 'unprovable,' that certain congeries of words aren't more effective than other combinations in helping word users to desired destinations. And we must continue to try to persuade and convince in areas where we can't prove and demonstrate irrefutably because those are the very areas crucial in trying to live life with dignity, decently and, perhaps even, with nobility.

"I feel like I need to listen to some great music before I hit bed—how about Schumann's First Symphony, the "Spring Symphony,'—a good antidote to November."

CHAPTER NINE

MARTIN DIDN'T EXPERIENCE A panicky sensation, nothing in that neighborhood even, when groping in his mail box he found the message to call Dean Weymouth. But he did allow himself a slight tinge of uneasiness. After all, he didn't anticipate that the Dean would have anything heartening or even mildly stimulating to say to him. He and Weymouth while perfectly polite and cordial to each other simply didn't have much in common. There just weren't many points of intersection. The Dean respected Martin for doing a good job in the classroom and keeping up a more or less steady stream of very solid, if not wildly brilliant publications, while Martin respected Weymouth for being a deft diplomatic administrator who kept the ship chugging ahead on course with a minimal amount of mishaps or dysfunctions. When a problem did develop Weymouth pounced on it pretty immediately and almost always was able to work out an expeditious and fair solution which brought the ship back to an even keel.

When Martin called the Dean's secretary, the always cheerful and genuinely helpful Marsha Waters, she told him to come right up if he liked since the Dean was in his office and not being assailed by even a single faculty or staff member, or any other complainer, whiner or petitioner. So, within ten minutes of finding the message, Martin was seated opposite Weymouth's massive wooden desk. That's the way

Martin liked it. He was obsessive about dealing with messages from on high as quickly as he could. He reasoned that if something was on your boss's mind he might as well find out what it was, take care of it as soon and as effectively as possible and 'get it behind' you, as the politicians had become so fond of saying.

Martin hadn't been able to settle into one of the comfortably cushioned winged chairs before the Dean had bustled out from behind that formidable wooden structure , (no contemporary steel or glass for this traditional type commander,) and grabbed Martin's hand, pumping it enthusiastically as he assured Martin that it was such a pleasure to have the chance to talk with him. Once they were both back in seats Weymouth didn't easily let go of this theme.

"Yes Martin, you know we just don't seem to run into each other too much, where we can just shoot the bull, or whatever. It seems I'm always involved with some detail or picayune point, of one sort or another. I don't often get the chance to just gab with a faulty member, you know as a person, instead of someone who teaches Trusts or wants to teach Anti—Trust, etcetera. I mean you are people, human beings too, aren't you?" Weymouth smiled broadly and twinkled his eyes to un -mistakably indicate that this last comment was meant humorously. He'd found, over time, that it was imperative to signal when humor was intended as not every faculty member had a sense of it. There were some extremely solemn, earnest, grim, even dour, law professors.

"Oh, I think at least some of us are, Dean, but I myself wouldn't get hyperbolic about the exact numbers, "Martin deadpanned. Weymouth compelled himself to chuckle much more heartily than Martin's remark warranted.

"Speaking of talking about civilized human being things, in contradistinction to law professor issues, have you had a chance to look over this season's symphony schedule? One or two things caught my eye."

Once Weymouth had somehow found out that Martin was passionate about classical music he'd indicated to Martin that he, too, was a devotee who made it a point to attend at least several Chicago Symphony Orchestra concerts, as well as various recitals by distinguished soloists, each year. Martin didn't doubt that he did go to a fair number of concerts a year, but Martin had never been convinced that the motive was music. It seemed that the Symphony performances were one of those Chicago things that had to be attended with a certain degree of frequency by the right people if they were to retain their right people status. Nevertheless, because he was a competent individual, someone who very much wanted to be thought competent regarding anything with which he dealt, Weymouth, irrespective of what his actual depth of knowledge or artistic appreciation might be, could maintain a fairly fluent, reasonably sophisticated sounding conversation about classical music and its leading performers. It had become a topic which Martin and the Dean could use as a sort of social lubricant for whatever business conversations unavoidable circumstances compelled them to have.

"Enough to keep us busy, I guess. Not a schedule to take your breath away but, as you say, some things look tantalizing. I saw that Claudio Abbado will be conducting for a few weeks. He always seems to muster a thrilling performance out of the orchestra; hardly matters what they're doing. And I saw that they'll even be doing the 'Eroica' with him."

"Oh yes, I noticed that particularly too. Better order my tickets promptly. Certainly can't afford to miss Abbado doing Beethoven with the CSO. Triple blockbuster!! And did you catch that later in the season Maurizio Pollini will be the soloist in the Schoenberg Concerto?"

This, Martin thought, was just perfect Weymouth. Picking out an esoteric and, for most classical music fans, a difficult twentieth century work, just to let you know that he was up-to-the-minute, au courant to the max, and not rigidly stuck in the familiar melodies of Mozart, Beethoven and Brahms. Martin speculated to himself that Weymouth had never actually heard the Schoenberg Piano Concerto, with Pollini or anybody else for that matter, but felt like he should act like he had, or, at least, as if he wanted to, desperately.

"Yup, Pollini's a real champion of Schoenberg. I'm pretty sure that some time ago, I saw in Rose Records, right downstairs, on Wabash Avenue, that he has a three or four CD set of Schoenberg's complete piano music. Not that I can afford to buy it, you understand, on what you pay me."

Weymouth allowed a tight smile that betrayed effort at the seams. "Well, Martin, speaking of me paying you ,I suppose that, pleasant as our musical discussions always are, really refreshing for me, we do need to get down to some business."

"I'm all ears if I have to be. But would my ears rather be hearing Abbado?"

Weymouth, in deadly serious mode now, not far from dismissiveness, just let that one pass. "Let me simply tell you, Martin, what's been going on and then you can tell me what you think. Mind you, I'm not taking any position here or putting on any pressure. I'm just going to pass along some things and then you can give me your version."

This doesn't sound promising, Martin mused. Experience has shown that once he says he's not putting any pressure on you immediately start to feel the pressure. What was it that novelist Gore Vidal said about President Nixon's "I am not a crook," asservation: if you'd ever had the slightest doubt about whether Nixon was a crook that much too much protest dissipated it instantly.

"Shoot, Fred—what crime have I committed?"

"No, no. No crimes ... But this is something that's just evolved over the last two or three weeks. Several students, I don't remember the exact number, three or four, maybe five, but you've got to be mindful of the fact that that means there are probably more, maybe quite a few more, who feel the same way ... Well, anyway, these students have taken the trouble to make specific appointments with me , once they were told, in no uncertain terms, that they just couldn't barge in here at the very moment the spirit moved them, to excitedly press a particular point on me. Now I think a fair summation of what they all said, in one form or another, and I don't need to remind you that some of our students are not paragons of articulateness and precision of speech, is that you intrude too much of your personal politics into your Contracts class. Oh, by the way, and no surprise, they all pretty much acknowledge that you're a fine teacher of Contract law—no complaints there—they just wish you'd stick to that, since that's what *they're* here for, and go easy, or at least easier, on the politics."

Martin couldn't help noting that Weymouth, in administrator-by-the-book fashion, had indicated that the students were quite forceful on what was bad; viz., the "politics," but had soft—pedaled whatever praise they may have doled out. For the good he used phrases like "fine" and "pretty much acknowledge," instead of modifiers in the "very good" or "excellent" vein. Martin, who over the years had finally learned to be more patient, instead of keen on immediately responding to anything anyone said, waited as Weymouth casually tented his hands to support his chin. Sure enough, the Dean filled the pause himself.

"That's really the gist of what they had to say. Too much politics, they felt. They'd rather have your skills spending more time on imparting Contract law."

Martin had also come to learn that he could ask questions which, in his younger days, he might have censored as excessively "pushy."

"So, Dean, I guess a question that naturally comes to mind is what did you say to them?" Martin supposed that he could have gotten even more aggressive by asking exactly who the complaining students were. But he was pretty sure, that for obvious reasons, Weymouth would have refused to disclose that information. So, pushing that way would only have resulted in Martin holding the bad—form bag. Besides, he didn't really care who they were. He'd heard this one before. More than once or twice, as a matter of fact. There were always some who felt that way. Who knows, maybe many. Martin's attitude pedagogically, (and perhaps politically, too,) had always been that it was their problem. And decidedly not, in any significant way, his.

"As you can well imagine, Martin, I just basically listened. Took no sides, made no judgments, of course. I said I understood what they were saying and that I would pass along their feelings to you. As I've just done."

Now, Martin could clearly sense, Weymouth would wait for Martin to say something, evince some reaction.

"That sounds pretty good to me just like that, Dean. I'd be happy to leave it right there. But I'm feeling that you want something more specific from me."

"Well, yes, I would be grateful ..."

"Let me give you an unvarnished reaction, Dean, right up front. Then maybe, if you want, we could go into this whole thing in a little more detail and depth. My instinctive, initial and very strong feeling is that it's exactly the kids who come in here complaining about my so—called political intrusions who are the ones who most need to hear something beyond A wins this case because the rule is ... Or B wins that case under Regulation 235, etcetera, etcetera. My god, don't they get enough of the conventional stuff to last them twenty—

seven professional lifetimes! You'd think they'd welcome an alternative perspective, almost *any* departure from the usual pap."

Weymouth's features had tightened from the more relaxed state they'd assumed when pleasantries about music were being exchanged. It's wasn't that he'd become palpably tense or aggressive but, at the very least, he'd morphed into a decanally serious mien. "But, Martin, apparently some of them don't."

"O.K., Fred, to drill a little deeper vein, I'd suggest that some of what they're objecting to isn't really much of a departure from what they say they want—it's just different. Legal reasoning, as its called, or analysis according to legal rules and doctrines *is* ideology—it basically pushes a rather narrow political point of view. But it's a conventional, societally endorsed one. What they so contemptuously call my political intrusions is just a critique of this conventional, dominant system. It's counter—politics to the reigning political wisdom. Of course, I like to think of it as speaking truth to power, but I'll acknowledge that that's neither much here or there. You know, everything is politics in the sense of affecting what happens in human experience. But the complainers seem only comfortable with political expressions that support the staus quo and they fiercely resist any changes to it. Almost as if it threatened "their way of life," Dean. I suggest that the stutus quo is far from perfect and in need of improvement, perhaps even thoroughgoing transformation, and this is the core of their grievance. My very strong suspicion is that in the vast preponderance of their classes, and I do mean *vast* preponderance, they get exactly what they want. But they want that stuff to wash over them, unvaryingly, soothingly, ubiquitously, do I dare say cloyingly. For God's sake, can't they open their alleged minds to the slightest smidgen of a competing viewpoint?"

"I'm not entitled to ask this, strictly speaking," Weymouth broke in, "academic freedom and all that, although some think it's more freedom or free reign for academics, but if you'd be willing to let me in on it, I confess tremendous curiosity as to the kinds of things which you do say, what exactly it is that evokes their so strenuous objections."

It immediately flashed through Martin's mind that surely the objecting students had provided the Dean with ample examples of Martin's purported delinquencies or aberrations. But he supposed that the Dean wanted to hear from the horse's mouth, just what Martin thought he was doing or accomplishing.

"Not at all Dean. I've got no problem, whatsoever, with giving you a graphic example of the kind of thing I'm pretty sure they're stressed by."

It did occur to him to ask Weymouth what the students had told him that Martin said, but he was pretty sure he'd get only the vaguest generalities in response. Anyway, Martin now felt himself working up some fervor and eagerness to wrestle with his adversaries. He was going into advocate gear, intent on convincing his boss just how narrow—minded, incurious and anti—intellectual that considerable cohort of his most unimaginative students were.

"O. k," Martin spit out, warming to the task, as they say. "In one of the cases we read, a Dayton, Ohio department store runs an ad in the local newspaper, it's in 1940, saying that they have one hundred seventy—five dollar sewing machines on sale for twenty—six dollars. Now, when the plaintiff shows up with his twenty—six dollars, and, by the way, there's evidence that he was one of the very first customers in the store on the day in question, the store refuses to sell him the twenty—six dollar machine. In the opinion there's a suggestion that high—pressure tactics were brought to bear to get him to buy a much more expensive machine, instead. The 'legal' question, as you would guess, Dean, is whether the ad 'offers' to sell the sewing machine for twenty—six dollars so that when the customer shows up proffering that amount he's 'accepted' the store's offer and thus concluded a binding contract between himself and the store for the twenty—six dollar machine. The court, however, says that this was not the story, because they deemed an advertisement in a newspaper not a legally binding offer, but, merely, a solicitation to receive offers from customers which the store, itself, is then free to accept or reject as it wishes. How convenient for business!! A totally objective decision?—I don't think so Dean! In any event, that's what students of the type we're talking about ..."

"I don't know that there's any particular type of student that we're talking ..."

"Then just let me say that there a lot of students who are *extremely* content to stop right there. Now they've got a rule which declares that an advertisement in a newspaper to sell something isn't a legal 'offer' to sell it. But then I simply ask some questions: what if the store never intended to let any customer have one of the advertised sewing machines for twenty—six dollars? Suppose they deliberately, calculatingly and with malice aforethought, so to speak,, ran the ad knowing it would bring many people into the store who otherwise wouldn't have come in, but knowing, all the time, that they would actually let no one have a machine for twenty—six dollars, but, rather, would try to convince anyone who asked about the advertised bargain to purchase a much more expensive machine, an almost two hundred dollar one. Then I ask why, *under such circumstances*, as per my hypothesized facts, should a court not hold that the ad is, indeed, a legally binding offer which the plaintiff in fact accepted by showing up with the twenty-six dollars she was willing to pay for the advertised machine. And I suggest that this type of decision by a court would be very welcome and re-assuring to businesses trying to maliciously bait and switch customers in such a totally manipulative way. Those are the kind of notions I throw out regarding a case like that. Pretty wicked, huh? Verging on the grossly irresponsible?"

"No, I can't say that there's anything ..."

"Oh, wait a second," Martin burst in, still in his agitated advocacy mode, intent on unmasking the students' qualms as fairly ridiculous petty ones. "I also say, if I remember to, that the fact that the case was decided in Ohio in 1940, probably also had something to do with the decision, which I characterize as nakedly pro—business, anti—consumer; the court supinely permitting department store managers to do whatever they think maximizes bottom line profits. Then I call their attention to a case in the book, which comes right after the 1940 Ohio one. It came up twenty years later, and in a jurisdiction, I can't recall exactly which one now, generally thought of as much more liberal than Ohio and the court found that a department store newspaper advertisement was, indeed, a legally binding offer. I emphasize to them that the time, place and who the judge or judges may be are all important factors going into the mix of a final decision. Twenty years later the socio—political environment was much more hospitable to consumer interests and much more receptive to imposing certain restraints on business activities .I suggest that a court could really go either way on whether a department store newspaper advertisement is an offer of legal consequence and that what truly underlies a decision, one way or another, are values that don't necessarily neatly fit into the doctrinal categories of traditional legal analysis. The ones which courts almost always try to convince readers of their decisions they are in fact using to reach their conclusions. Yes, Fred, I say all of those things, if I remember them all, and I very much do believe them. In fact, I think that teaching young law students without at least bringing such considerations into their consciousness is short—change teaching. But that's just my opinion. But it is my professional opinion—and I think I'm entitled to act on it."

"Oh, I don't think anyone is raising or contesting any issue about what you're entitled to do in the classroom," Weymouth said rather softly."It's just a matter of getting things as harmonious as possible between teacher and students. Iron out any problems or rough spots. Facilitate learning as much as possible. My job, you know."

The Dean unleashed a smile, but one not nearly as broad as he'd projected during the musical palaver. His eyes were hooded. "The students are the paying customers, of course." Martin felt he was almost on the verge of adding "In a school like this."

But Weymouth went on, "In a law school the customer's not always right. But on the other hand there's no need to antagonize, if it can be avoided …"

"Maybe it can't be avoided," Martin bit off, with some force.

But Weymouth didn't ruffle. "Most of the time I think it can; just a word here and there to people of good will. But that's all I really have at my disposal, some reasonable words. But I can't coerce; nor do I want to. And, it seems to me, that there's no need to—even if it were possible. Yes, Martin, the kind of thing you've just told me about is, naturally, well within standard law professor discretion and pedagogical technique. Certainly, at least, at the better schools, ones such as you and I attended, if it's not, necessarily, the dominant norm at many of the others."

On previous occasions Martin had noticed the Dean's deftness at somehow seeming to reflect, almost echo, the position of the person to whom he was speaking. Or, at least, finding something in common with that person. And that was even when Weymouth was actually taking a position contrary to the other person or essentially being critical of him or her.

Weymouth continued, "So, I think the great majority of these student—teacher conflicts, so—called, are highly amenable to reconciliation, harmonization, call it what you will, by a little good faith and effort to understand from each side."

Martin was now getting caressed out of whatever aggressiveness he'd been able to summon by Weymouth's tenacious, yet honeyed, insistence that the basically insoluble could be solved—or at least made to vanish from the Dean's problem basket. "Frankly, Fred, I don't think I'm having any trouble understanding where the objecting students are coming from, as they themselves would be likely to put it. Like I mean that's how like they would probably say it. I just don't agree with them that legal education should consist of the delivery of a series of cut and dried rules which are always certain to yield an easily discernible pre—determined and pre-determinable result. I think they're sorely in need of being disabused of that notion, not re-inforced in it. I guess I strongly feel that I'm doing a pretty good job the way I'm doing it and I'd like to keep going that way …"

"And no one's saying you can't, " Weymouth said steadily, while sneaking a not completely furtive glance at his watch to indicate that he'd spent enough time on his pitch and that he didn't think that going on would bring Martin to a place other than where he was right now. "I suppose I would merely counsel a little sympathy on your part for the students' point of view. Maybe you could just accommodate that, somehow, to some degree, so that they feel you are being responsive and that you're not just riding roughshod over them."

Martin appreciated that the Dean was now, almost desperately, searching for some common ground with Martin so that he could feel that they'd come to some "agreement" on, a "resolution" of the problem. Perhaps he even needed to report something like that back to some of the complaining students. Martin himself wasn't averse to coming to this type of nebulous understanding. He'd noticed that the older he became the more he was inclined to stress areas of accord rather than discord. He tended to recognize, also, that while you might need to do what was integral to your significant purposes, to your overall perspective, and, so, was not really available for compromise, there was no need to be self—righteous or dramatically and adamantly unyielding about it.

"Maybe I could very directly and concretely explain why I do call their attention to factors which I emphasize as usually unacknowledged but very real influences on case outcomes. I could try to clearly communicate how those things are intensely practical at the same time they might be considered merely critical or ideological. Try to make them see that in a very real, hard—headed way that they are often crucial elements in determining just why a case comes out as it does. I could try to get them to see why listening to my diatribes might actually help them become better craftspeople, more effective practicing lawyers."

"Something like that sounds fine, Martin," Weymouth moderately enthused. "I'm sure that once you brought them into things that way they'd be more than willing to meet you half—way, at least."

As Martin got up to leave he realized, yet again, that deans characteristically didn't care so much about whether people for whom they were administratively responsible disagreed or were antagonistic—so long as it seemed there wasn't too much dissidence causing unacceptable levels of static. Machiavelli's tenchant observation came to mind: "It is not so much how things are that is important but, rather, how they seem to be."

"November_____

"Now what the hell am I supposed to do—spend hours and hours parsing his words and intricately trying to figure out what Weymouth was *really* saying to me? Was he actually warning me to damp down the 'political' analysis and rhetoric , or was he just going through motions which he had to go through to satisfy and abate student pressures on him? I'm sure not especially perceptive at doping these things out. Frankly, it probably doesn't matter too much as to what he was *really* saying and doing since an obdurate son of a bitch like myself isn't going to change what I'm doing. Or not much, anyway. But a teacher does like to know just how ferocious the opposition is—whether sticking to one's intellectual guns will provoke unpleasant confrontation, or just result, as per usual, in playing itself out, without too much more attention, from anyone, to it.

"This, amongst many other things, makes one understand that there are times when precision is not really wanted. Perhaps, indeed, almost the opposite—ambiguity. For instance, a negotiation situation in which the parties were, at the outset, significantly at odds on certain points, but which gradually evolved so that solid agreement has been reached on most of them—in fact on the most salient of them. The parties want very much to proceed as though a complete agreement has occurred so that fruitful action, execution, can begin. In such circumstances the negotiators may refer to the unsettled point(s) in vague, imprecise terms so as to conceal any real substantive differences which persist. They might use language which cloak(s) the issue(s) in the cloudy possibility of consensus, minimizing friction points, so that dis-agreement is de—emphasized rather than highlighted. Lack of rigorous precision here facilitates continuity and, ultimately, mutually beneficial action; (implementation of the "agreement.") Linguistic haziness allows life to proceed productively, whereas sharp, crystal clear articulation of differences might barricade progress. Might cause 'To the barricades.'

"Occasionally, unfortunately, words perform other than as intended. Sometimes with disastrous consequences. (As distinguished from words having been intentionally employed to produce unruly results, or to say things from which unsettling consequences could have been reasonably forseen as possible or likely.) Context, again, may be deeply implicated in instances of serious verbal misfiring. Words which themselves are characteristically neutral, surely not typically barbed might be interpreted as offensive and searing if the auditor or reader is, e.g., feeling especially sensitive or vulnerable when exposed to them. Maybe someone says, "Oh, I'm really bad at mathematics" and a listener responds with "Oh, I know," meaning only that the listener, too, is math challenged and, therefore, knows exactly what the speaker means. The original speaker may, depending on mood, (mis)inflection of response, etc., feel this as unduly enthusiastic agreement with what may have been intended not so much as an authentic statement of self—deprecation as one of self—effacement or reaching out for re-assurance. So the original speaker might feel stung that her listener did not suggest that she is really adequate at math and thus, possibly, retort, "Oh, actually, I'm not that bad, I get by." If the conversation continues in a manner of assertion, denial, counter—assertion and so forth a friendship might be strained or, even, ruptured, at least temporarily. All from innocent words.

"That words aren't always exclusively pleasure-giving is also demonstrated when they're instruments by which unpleasant moments in the past are re—experienced—with renewed, even increased, pain. Additionally, sometimes when we recall a scene acutely embarrassing or hurtful to us we conjure alternative words we could have used to have made the recollected experience better or , at least, to have mollified the disturbing character of what actually did occur. When we do think of superior words then they become instruments of laceration and the ones actually used, at the time of the incident, flog us again, in comparison to these preferable ones which might have completely taken the sting out of the fiasco or near fiasco. As the word(s) we should have said is (are) so much better than what we did say so is our injury multiplied. Thus(better) words punish. They actually hurt anew, and perhaps more painfully to boot.

"As for the concerns of Weymouth, let's face it, my 'political' rhetoric, stance, observations whatever one calls it, is not negotiable. It's only by critiquing the system as it is, by pointing out how it should be changed to be less exploitative of, and fairer to, the have—nots, that I feel at all good about what I'm doing. Take this away and I'm just training the enemy in skills and techniques which they can apply to combating and eviscerating the ideals and values in which I really believe.

"Another way to try to redeem the universe, oppose all the ugliness and hatefulness, is by reminding others of the redemptive aspects of the world that does exist. Where there is integrity, inspiration, decency, kindness, compassion point it out, highlight it, so that it may be inspiration, solace, motivation, happiness, instigation for others. Where there is great art or magnificent artistry which perfectly portrays the human condition powerfully , that salves it, speaks against the flagrant injustices that ravage it, with forcefulness, vigor and indomitability, always celebrate and glorify it so that others can maintain hope and resolution. That's why I love to clip out examples, reports, squibs, what have you, from newspapers, magazines, any ephemera, and send them off to friends, even just acquaintances. I hope such things ignite them, fortify them, make them want to go on in aspiration and with respect and admiration for those who, in one fashion or another, have fought to mend, i.e. to re—create the world. Yes, from the Hebrew heritage of "tikkun, " to repair the world. Of course we'll all fail , but that sobriety provides us not the slightest dispensation to not try to struggle and assist as much as energies and realities allow.

"Beautiful words are the humanities; philosophy, speculation about human nature, theories of society, literature and history which reveal ourselves to ourselves. Science's language has to be much more exact. It tries to describe at least some of what actually is with utter precision and accuracy. Ideally with total fidelity. To be impelled toward both Science and the Humanities is to be somewhat torn between two fundamentally contrasting approaches. An apercu of a poem is in large part a meaning—less, (or non—meaning) statement for an 'objective' minded scientist . A noxious character ruled by tremendous greed, created by a playwright, does not inform a scientist how to fashion a more appealing psyche for such a fanatically gripped, tormented individual. However, while science with its great precision and powerful constructs can repair and cure physical hearts it does not have much to tell about how to avoid or remedy the broken hearts so often produced by the vagaries of the human condition. To be drawn to both science and the humanities is to verge toward a split, conflicted, divided, torn personality. In ART AS EXPERIENCE John Dewey wrote: 'Science states meanings; art expresses them.' (Despite his sometimes tremendously convoluted style, Dewey was also a master of stoking a tremendous amount of powerful, suggestive material into a single sentence.) Art can evoke deep emotions and heartfelt responses. But it can't categorize, rationalize and systematize those responses into a coherent methodology of investigation and discovery.

"Unfortunately, the power of words is diluted by the fact that they compellingly appeal to relatively few. There's a scarcity of souls for whom they are crucial. Most people use words quite loosely and respond to them only sluggishly. An approximately accurate word, (even one pretty far off the real mark,) instead of a precisely hit-the-nail-on-the head one is a ho—hum matter to many. Most individuals are not affected by words so intensely that they dwell on the cognitive, or, perhaps more important, the emotive meanings of single words, phrases, sentences. The vast majority of people are not poets or poetic in their responses and reactions to words. This piles higher the difficulties words face in their mission of transforming the world. They, once again, are forced to operate in the face of insensibility. This is not because people are morally faulty; it is just how they and the world are built.

"Another issue is that too often the crafter of words is much more taken with what she has written , the language she has shaped and manipulated, than are most of those who will come to read her words. Those ardent about words tend to fall in love with the ones they've worked into an extended exposition or project, to believe that the final product is important, powerful, perhaps even 'moving.' But the emotion may be more, or only, in the author rather than in the reader. The writer loves words, in general, so much and her own, in particular, so intensely that she is loathe to recognize that they may not create the intended impact on those who come to read them.

"Science seems more potent than the humanities because the knowledge it can, literally, discover seems unending, infinite. There is always another interaction of different molecules to be described and analyzed. Contrastingly, it feels like the Humanities already know all they can and are now confined to presenting and displaying, in a fresh format, what they have already, usually long ago, discovered , dertermined and voiced. In a way they are merely a continual re—hash of their past achievements. Science, however, can continue describing fresh concrete facts about the universe today, at this very moment, and at sub—microscopic levels. It continues to reveal truths about ions, processes, phenomena and sometimes the application of the knowledge thereby gained, to actual human affairs, is exceedingly impressive—e.g. when a new drug therapy for a devastating disease which has plagued mankind for millennia is discovered. Work in Science is intricate, intense, intelligent, informative, intentional, (O.K. that's deliberately alliterative,) in the sense of highly purposeful. Occasionally it's markedly inspirational. It gives us the sense that we can grasp and somewhat control the physical environment which surrounds us, sometimes seems to overwhelm us. Banting and Best discovering insulin—giving life, rather than death, to millions. Extraordinary!! Magnificent!! If we are not masters of the universe, nevertheless we possess some means by which we might master it. While metaphysicians, humanists and other speculators can only argue, with no definitive conclusion possible, about, so to speak, how many angels might be able to dance on the head of a pin, scientists can inform us, with ever growing methodological security, as to exactly how many billions of microbes, of exactly what specific composition, fit on a given pin. This infuses science, as well as our confidence in it, with a great sense of muscularity and control. At just about the middle of the nineteenth century that great English Romantic, Alfred Lord Tennyson, wrote 'Knowledge grows from more to more.' Science still merits that judgment—except even more so.

A fundamental problem for those who love to play with and write words is that sometimes the desire to fashion, shape, caress them is there, but substance, exactly what to say with the words one is impelled to palpate is wanting, absent. The sheer love of language inspires the impulse to employ it, but the prospective writer or speaker doesn't always have something reasonable to articulate with the words. This syndrome can lead to weak statements, indolent formulations, muddled points.

"But what one can always hold on to is unswerving belief in the worthiness of certain ideals. Futility of attainment needn't douse indomitable fervor. Defeat after defeat, in the realm of the practical, in no way validates or permits abandonment of the shining merit of the ideal. The justice of it stands proudly and vigorously so long as our passion continues to fuel it. We can go on believing that we are unquestioningly, unquenchably and eternally right, regardless of how real—world ineffective we and/or our cohorts are. The ideals are perpetual treasures , ours to always have, retain and cultivate irrespective of practica triumphs orl successes . No defeat is final if we maintain inspiration and determination. What is it that Churchill said? "In victory magnanimity, in defeat defiance." No matter how discouraged and rebuffed we may come to feel the transcendent jewels of our fundamental, deeply cherished beliefs shall gleam for us forever.

"Now I have to face the reality that the students who run to the Dean and complain about what I'm doing in the classroom, how I'm teaching, how I'm assailing and sullying their pure capitalist ears with sacrilege, are almost surely lost causes .Lost souls? They don't want to hear it at all, and if they are forced to hear it they're going to try mightily to just shut it out completely and not give any possible credence to anything that might somehow seep through. But I always have to remember that it's for the others—for the ones whose minds are still open enough to be affected by what a teacher sincerely says, by what he dedicatedly tries to show them. By what he teaches.

"Hey, you know, (whoever 'you' might be,) I'm entitled to talk this over with a simpatico soul, right? Why shouldn't I call up Mary Hanks and ask her what she thinks Weymouth was really saying, what he was intimating. Threatening? From what I pick up around the corridors, and from my own intuition, it seems that she also, at least to some extent, is a teacher who occasionally criticizes the what is instead of just pointing out that the is indeed is, with the expectation that one and all will be immensely pleased and gratified by her reveling in the warm bath of the status quo. So maybe she'd be interested in my little tete a tete with the Dean and just what it might signify in terms of pressure for the 'unconventional' teachers. After all, she's *got* to be thinking about tenure and how to ensure that fifty per cent plus one, at least, of the faculty come to believe that she deserves it. Q.E.D. And who knows, through her presumed interest in this professional topic maybe I could even inspire some non—professional interest by her in me. I would greatly like to stroke those supremely shapely, nylon sheathed legs.

CHAPTER TEN

MARTIN WAS FEELING PLEASED with himself. It had taken him only a single day to gird his resolve to call Mary Hanks, Assistant Professor of Law. He'd been on the lookout for her when he was at the law school earlier today. But he hadn't run into her, nor had she been in her office the two times he'd rapped at her door. It's probably better this way, he thought, as he went to the phone to dial her home number, which he'd already memorized since he'd been mulling over calling her so much. It could be awkward to gab about sensitive school matters right on the premises. Someone whom you really didn't want to overhear the conversation might just wander by. Worse, someone like that might actually try to intrude him or herself into the "business" conversation. Martin fervently didn't want that. He wanted this to be as private a conversation as possible between Mary and himself. So the telephone was really the best way to do it. That method also had the fringe benefit that he wouldn't have to concentrate on making sure that it didn't seem as though he were staring at her, or "looking her over," or anything that flagrantly in the man—woman vein. He usually tried not to do that sort of thing, which so many men seemed to do almost automatically when speaking to an obviously attractive woman. But how did he know that he was always, or ever, successful. Perhaps he was perceived as leering anyway. A leering "older" man.

He definitely hoped that she was home this evening. His resolve up he would hate to have to fortify it, maybe several times, through busy signals or, worse still, no answers. That might even entail the effort to carry the resolve over until the following day.

However, the phone rang only twice before she said a crisp, but not unfriendly, "Hell-o."

"Hi, Mary, this is Martin Steen, you know from school." Immediately he thought, and felt, how absurd he sounded. She very well knew who he was. Why did he, like a bumbling fool, a totally insecure adolescent boy, provide the superfluous "from school" identification.

"Oh, hi Martin, how are you?"

She sounded surprised, but not blatantly displeased or nonplussed.

"I'm not any worse than usual. How are you doing?"

"Masterfully evasive lawyer—speak, Martin. 'No worse than usual' could run the gamut from fantastically superb to abysmally horrible."

"You caught on to that right away, didn't you." At least she had a response. Most people on whom he tried that shtick chuckled nervously or non—commitally, at best, and a fair share got concerned looking and serious sounding and inquired whether there was anything wrong or something bothering him."

"Actually it's neither one of those states, but I'm O.K."

"Good, that's re-assuring."

She was playful, wasn't she, Martin registered.

"I'm grateful for your feeling re-assured over how I'm feeling. But now that we've established how momentously important just how I'm feeling is I bet you're wondering why I'm calling."

"Well, I'm not yet at the edge of my chair with curiosity, but I guess I'm sliding towards it."

Martin started musing as to whether this meant that she was growing impatient, that she really was not wanting to continue talking and was starting to wish that he'd get on, and over, with whatever it was that had prompted his call. But immediately, as though with a new—born burst of energy and self—confidence, he demanded that he drop such defensive, negative, absolutely self—defeating thinking. What the hell did he have to lose here, anyway. He was just talking to a colleague. So what if she was also an attractive, very attractive, woman.

For God's sake! Why not try acting normal for once instead of so damn contemplative!

"Since you demand that I instantly get to the point rather than prolong our pleasantly aimless chatter …"

"I wasn't trashing the pleasantly aimless chatter by any means," she broke in.

'Well, that's good, I'm glad to hear it. Pleasant can frequently be in short supply. But, to tarry no longer, I was summoned for a conversation with the Dean yesterday and I thought you might have some slight interest in being filled—in about it, since I've heard, in the corridors and elsewhere, that you, too, are someone who, in your classes, occasionally slings an arrow or two of criticism towards our revered legal system ."

"That may well be the case. But I sincerely hope that I haven't grown so timorous in my advancing age to the point where I confine it to just one or two criticisms. If that's true I'll have to make a very concerted effort to up the ante."

"Mary, go easy on the advancing age stuff. If a vital young person such as yourself, barely in your mid—thirties—which of course I know only because I saw your resume when you interviewed here, you certainly don't look it—can be considered as advancing in age, using your words, then no amount of diligent dictionary scouring can possibly come up with a sufficiently gentle euphemism to denote a doddering codger like me."

"You should *not* advertise. I hadn't noticed, at all, that you were in that category."

"That's good. Lincoln would be pleased—at least you can still fool some of the people some of the time."

"So that's all I am to you—just one of the crowd? … Oh, what the hell, if no one notices that you're in a category then maybe you're not in it. Why not look at it that way. Surely some philosopher has written an excessively learned treatise entitling you to look at it that way."

She really was adept at verbal play, Martin thought. And he very much liked the ever so slightly flirtatious, "So that's all I am to you— just one of the crowd?" He still hadn't gotten to the purpose for the call. But, he calculated, why not persist in the banter. He enjoyed that sort of thing, got much too little of it with his relatively cloistered existence and she seemed to like to mix it up a little too. He could try some more.

"Well, I must admit that I know of no classical philosopher who would go so far as to entitle each person to his own view of reality except, perhaps, that very indulgent Scotsman, Bishop Berkely. You know, the guy who insisted that each person's perceptions were *her* reality, causing Samuel Johnson to remark, when he smashed his foot against a formidable rock delivering himself great pain, 'Thus I refute Bishop Berkely.' Nevertheless the authority of that incisive contemporary thinker, Mary Hanks, is imprimatur enough as far as I'm concerned."

"I approve of the switch from 'him' to 'her' and, also, I accept, gracefully I hope, my sudden, or is it just imminent, elevation to philosophical eminence. I'll have to start conjuring up my next brilliant insight and thinking about what to entitle the paper in which I flash the superlative apercu before the eyes, or, rather, the brains, I suppose, of the most rarefied intelligentsia."

"Mary Hanks, you seem to be a formidable yuckster. I didn't know it was coin you minted but it sure is welcome and refreshing to run into one now and then. A vanishing breed, definitely. In any event, I'm just stalling now. You've got me so off—balance that I don't have a come—back. Oh, of course there's one I could press into service if urgently necessary but it's weak and not really in your league. So, a round to you. But now you're obligated to listen to the grim encounter I had with our leader, F. Weymouth. Therefore, I now assume my most serious and sober law professor mode and inform you free of charge."

"If we absolutely, definitely, there's no way out have to get serious then I suppose we must."

Martin described his conversation with the Dean and Weymouth's recitation of student complaints about Martin's "political" teaching. He tried hard to report the relevant parts of the conversation as accurately and completely as he could and must have gone on for a solid five minutes or more without Mary Hanks saying anything other than an occasional "uh—huh," or, "I see." As he neared finishing up he started speaking more rapidly and animatedly, as though anxious to hear her reaction.

"Well, that's about it, as best I remember it. I was wondering what you make of it all. Do you think I'm being muzzled, or, more importantly, that any of us who dare to try to upset the apple cart of the legal system's status quo, even an iota's worth, are being told to watch what we say from a gate receipts point of view? By which, naturally, I mean the paying customers, the students that is."

"Whatever he's saying, and what mere normal mortal ever knows what an administrator's *really* saying, it doesn't sound like completely unblemished good news, does it? But let me tell you, while I'd very much like to discuss all of this with you, right now I need to read three long cases in order to be able to teach my classes, tomorrow morning, at a level just barely above rank incompetence."

Aha, Martin thought instantly, here it comes, the very polite brush—off. She was willing to indulge me amiably for a few minutes, even chime in some bright toned repartee and patter of her own, but that's it. She's done her social work bit, maybe trolling for tenure too, and now she's starting to get bored. His heart and spirit slid downward and fully knowing what she'd be saying he hardly was listening to what she did say.

"So I really should get to those cases and off the phone this very minute. In fact I definitely have to do that. But I find your encounter with Weymouth very interesting, indeed, and I'd really like to bat it around a bit. Can I propose something?"

Those last few words brought Martin back from wallowing in emotions imprisoned in the wintry torpor of a failed attempt.

"Oh, sure, go ahead, propose away. What's a lawyer for except to hear proposals?" he said flatly . He was through being dynamic and upbeat, superfluously. A lost cause is a lost cause.

"O.K., I hope you'll dispose favorably on my proposal. Here goes: tomorrow, believe it or not, even though it's November, it's supposed to hit 70 degrees. Another demonstration of the utterly unpredictable meteorological happenings in Chicago. As the saying goes, I've learned, since coming here, if you don't like the weather wait five minutes—it'll change. But, better yet, if you're not one of those grumpy formalists, so tiresome in the law, as well as elsewhere, who declaims and rants against unseasonable weather, the day after tomorrow, Saturday, we're promised sunshine all day long and temperatures into the high sixties."

Martin, not able to keep his mouth shut for too long and, also, not wanting to reveal just how discouraged he'd become, interjected: "Actually, that's one area where I am a formalist. It's supposed to be coldish in November. Things should be what they're supposed to be;

the weather included. I'm from the old school—not exactly surprising since I'm oldish—if it's hot when it should be cold, or vice-versa, it makes you sick. The big swings from hot to cold, back and forth, just toss my sinuses around unmercifully. So, how's that for a crotchety reaction to a weather aberration that most people, yourself included apparently, absolutely delight in. Nothing personal you understand," Martin finished, trying to daub a little energy on to his voice.

"That is pretty zesty on the crotchetiness. Approaching mild irascibility, I'd estimate. But you haven't even heard my proposal yet. Who knows, maybe that will induce some even more intense paroxysms of crotchetiness. Might even qualify as curmudgeonism."

Martin, couldn't help himself. He laughed. "That's right, I shouldn't get too worked up prematurely. I should hoard some crotchet ammunition in reserve. Just in case I need some real toxic spleen."

Now Mary laughed, maybe it was even a giggle. "Fools jump in … So, as I was saying—and I won't interpolate, 'Before I was so rudely interrupted,' even though I could make a good case that I was— with the temperatures going to be in the high sixties on Saturday, but with still a nice smidgen of November sharpness in the air, and all of it spangled with crackling sunshine, it will be, I can say without fear of contradiction—I hope, an absolutely smashing day for a stroll through the Lincoln Park Zoo. At least that's the way it would look to all non— crotchets, I'd bet. I thought that we could continue our discussion of the censorious intentions of our leader, Weymouth, under those pleasant conditions, in that enchanted atmosphere. The machinations that seem to constantly go on in a law school I've found often put one in mind of Wonderland, anyway. So why not deal with them in a delightful, fanciful, almost wondrous setting? But I suppose a crotchet would only be put off, appalled perhaps, by this too nice, almost unreal pleasantness. Still I'd love to talk you into it."

Martin's spirit braked it's downhill ride. Not only was she not dealing out a deftly finessed brush—off, she was, at least in the lexicon with which he'd been brought up, actually asking him for a date!! If that was too hyperbolic ,she was, certainly, doing no less than strongly suggesting they have one.

Verve flowed back into Martin's vocal cords. "Either I carelessly let my lifetime membership in the crotchet club lapse or you have remarkably persuasive skills of advocacy, beyond even your professional ones. Because, without having to say another thing, you've not only talked me into it, but you have me believing that it's an irrefutably compelling idea. How else could one even conceive of spending such a Saturday afternoon but, exactly as you've suggested, by a leisurely amble in the zoo."

"Good, then it's settled. How about if we meet at say, the elephant area, about one ? Is that o.k. for you?"

"That's absolutely great, superlative for me. And I don't want to hold you up any longer now, I know that you're palpably yearning to start reading and analyzing those three fascinating cases you mentioned, but how did you know that elephants are my favorite animal?"

"Because they're so intelligent and noble? How's that?"

"That's very good; superb in fact. I'm not going to argue with that. Not in the very slightest. But you could have mentioned their magnificent memories also."

"It was implied. O.K., elephant man, don't forget to be there at one on Saturday."

"I think you can definitely count on seeing me on that noble, memorable day."

"November 18th

"Holy shit!! I can't believe it. Would anyone believe that I have a date? That's right—a date; about a day and a half from now.

"So what am I going to do –think about it constantly between now and then; plot out what I'm going to wear, wonder what she's going to wear, (I do hope that she wears that spectacular blonde hair long,) try to come up with stimulating topics of conversation, wonder about how long we're going to stay at the zoo, worry about whether I should have something planned to do après le zoo, in case things go well, so to speak????? No way. I'll just play it with the casualness of maturity. Age at least teaches not to anticipate too optimistically, not to expect too much. The lower expectations are the less disappointment there can be.

"But, truth to tell, there is a tinge of being seventeen again in the way I feel now. She does want to go out with me, it was lots of fun, after the PRESSURE wore off, to talk to her on the phone. She's very articulate and sharp, she can be funny, and, by the way, I most definitely sense my heart leaping a bit when I envision her fine, but also full, figure and the very pretty open features against the backdrop of that astonishing hair. I had no idea my heart could still vault like that. I thought and assumed that forty—eight year old hearts have lost their spring forever—there are no more springs for them, only autumns plus—just as with forty—eight year old legs . (Can't go up for those rebounds on the basketball court any more. Yeah? How do I know? When was the last time I played?)

"So, journal, dear diary—how do you like this for a surprise. I'm actually feeling pretty good right now. Believe it or not, I'm looking *forward* to something—not just badgering memory to summon some past satisfaction or mild contentment. (Usually very past.) I have every reason to believe that Saturday will be a pleasant experience. It might even rise to the level of fun. Perhaps there'll even be moments of happiness.

"But, on that inevitable other hand, let's just hold on here for a sec. Let's not get overly carried away with the euphoric possibilities of life. In addition to the fact that the encounter with the seductive Professor Hanks could just as well turn out disastrously, or disappointingly, rather than exhilaratingly, what happens, even if it's totally delightful? That's not the beginning of the world, to maim a phrase, is it? Happiness is a sustained sense of well being and gratification, not a one-shot upper. And, it seems to me, that that kind of satisfying, generally uplifting sense has to be rooted in productive work which you, yourself, respect. Something which, most likely, involves some meaningful service to, or communication with, others. I.e. other *human* beings. As in 'human' and 'being.'

"Oh, but aren't we waxing way too philosophical right now? Maybe it's philosophy, cerebration itself, that's the enemy of true happiness . I'm feeling very good right now. There's something I'm going to do in a day or so which I've got some reason to believe is going to give me distinct pleasure. Why not just let it go at that? Why not be happy when you are? Damn it!— that's just what I am going to let it go at.

"My emotional mood is tingling right now and, screw it all, I'm going to enjoy, I'm going to cherish, in fact, damn it, I'm going to absolutely wallow and revel in that invigorating tingling. Mary Hanks has already given me some 'happiness.' She's made me feel good, positive, optimistic, energetic. Instead of like I just about have enough shreds of energy to let me hold on. In fact, I'm feeling the kind of exhilaration that craves re—enforcing itself. So, I'm going to give in to it—I'm going to listen to some flagrantly exhilarating, exultant music. It's Beethoven's Seventh Symphony, A-Minor, Op. 92, (Wagner called it 'the apotheosis of the dance,') that's calling to me. It's been so long since I played my Bruno Walter/New York Philharmonic recording of it. Certainly not since Anna died."

$$\sim\!\!\circ$$

Naturally Martin left his condo apartment, on Sheridan Road, with plenty of time to get to the zoo punctually. However, since Saturday did turn out to be a bona fide beautiful day it seemed that everyone in Chicago had emerged into the out of doors. "They'd" all come out of their doors. Traffic was more clogged than usual and the bus took more than thirty—five minutes to make what should have been a fifteen minute trip. So it was already 12:55 when Martin, with quite a few others, many of whom like him had had to stand in the overflowing bus, finally got off. And by the time he was actually nearing the entrance to the zoo he was in jeopardy of getting to the elephant building, about a hundred yards to the Northwest, a few minutes late. As he strode briskly toward the gate, his arms pumping , almost like someone trying to ensure that his walking met aerobic standards, he glanced to his left, at the rear of the statue of Freidrich Schiller, thinking about how movingly Beethoven had set the German's poet's words about all men being brothers to the final movement of his incomparable Ninth Symphony. Perhaps, Martin mused, the most glorious music ever composed. Just at that moment he saw Mary also walking rapidly toward the "Lincoln Park Zoo" sign.

Practically involuntarily his right hand shot up waving a greeting and he called "Mary," just as she smiled , bending her left arm at the elbow so that she could make a lateral waving motion, her wrist her hand's pivot. Martin took her in very quickly, as they came toward each other, and was acutely disappointed to see that the alluring legs were in flat black shoes rather than the medium heels which showed them off so beckoningly in the halls of academe. Nevertheless, even such a sartorial ignoramus as himself immediately recognized that the flats went very consistently and precisely with the beige blouse, dotted with a faint blue pattern, and the rich, dark blue calf—length skirt.

Martin was glad that he'd been courageous enough to dress casually in chinos, (his one untattered pair,) his battered loafers and a long—sleeved plain white Oxford shirt, buttoned down, of course, at the collar. This had to be the first time that Mary had seen him tieless. Not to mention not in a suit, or, at the very least, a sports jacket. He had the impulse to say how strikingly fresh and appealing she looked on this summery day, on the threshold of winter. But he appraised such a remark as too forward and aggressive sounding. However, there did flash across his mind a sentence that the French novelist and Nobel Prize winner, Albert Camus, had once written: "In the midst of winter I found that there was within me an invincible summer." He was groping for some innocuous yet appropriate opening comment, but she spoke first.

"Martin, you look so nice in those casual clothes. I don't think I've ever seen you in anything but a male law professor uniform—you know jacket and tie—before this moment. You should do it more often; you look, so relaxed."

Slightly emboldened by this compliment he felt he could take a risk. " I even sort of feel relaxed. Much more than I normally do. You must be a tonic, Mary. You look very fine too. Definitely augments the tonic effect."

He paused for a moment as they smiled easily at each other, like two people who only minutes after meeting for the first time know that they will like each other quite a bit. Then, very quickly, almost sotto voce, he shot in: "Maybe we should do this more often." But, without waiting for an explicit reaction from her, he hurried on: " I relaxed immeasurably when I saw that you were just as slightly late as me and that I wouldn't arrive at the elephant house as a delinquent with you, tapping a foot, already irritated with me. Now it's not that I haven't been given to understand that I can inspire quite a bit of irritation, but it's not usually by being late. Punctuality, in fact, is one of my few and chief strengths. If a strength it be."

"Oh, I don't know. I don't think so. I sense you have other strengths."

"I appreciate your perceptiveness. Not many folks are so discerning.," he raised his eyes theatrically, "or, perhaps, misguided," he added, dropping his voice.

'Well, it's not often that just how perceptive I am is discerned by others. Least of all my students. Not to mention my colleagues. So I appreciate your insightfulness too."

Martin was very glad that she so easily fell into the kind of flippancy which he'd so enjoyed with her, over the phone. But he sensed that there were limits as to how far they could go with such bantering, that they needed to expand beyond repartee.

"Now that we've solidified our mutual admiration society , dedicated to lauding each other's hidden virtues, even the not so hidden ones, we probably shouldn't keep the elephants waiting too much longer. I doubt that what's now developed into our flagrant tardiness can be concealed from them with casual glibness, as is our wont," he said. "They're too smart for that, no?"

"Oh, absolutely right, I'm certain it can't. They have unerring antennae for decency and responsibility. They'll know we've let them down."

He touched her very lightly on the elbow , to nudge her up the path toward the Regenstein Habitat For Large Mammals, where, he recalled, the elephants were sheltered. As they strolled they discussed the current extra added attraction of the elephant house—the opportunity to observe the new baby elephant, born only a month ago. In fact, as they walked, they saw notices affixed to trees along the path informing of the exact birth date and birth weight of Patsy, and identifying her parents as Onyx and Bozie . And also assuring the public that Patsy was on display during most of the hours during which the zoo was open.

When Mary and Martin entered the habitat, along with many other zoo—goers eager to see just how precocious Patsy was, (the newspapers had reported her as *extremely* precocious,) they turned toward each other and laughed at the very strong odor pervading the structure.

"One forgets this cost of consorting with the elephants, doesn't one," Mary giggled , pinching her nose with two fine, long tapered fingers with clear colored nails.

"That cost is relatively low considering the pleasure you get," Martin assured.

They ambled past rhinos and other creatures of considerable bulk, stopping momentarily to gaze and peer, on their way to the elephant area.The tremors of noise emanating from there, generated by the congregated throngs, preceded their actually catching sight of the massive, noble animals. Because of the numbers of people crowded up to the area where the elephants were restrained, by thick steel wires, once the elephants did come into view Mary and Martin still couldn't get as close as they would have wanted. Even at the fringe of the curious group they were jostled and pushed.

"They are so sovereign looking, aren't they?" Mary exclaimed.

"That's a great descriptor, Mary. That's exactly what they are—sovereign. Sovereign, noble, imperial; nothing's in their league. And look at little Patsy. I mean she's learning the appropriate bearing. She seems to have quite a bit of the majestic strut already."

"She *is* cute. Aah, look at how cozily she nuzzles up to her mom's leg."

They watched, admired and commented enthusiastically for a few more minutes, as people came and went and kids shrieked, laughed and cried. But there wasn't all that much to see as the elephants had to be relatively quiescent in their confined space and couldn't do too much. In fact, about all they could do was walk haltingly, back and forth, scooping a trunkful of water every few minutes. The three mature elephants kept giving attention to Patsy who seemed to be thriving on it. Nevertheless, even this new born youngster seemed too lackadaisical and appeared to be just shuffling through motions.

"They really shouldn't be here, should they?" Martin said in a subdued voice. " They don't have enough to do. No challenges. They should be out somewhere where they should be doing what they should be doing."

"I suppose that's right," Mary agreed, quietly.

"So," Martin continued, jacking his voice up a notch, " that means we have a moral problem. By coming here are we really contributing to the illegitimate subjugation of these wonderful creatures? Is our taking advantage of the opportunity to observe them implicitly endorsing the whole idea of keeping these magnificent animals in captivity? I bet you didn't know that going to the zoo was fraught with so much ethical peril," Martin remarked, looking directly into Mary's large hazel eyes.

She gave a brief, but throaty chuckle and acknowledged, "You're right, I didn't know that I was treading such an ethical precipice when I suggested that we might enjoy ourselves by coming to see the elephants on a dazzling day. In view of this trenchant question, that you've so inconsiderately raised, should I understand that we've stopped enjoying ourselves or that, at the very least, we don't know if we're enjoying ourselves any more? And that we're in serious moral turmoil that it's imperative we work through?"

"I don't know. As a good law professor, one of the few things I think I am pretty good at, I merely raise questions. I was hoping you could enlighten me."

"Are you suggesting, by intimating that I might answer a question, that I'm a bad law professor?"

Martin laughed easily and said, as he firmly took her elbow with his right hand, while motioning to the way out with his left hand, "I am suggesting that we've reached the point of diminishing returns as far as the elephants go and that perhaps we should move on ..." He became conscious that grasping her elbow had fluttered some excitement in him.

They left the Large Mammal Habitat and walked a few steps down the path along which they'd come before. Several yards further was a refreshment stand, a few people were standing in front of it, selling popcorn, ice cream, soft drinks and such. Martin pointed and asked whether she'd like something. She shrugged non-commitally and he suggested they share some popcorn. She acquiesced. After buying the $2.00 medium size, as Mary tried to foist a dollar bill on him, Martin gestured at the grassy plot surrounding the Schiller statue and asked if she'd like to sit on the grass there, as others were doing, while they applied themselves to the popcorn.

She nodded cheerfully and walked toward the front of the statue while Martin followed, balancing the popcorn container. She located a few square feet of unoccupied grass and, arranging her skirt with a broad sweeping motion, guided herself to a sitting position, legs stretched out in front of her, crossed at the ankles. Martin was disappointed that hardly any of her beautiful legs showed. After quickly peering to determine just how much loose soil or other debris there was on the grass, he handed the popcorn to Mary and, hoping that his bones weren't creaking audibly, eased himself down beside her. She grabbed some popcorn and pushed it into her mouth as she extended the container toward Martin. He, too, fingered a handful and started contentedly, if still nervously, munching.

They'd wound up about a hundred feet from the Schiller statue, more or less facing it at a forty—five degree angle.

"This popcorn's good, isn't it" Mary remarked after a minute or two of sampling, stuffing and munching.

"No, not bad at all for zoo popcorn."

"Oh, I wasn't aware there're highly calibrated gradations of popcorn quality and that zoo popcorn is down toward the bottom rungs," she said, turning towards him and smiling that maximum wattage, all –out smile. Hackneyed as it might be "radiant" was the word which crossed Martin's mind when she turned it on him.

"I don't know that there are. But *if* there were, wouldn't zoo popcorn be suspect; at least likely to rank near the bottom?"

She just kept up the smile. Martin , using the hand that wasn't holding the popcorn, motioned towards the Schiller statue.

"Do you think that he's miffed that he may well be remembered more for the fact that Beethoven set his 'Ode to Joy' as the last movement of the Ninth Symphony than for his own work as a dramatist? After all, he was one of the leading exponents of the *Sturm und Drang* school's cries for political freedom."

"I, personally, would say that it's a good bet that he doesn't mind anything any more or think anything. But if he did, maybe he'd feel that Beethoven had made more effective use of his material, in the overall cause, than he himself did, or could have done. In any event, I don't know much about *Sturm und Drang.*"

"Nor do I," Martin admitted. "But I do know that I love Beethoven's Ninth. That I unequivocally know."

"I knew it, I just knew that you were going to be a classical music aficionado! You are, aren't you?"

"Guilty as so vituperatively charged. Completely. Definitely, no qualifications possible. How about yourself? I'm hoping fervently."

"I like a good bit of it and I know *some*thing. But I'm sure, I can tell just from the throb in your voice, that I'm not in your league."

"I don't know just how major a league that is but I'm sure that you have great potential. Once you're in to it, to any degree at all, you're on your way to being an addict. Now the Ninth Symphony is absolutely irrefutable. I can't imagine it being resisted by anyone, although I'm sure it is. Of course it is—obviously. But what about the other LVB symphonies, as we faux cognoscenti like to call him. Which are your favorites?

She mentioned the Third, the famed "Eroica," Beethoven's own preference, and also the Fifth and Seventh. And they were off—telling about their favorite composers, the works they loved best of all, the interpreters they most respected. Like two early teens excitedly disclosing and trading their treasured childhood experiences. Mary, in fact, didn't know anywhere near as much as Martin did, not too many non—professionals did, but she unmistakably conveyed a real appreciation and delight about those works she had made her own. And, naturally, Martin found whatever ignorance she did display as endearing. He could teach her. He had always loved teaching Anna things. He loved teaching, period. That which was worth teaching and transmitting.

Not surprisingly, Mozart was high on Mary's list. Wolfie came right after Beethoven. His late symphonies, some of the piano concerti and also operas like "Don Giovanni" and "The Marriage of Figaro." Martin was disappointed that she didn't seem to know much Schubert. She more or less stopped with his legendary "Unfinished" Symphony and the "Great" Symphony, the Ninth in C—Major, and was basically unfamiliar with the transcendence of the last three piano sonatas or the Impromptus of Op. 90 or the "Moments Musicaux," those absolutely exquisite and poignant piano pieces. Not to mention the six hundred plus songs, some of which were incredible masterpieces in themselves. However, she did love the spectacular "Wanderer Fantasy," so difficult to perform that Schubert himself once, at the keyboard, threw up his hands and exclaimed "Let the devil himself play it." Since Schubert was definitely Martin's second favorite composer,—sometimes he even verged on rank disloyalty and when particularly affected by one of Schubert"s achingly lovely passages allowed himself to speculate that Schubert might surpass even the colossus, Beethoven, but he always returned to his senses when he thought of that supreme master of dramatic complexity— he became especially animated in extolling Schubert's incomparably wrenching phrases and stayed just this side of frenzy in enthusing about the works which Mary should get to know, or know better. On the other hand, she surprised him, very appealingly— much that she said or did appealed to him— with a quite sophisticated take on Robert Schumann ,proclaiming her love for each of the four symphonies as well as piano compositions such as "Kreisleriana," "Davidsbundlertanze" and "Kinderscenen." (And it wasn't only the exceedingly familiar "Traumerei," Vladimir Horowitz's signature encore, that she loved from the latter collection.) Martin then demanded, all the more strenuously, that since she knew Schumann's piano works so well she absolutely *had* to expose herself to the great, great late piano works of the infinitely great Franz Schubert.

They also agreed that of living pianists those two remarkable octogenarians, Rudolf Serkin and Claudio Arrau were superb artists, as their distinguished contemporaries, Horowitz and Artur Rubinstein had also been. Martin practically beamed with satisfaction when Mary said that both Serkin and Arrau were peerless interpreters of Beethoven piano sonatas with Serkin, perhaps, just a bit more compelling—if that were possible. Martin actually shook his fist excitedly, the way top athletes who've just scored an important point or made a great play do,and blurted out, "Yes, exactly!! That's just the way I feel. Serkin's always been my very top favorite ever since I saw him do the 'Emperor Concerto' with the Boston Symphony, when I was in law school. He *makes* you listen, the pull is inescapable. That's what Isaac Stern claims: that a great composer or a great artist *makes* you listen—you've really got no choice. You're compelled."

"Speaking of Isaac Stern, not a bad violinist, not a bad violinist at all," Mary spiritedly interjected, focusing the brighter than a thousand suns smile directly on him."In fact, one hell of a tremendous fiddler, maybe one of the very greatest of this century," she continued.

"I'm not going to argue with that," Martin agreed. "Tremendously passionate player. And he gets you to be passionate about what he's being passionate about. I once heard him say, in a television interview, or something like that, that the music is *between* the notes. Playing the literal printed page, black marks on white paper, is to miss the real music. There's no question that he certainly excavates the true music, the art. But as far as great violinists of the twentieth century I don't think you want to foerget about brilliant performers like Fritz Kresler and Yehudi Menuhin and Mischa Elman and, of course, the standard top choice—Jascha Heifetz. Although I confess, I, myself, am not that huge a Heifetz fan. Naturally I admire and enjoy him quite a bit but I find that I just don't *love* him, the way I do Kreisler for example."

"Mea culpa, I have to admit I just don't know Kreisler that well. I've heard him, here and there ..."

"You're too young again ..."

"But Heifetz is so strong in his playing. That powerful tone so dominates the music."

"Maybe that's it. Maybe he's too much about Heifetz the supreme technician and not enough about expressing the music's inner values. I don't know. I just hear a ferocious pyrotechnical grasp there, something that's a bit too clinical. To me it comes across a little cold. Kreisler on the other hand has that inexpressibly warm, glowing , heartfelt, soulful sound. Kreisler's dad, a doctor, who started him on the violin once said, 'That tone, that tone; maybe I gave him that tone.' But speaking of incomparable violin tone, let's not forget what was perhaps the most impressive tone ever produced by a violinist. I mean Mischa Elman's. He was pretty much the number one fiddle player until Heifetz displaced him in the twenties. But, like I've said, I'm not at all sure that the vox populi knew what it was doing with that preference."

Wasn't there another great Russian violinist of that vintage, Efrem Zimbalist?"

'Right you are, Mary," Martin practically shouted. "The real Efrem Zimbalist, the father, was a world class fiddler and not an actor who played on '77 Sunset Strip' in the fifties. That was Efrem Zimbalist, *Junior* , the son. Mary, you're bidding fair to enter the world of the cognoscenti with that one. But don't forget Nathan Milstein when compiling your list of great violinists who emerged from Russia early in the century."

"Don't be condescending, male chauvinist pig," she mock pouted. "Actually, I think I like the violin even better than the piano. That's disloyal, because I played the piano for a few years as a kid and I really do love the range of sounds it can make, from the boomingly deep to the most fragile tinkle. But the violin is just so ... so ravishing. It sweeps one away, and, well, it just quite seduces me."

Suddenly Martin wished that he could still play the violin.

They compared notes on just how much progress they'd made in their childhood music lessons: Mary on the piano, she'd gotten to a Chopin Prelude or two, Martin with the violin, he'd never gotten beyond some very simple student concerti. He confessed that his love of music far exceeded his ability to perform it with any competence whatsoever.

They'd gone through the popcorn and Mary had allowed herself to stretch out fully on the grass, on her back. The sun was so bright it sharply glinted off one of the metallic buttons on her blouse. It also caressed Martin with its warmth and he realized that at this moment he was feeling very warm and contented emotionally. Still sitting upright, legs straight out, palms of his hands pressing the grass, he gradually sunk down so that he too was on his back, fully stretched out on the grass.

Their chatting continued. They reinforced each other in feelings of just how uplifting, as well as soothing and consoling, great music could be. Each mentioned times when depression was very difficult to repulse but music had come to the rescue, an immeasurable balm in initiating resilience, restoring spirits. It had shown, multiple times, that it could penetrate and disperse ebony moods so leaden as to seem never likely to depart. Martin told her how he'd once heard the great English mezzo—soprano, Janet Baker, give a little talk at a "Meet The Music Makers" event, prior to a Chicago Symphony Orchestra concert, in which she'd remarked "Music comforts, music consoles, music is healing," and how he'd never forgotten those words, how they proved, in his own case, so resoundingly, so durably, accurate.They also discussed how if you were feeling good you were propelled toward beloved music as a way of underlining a sense of joyfulness or well being.

Martin was feeling very good now, he even sensed that he could drowse off in the sun's beneficent rays. Thinking, however, that Mary might well interpret such an occurrence as ennui on his part he, instead, pulled himself back to a sitting position, resting his chin on his knees, arms encircling his legs.

Mary cupped her hands around her mouth and simulating shouting said, "You up there, let me ask you a question. Here we are in the shadow of Schiller's statue and we've talked about Beethoven using Schiller's 'Ode To Joy' and its theme of all men, all people I suppose I should say, being brothers—and sisters—as the exultant finale of the Ninth Symphony and all the rest of it—very inspiring and all that. But do you find that you can bring any of that grand theme, or any other grand theme for that matter into your classes, your teaching, in an effective, productive way? I'd love to affect the world for the better, a little bit at least, through my teaching. After all, that's one of the strong reasons I went into it, instead of racking up the big bucks with a law firm or such. You too, I bet. But it seems so futile, so often.The students, or at least the vast majority of them, don't seem interested in anything but honing technical skills to the mania of reaping lots of filthy lucre."

Suddenly a rubber ball glanced off Martin's right ankle. Thirty or forty feet off a family of three had spread some blankets under a picnic lunch. The little boy, around three, had been playing with the ball, rolling it around and more or less tossing it to himself, while his parents chatted. Finally it had gotten away from him. He'd toddled half way towards it but had stopped in shyness once it had hit Martin's ankle. Martin retrieved the ball and held it out smilingly to the child. But he wasn't intrepid enough to continue advancing even though his mother and then his dad had urged him to keep going and "get the ball from the nice man."

After turning to Mary and whispering "It's not often that the young call me a nice man," Martin maneuvered himself onto his knees and held the ball out, invitingly, further in front of him, toward the timorous three year old. When the toddler just kept staring wide—eyedly at Martin, refusing to take another step, Martin finally called out heartily, "Here you go," and pushed the ball in a very gentle roll towards the tyke. It stopped just inches from the little fellow's shoes and with a very hearty expostulation, somewhere in the laugh family, he bent over, picked it up in both hands and very quickly turned and ran back to the blankets on which his parents were sitting and, now, smiling broad smiles. They vigorously applauded him and daddy gave Martin a big wave of thanks.

"You functioned swimmingly in that little domestic tableau,"Mary remarked brightly.

"Anna and I were never able to have any kids of our own, so I guess it's easy with other people's," Martin responded. "No pressures, no responsibilities, you know," he continued. "But getting back to what you were saying, Mary, I mean it being so difficult to dent our students' obsession with filthy lucre, as you so delicately, or not so delicately, put it. You know, in behalf of concern for public service or some broad policy aimed at improving things which need improving …

"Right, do you find that you can't get through either? Let me tell you—you certainly have quite the reputation for trying. Whether you know it or not, some of your colleagues, moi included, call you the conscience of the faculty."

"No, I didn't know that, I didn't know it," Martin said slowly. More spiritedly, he continued, "Never can tell what goes on behind your back. I'm not sure that it's meant to be flattering rather than satirical, but, as we lawyers are taught to do, I'll interpret it in the light most favorable to myself."

"Oh, please believe me, it's very much meant that way—at least by me and others whom I've heard use the term."

"I am flattered. Touched, really. But to get back to your frustration over how little you seem to be able to influence the students' pre—existing orientation and sensibilities. Or lack of sensibilities. Unfortunately, you're all too right. At first they're tremendously overawed by the mystique of law school and look up to us as almost god-like, goddess-like, too, in all sorts of ways. They have the openness, the willingness to be guided, shown, of the insecure. However, they seem to catch on rather quickly, say somewhere about the middle of the first year, not too long from now in fact, that the professors really aren't such a big deal at all. They're simply the conduits who pass along the technical info students have to master in order to come up with the best paying jobs they can find. In fact, I had a young woman," Martin almost startled at his "I had a young woman" phraseology, "a first year student, in my office, only a few weeks ago, basically admitting that—of course she didn't express it quite *so* bluntly—to my face. So, bottom line, I think we have to be realistic and accept that we're not exactly champions in the transform the world game. On the other hand, I don't want to acknowledge abject, totally frustrating defeat. It's never time to say die. If you've got any public spiritedness at all in you you're impelled to try to change civic life for the better. But you come to realize, as you grow older while you struggle to do so, that you're not really making any tangible, discernible progress and that the odds are stacked pretty high against your luck substantially changing. I suppose the only solace is that very incremental gains are gains nevertheless."

"The picture's that grim, is it?"

"Admit it, you, yourself, suspect that that's how gloomy it is. There's no doubt about it, the exasperation gets to be pretty agonizing. Right smack in the face of your passion to get something accomplished, to move something forward, you're made to feel totally powerless. You're forced to start recognizing that you're not going to succeed."

"I don't want to accept that," she said softly, her head shaking from side to side, the blonde hair flowing.

Her earnestness enhanced her considerable natural beauty. It suggested an angelic, ethereal quality, usually present in only young women still in their twenties .Martin wanted to, oh so lightly, draw the very tips of his fingers across her high cheek bones, then her eye lids. He just gazed at her, for several, what seemed very long, seconds before responding.

"That's exactly the right reaction! I don't want to throw in the towel, accept the game as lost, either. And we shouldn't. We have to keep on trying. It's our obligation. What is it that Beckett wrote in 'Waiting For Godot'? 'I must go on. I can't go on. I'll go on.' Or something like that, anyway."

Her face remained taut with seriousness. But she infused some energy into her voice. "I'm so glad to hear you say that."

"Oh, definitely, it's the only way to go. By no means does reality take you off the moral hook. I once heard Father Daniel Berrigan, the great anti—war Jesuit priest, give a talk—in fact I had the honor of introducing him, one of the peak experiences of my life— in which he commented on just such a hopeless attitude of 'I'm not going to be able to change anything, or make a real difference.' He said of course you're going to fail but that gives you not the slightest dispensation to not try mightily. That much you can do and that much you're morally obligated to do. What you can't control, despite best efforts, you can't. But as to what you can do you'd be morally delinquent if you didn't. Or, as some philosopher once said, or certainly should have said, 'Just because you can't do everything which needs to be done is absolutely no excuse for not doing anything that needs to be done.'"

"That's true, and a little comforting, I guess," she said, with some determination. "But I still wish I could feel some tangible control."

"Not only feel some, but have some. But how can you, realistically? Take a look at how huge and ungainly the world and its infinitely numerous problems are and how small and relatively powerless you are." Martin almost added something like "Despite being exceedingly well formed," but, of course, didn't dare.

"I'm sure that you're very probably all too right, but I don't know that I'm ready to bow to accuracy. I'll have to sort things out. However, talking about small and considering that you can't let yourself sink into the morass of such portentous questions for too long, without getting seriously depressed, what would you say to walking over to the Penguin House and watching those strutting fellows for a bit? They're so cute. They almost seem to know that their dressed formally. They act like they're determined to conduct themselves with dignity."

"A capital idea. I like penguins too." Martin paused, but then sheepishly said "Your idea is definitely *not* for the birds."

She wrinkled her perfectly shaped nose in condemnation. "Martin, even you should have kept that one under water."

They ambled slowly back toward the penguin house which they'd passed on their way down from the elephant habitat. As they passed the refreshment stand again Martin remarked that it sold ice cream too and asked Mary if she'd like a cone of some flagrantly sinful flavor. She confessed strong temptation but declined on the grounds that the apex of the day's warmth and the sun's brightness had been about an hour ago. By now the sharp teeth of a Fall briskness had started gently, but persistently, gnawing at the air. Martin acknowledged his gratitude to her for dissuading him from absorbing unneeded calories. Very gingerly she patted his slight paunch and assured him, just as they reached the penguin house, that he didn't have to worry too much about calories. But she repeated the word "too."

There were only two other penguin devotees there so they pretty much had the appealing creatures to themselves. They laughed in tandem when they read the informational sign which advised that if the penguins looked scruffy it was because they were scruffy, since this was the molting season. They began pointing out to each other just how bedraggled one and another of the feisty birds really was.

They read another sign which proclaimed that a penguin could stay under water for as much as six minutes at a time and then proceeded to periodically elbow each other to call attention to a penguin which had just submerged itself so that they could monitor how long it stayed down. When neither a particular one nor successors which they kept tabs on came close to the six minutes promised they agreed that the sign was unduly boastful of the zoo's attractions or that the penguins they happened to have observed were weak in prowess.

Martin felt more and more relaxed. More relaxed, he was sure, than he'd felt in a long, long time; probably, actually, since well before Anna had died. In the semi—darkness of the penguin house he was able to furtively glance at his watch and was completely shocked to see that nearly three hours had passed, as time goes by, since they'd waved at each other. He was confident in the proposition which, from the time he knew he'd see Mary today, he realized he might make and which now, almost spontaneously, he did decide to broach.

"Mary, you know there are a few more lovable creatures we could check out here, but it's edging towards dinner time and we haven't even discussed the infinitely various and complex meanings, connotations and ramifications of my meeting with our esteemed leader, a veritable dean of deans, the sometimes honorable Frederick Weymouth." He was feeling positively jocular.

"Yes, Martin, we haven't even opened the agenda of this meeting, the reason I called you here. We've been naughty and discussed frivolities and what not. And even had fun—I think."

"I'm absolutely sure of it. In fact, most fun I've had in a long time," he said, his face settling into a serious cast. "Actually, I was thinking, why don't we combine business with some more pleasure . We could head somewhere comfortable for dinner. Casual though, not formal or anything, and chew over the myriad evils that riddle our place of business, otherwise known, in duly sinister tones, as the law school." There was twinkle back in his voice, as well as in his eyes, as he finished with what he hoped was his flippant flourish.

Mary's face sharply registered surprise. She seemed about to open her mouth but, as though thinking again, she hesitated a few seconds before she answered.

"That sounds like a great idea, Martin, and I'd really love to do it.

But, and I suppose this is going to sound utterly hollow, I really do have a previous engagement which I just have to keep. No excuses possible. I'm very sorry about it all … I …"

Martin was flabbergasted, shocked into virtual silence. He thought they'd gotten along so well, swimmingly,(in his, and hers too, apparently, antiquated parlance.) Why would she pull this hackneyed, completely out-of-left field, unexplained, brusque style turn-down on him? She might just as well have said that she had to go home to wash her hair.

"Oh, no … no …" he managed to mumble and mutter. "Don't worry about it. I should have given you a little more than a few seconds notice. Very thoughtless not to have …" He was afraid that he'd reddened and that perspiration was dotting his forehead. A bumbling adolescent refused a date that he'd finally contrived to ask for. Well, he thought, he might as well have been an adolescent as far as what he seemed to know and understand about things.

Looking at her watch, Mary, with some urgency, said, "In fact, I'd better start dashing now if I'm going to be punctual. I really do have to skip over to my car—I had to park a few blocks away—and get moving. Listen, it's truly been grand. We have to repeat." Quickly looking at her watch again, avoiding his eyes, she repeated: "I really do have to get going. I'll be seeing you."

"Sure, sure, go ahead, I understand." Martin was so shaken and hurt that he neglected to even offer to walk her to her car—as though she'd want him to or, even, if that's where she really was going, he speculated.

As she, literally, half ran off she suddenly turned, forced a smile, the non—radiant type, and waved with her left hand. In automatic, unthinking response, Martin slowly raised his right arm as prelude to perfunctorily returning her wave. But before he could execute she had turned her back to resume her half running, half walking retreat from Martin and toward the zoo exit. Almost involuntarily, largely out of practiced appraisal, he noticed her full, perfectly shaped calves and the delicately turned ankles.

He also realized that the flirtatious November sun was just about gone now, the light much paler. The temperature had dropped quite a few degrees and a grey—black cloud formation was creeping toward the zoo and the high rise apartment houses that stretched interminably, in both directions, on the opposite side of the street. Martin started wondering how frequently the buses would be running at this hour, how long it would take to get home, and also whether it would have become so chilly by the time he got there that he would start to feel cold in his shirt sleeves. About one thing, however, he was deadly certain: the cellophane day at the zoo, with the lovely, bright, alluring Mary Hanks, was definitely over.

"November_____

"I hardly know what to do, except be really pissed off. I practically choked on the veal scallopine with rigatoni, gourmet brand, frozen dinner I just slammed down my gullet and it snidely avenged itself by spreading instant indigestion throughout my stomach and chest. 'Pissed off' is actually too meek a term. Too often it's used to express only minor irritation or being put out over a relatively trivial or frivolous matter. Angry is what I really am. Damn angry, in fact. And hugely disappointed.

"I thought things were going so well and they turned out, abruptly, so unsatisfyingly. What do I mean 'unsatisfyingly'? Highly frustrating and exacerbating is more like it. I would have bet a lot that she, too, would have wanted to extend and expand the warm, easy feelings we'd come to—by going to dinner, talking some more, getting to know more about each other. And lest I be thought an inveterate lecher, or something, I don"t mean by that physically significant activities, or anything at all in that vein. Just a continuation of the rather smoothly flowing companionship we'd initiated during the afternoon. I mean we were laughing and jabbing each other in the ribs in the penguin house … Instead, she ran off like she'd hit her quota of charity work for this week—end and couldn't wait to get out of there—to her real life.

"A real life that maybe included a real date, with someone much more her own age. She might have been actually telling the truth, strictly speaking, and did have another appointment , never having even given a thought to spending more than a very few sunny afternoon hours with me. Maybe she did just have to run home and get all 'dolled—up,' very seductively no doubt. (She looked pretty damn seductive to me, already; the more I get to know her the more seductive she becomes.) But, then, she cut it very thin, didn't she? Is it that she just never imagined, in her most extravagant dreams of beneficent social worker, that the afternoon with me might go so well, that it could stretch on, somewhat open—endedly, develop its own very pleasant, comfortable, forward rhythms?

"Well, certainly part of the reason, maybe the biggest part, I'm so furious, so damn exasperated, is that, obviously, I like(d?) her quite a bit. I'll admit there"s plenty of physical attraction for me. Her face is shining, her features open, verging on perfect and she looks so softly full—bodied to touch. But I'm not just a sexually frustrated, deprived, whatever, dirty old man—I don't think. I'm pretty sure it goes beyond that. She's intelligent, she's lively, converses animatedly, she can be funny and appreciates humor, (even mine,) she *wants* to laugh and she seems to have the luminous aspirations of an idealistic college sophomore. Quite a package!! And packaged so desirably. Not to mention that she's a classical music buff. And one with just the right mix of knowledge and ignorance. Enough knowledge to be able to talk about it sensibly and sensitively, and enough ignorance to be very appealing, (she's got LOTS of appeal,) in her willingness to learn from someone who knows somewhat more—like me, for example.

"And, undeniably, we had fun. We did laugh, we chatted about some interesting things, we talked about some serious things and there seemed to be a lot more to laugh and talk about. (We had so much to discuss that we didn't even get to bullshitting about my meeting with Weymouth and exactly what the hell all that nonsense meant.) And who knows what could have developed. I was certainly wanting to touch her, to stroke that alluring proportioned softness. And she, for her part, seemed very warm and open, (pardoning the double—entendre,) until, in one of the most precipitous volte—faces , (volte—feces?) I've ever seen, not to mention experienced, she just completely shut down and left. I recognize that I haven't had much experience with women in general, but I'm almost fifty years old and not entirely unperceptive or thick. Most of the time I correctly 'get' what messages, the 'vibes,' people are giving off. She sure seemed to enjoy being with me for a few hours. She was receptive not rejecting. Or she's one hell of a great dissimulator!

"Could it be that that was exactly the problem? She not only enjoyed being with me but started to feel that the whole thing might be getting just too enjoyable for both of us—that it might lead too far? Maybe she's committed sexually. For all I know she's in a deep, all-around relationship and just didn't want me and herself to go any farther. She was willing to go to the zoo, on a sensationally beautiful afternoon, with a tenured professor, whom she finds not unpleasant, and who'll l participate in the decision re: her promotion and tenure , but she surely didn't want any 'relationship' to come of it.

"But you know, o august journal, I don't really think this last is it. She could have buttered me up for pragmatic purposes, in many ways, without making the zoo date. For instance, she could have just dropped by my office occasionally to BS about school, she could have phoned me up once in a while, asking advice, etc., etc. I think, to some extent at least, she did like me as a person, wasn't just 'using' me. She doesn't come across as a 'user'—too clean of purpose for that. On the other hand, that doesn't mean she wants me caressing her delectably rounded ass.

"I guess what's really got me upset now is that I finally risked—and look where it got me. Another one in the loss column. I let my heart off its closely held leash a little and all it got was bloodied and battered some more. I liked her, wanted her to like me and that's exactly what seemed to be happening, until that almost cruel ending. Not designed to encourage one of my already generally timid disposition to keep on taking risks. If something which started out as auspiciously as l'affaire, (no pun intended,) Hanks didn't work out perhaps it's sheer doddering foolishness to think that I can still get payoff on risk taking. Maybe at this point, at the age I am and getting to be, one only loses on risks. They're all risk and hardly a shred of hope.

"Nevertheless, there's no question that I'm very considerably attracted to a woman like Mary. I like being with her: I want to be with her. And it's not as though life is so pretty, pleasant and fulfilling if one shies (as in shy) away from getting involved. In fact, it's largely gruesomely grinding, dull, boring, joyless as it's been going along for the last few years. With Mary I actually felt some excitement, some brightness, some wanting of something—other than to be left alone. It may be the most trite of clichés—but she made me feel alive again.

"Yet it seems to have come to nothing—worse, ashes of frustration—this time around. But I suppose one can't let that stop one. You have to keep on trying in this area, too. Just like I told Mary that you have to persist in trying to make an impact on the world, keep plugging at imprinting a wisp of social improvement. To quote that super redoubtable wordsmith, good old Sam Beckett, again: "I must go on. I can't go on. I'll go on." Or another of his; viz., 'Failed? No matter. Fail again. Fail better.' But I sure as hell don't feel like going forward right now. I feel like I've been smacked back, and pretty hard at that.

"I guess I'll get over it. As they say, 'This too shall pass,' and all that other heartily upbeat claptrap. Oh, anyway, let's not treat this as some sort of monumental tragedy. There's plenty of crushing specimens of that sort in the world—and this doesn't come close to qualifying as one of them.

"But I do have to mobilize some energy to deal with Mary the next time I see her. The nonchalant spurned swain routine. I could well see her in the office on Monday. Not looking forward to that. Not by any means. What the hell do I say when I run into her in the halls, or wherever? Some inane folderol like,'Oh gee, that was really nice Saturday afternoon; we'll have to do it again some time'? What I'd really like to say is: 'Why, God-damn it, did you leave so abruptly on Saturday? What were you so terribly late for? I thought we were having a delightful time and wanted to expand it into more delightful time. What was *your* problem?' That wouldn't be too diplomatic or smooth, would it? But why should I waste time, (as though I have so many other things to do, right?) thinking of the exact words to say to her when I meet her. Maybe I won't run into her for a while. It's not like it's a guaranteed everyday occurrence. So maybe I'll never have to say anything—the whole thing will be in the past and forgotten. Or, better yet, let her think of what she should say to me, if it turns out that anything need be said. She's the one who acted inappropriately. Or, at least, strangely. Let her make the excuses, or small talk, whatever. I'm so disappointed, upset, mad that I don't want to do anything. I don't think that even great music can soothe this savage breast."

"Thoughts on Contracts and Life, the morning after.

"Words can be made precise, but they're not always to start with. Part of their impact is context and inflection. The very same words can mean differently, depending on the environment in which they're uttered/used and just how they are articulated. A simple example: suppose a rabid classical music fan, strolling past Carnegie Hall, sees a poster announcing that the great pianist, Alfred Brendel, , is to play Beethoven's monumental "Hammerklavier" Sonata in a week's time, his only New York appearance during that concert season. This music lover is especially excited because he's recently read an article reporting that Brendel has said that he will stop performing the "Hammerklavier" after the current season because he finds it too taxing and distressful on his problematical back. The music lover is so pleasantly enlivened by the prospect of being at this magnificent artist's Carnegie performancethat he expostulates a spontaneous "Wow!!" His enthusiasm is keyed so highly that he stops the first person he spots coming down the street, eager to share his buoyant feelings. The approaching person, it so happens, although a man, has exceedingly long hair, is wearing tie—dyed jeans and his favorite music, in fact, is "heavy metal." When told that the internationally revered soloist, Alfred Brendel, is going to appear at Carnegie Hall to play one of Beethoven's most famous and celebrated creations, the daunting 'Hammerklavier' Sonata, the 'rocker,' with acid dismissiveness and derision in his voice, says very weakly, 'Wow.' Same exact word, but two different contexts and two greatly varying modes of voicing the word. Result: two *very* different meanings which could hardly be more contradictory or farther apart. Words surely do not gyrate innocuously in a vacuum. Their users have to be conscious of this if they want to maximize communicative precision and power."

Notwithstanding his assurances to himself, on his way to the office on Monday morning, that the burden was not on him, Martin mentally reviewed some scenarios of just how he would react to Mary Hanks if he happened to meet her in the corridors or elevators. He was grateful he didn't have to resort to any of them. He made it to his office without encountering anyone with whom it would be necessary to chat. That was one distinct advantage of getting there well before 9 A.M. There weren't too many , or, often, any , people there yet—those you had to talk to, or those you didn't.

He'd been at his desk less than ten minutes, desultorily looking over the few pieces of non—junk mail that had come in since he'd been there last week, and trying mightily to generate the fortitude to briefly glance at the notes germane to his next Contracts class, when there was a light rap at the door. He got up to open it with the irritable expectation that it would be some faux—eager student with some trivial , silly question. It was indeed a student, but not quite what he'd expected. Not at all. It was Jenny Hauser who stood there. In high—heeled black pumps, a very tight maroon sweater and a, seemingly, even tighter wool navy blue blue skirt. She looked brilliantly attractive. "Smashing" had to be the word.

Martin hoped that he didn't appear, literally, knocked over as he stepped back and motioned her to come in.

"If I'm not disturbing professor."

Immediately there shot through Martin's mind "You look plenty disturbing" but what came out was "No, not at all. I really don't feel like much doing what I keep on trying to gear myself up to do, anyway," he candidly acknowledged. "In other words, I don't want to work myself up to work," he continued with what he intended as a smile. "What can I help you with?"

She closed the door as Martin turned and walked back behind his desk. Then she slowly walked over to one of the chairs opposite Martin's desk. He noticed that she wasn't carrying any of the text books, notebooks, or any of the the other paraphernalia that were the unmistakable indicia of a first year law student. She looked directly at Martin as she sat and crossed her right leg over her left. Her well shaped legs looked splendid between the high heels and what was left of the skirt after it had finished moving up her thigh. Martin judged that, in point of clinical, esthetic fact, her legs were exquisitely curved. He had, as usual, tried to avoid looking, but, for once, had failed. There could be no doubt—he had succumbed to temptation.

She proceeded to ask him a question about some minor point concerning offer—acceptance, one he'd mentioned fleetingly at the very end of the last class session. But the question really wasn't one—her way of raising and phrasing it showed that even she had basically understood the simple, straightforward information he'd wanted to impart. He assured her that she had comprehended what he'd been driving at and even added some bland words of encouragement as to her increasing grasp of the principles of Contract Law.

"Oh, thank you, professor. Thank you so much," she basked. She then recrossed her legs and this time Martin was conscious that the skirt had ridden even higher on the left thigh than it had before on the right. But this time he triumphed in the battle with himself to not stare at just how high. Her tight sweater and the even more so skirt announced that she was sufficiently full—bodied as to seem almost overloaded for her medium frame. Almost, but, definitely, not quite. She stopped at voluptuousness without slipping over into undisciplined sloppiness. As he and his adolescent pals would have had it, long ago: she was "built." No use denying it—she was a powerfully appealing and desirable young woman.

She appeared as though on the verge of saying something, yet not quite able to articulate it. Martin. almost frantically, sifted his mind for some feasible shard of conversation but came up basically blank since he'd already asked how he could help her and she, presumably, had disclosed the full extent of her current needs vis a vis Contracts scholarship. Finally she cracked the thin shell of silence to say what she seemed so diffident about bringing up.

"You know, professor, there's only a few weeks left in the semester before final exams …"

"I know, I'm glad to see that you're aware of it …"

"Yeah, right … Well, I thought it's like really time to start reviewing seriously, you know in earnest …"

"Absolutely, no doubt about it. I'm happy that you're being so diligent …"

"Well, long story short, I have a friend whose family owns a cabin up in Wisconsin. But it's not too far, only about a three, three and a half hours drive from here. And they're not using it this coming week—end, and it's heated and all, so if it gets as cold as it's supposed to be this time of year that's no problem … Well, anyway, I thought it would be a great, quiet, sort of secluded place , no telephone or anything, to study and like really do some serious overall reviewing in my courses …"

"It certainly sounds like a place where, especially in late Fall, studying might be one of the more stimulating things you could do there."

"Yeah, really … Anyway professor, you were so nice to talk to me a few weeks ago, about job opportunities and that sort of stuff, and you've really gone way out of your way to answer my stupid questions and all, about things in your class …"

"Oh, not at all Ms. Hauser, don't mention it. I'm always glad to help students with their questions. It comes with the territory, as they say."

"Well, anyway, you are nice … in a lot of ways …" she giggled. "And I was just thinking. Like maybe you'd like to come along with me to the cabin … There's still some nice Fall leaves to see, probably, and it's real quiet, so you could read or do your research in peace … And there are even some nice restaurants not too far away, and it's all very peaceful and relaxing …"

As he often did with students who seemed not to have anything particularly significant to say, anything requiring much of his concentration, who seemed to be rambling just for the sake of going on, Martin had let his attention level sag to where it was just barely aware of what words the student was speaking and with at least a good part of his mental energy spraying thoughts elsewhere. So it took him a moment or two to sharply focus in on the fact that unless his concentration had dipped so abjectly that he wasn't accurately comprehending the simple words he was hearing, he was being offered the proposition of a week—end tryst with Jenny Hauser. That snapped him to recognition that he'd better immediately deal crisply with what in fact was going on before things got any more keenly embarrassing for Ms. Hauser. Despite how very tempting she looked he knew, virtually instantly, that there was no possibility that he'd participate in her little scheme. She was definitely, inarguably, a most provocative temptress, but he was sure, with that reflexive response of unshakable conviction, that he would not allow himself to fall to this temptation.

"Oh, that's awfully nice of you to think of me Ms. Hauser … It's very kind of you …" he stumbled and bumbled, while she stared at him straight on, large clear eyes widely alert and focused intently. "It's a capital idea and I'm sure it's a wonderful spot in the Fall, but I just can't do it this week—end … I've had something planned, for quite a while, that I just have to do … I just wouldn't be able to change it …"

Her features drooped a bit with disappointment as she recognized that a carefully crafted plan had not achieved its objective. Yet, despite her ingenuousness, in so many ways, she was veteran enough on this terrain to have been prepared to deal with mission failure.

"Oh, I certainly understand that Professor Steen; I didn't give you very much notice. I couldn't expect you to drop everything."

Martin, perhaps preposterously, was beginning to feel sorry for her sense of rejection, but he could only nod emptily, so completely nonplussed was he at what had happened.

As she pushed herself up from the chair, straightening and smoothing her skirt with one hand, she continued, her voice now taking on a slightly metallic and mechanical quality: "There should still be some nice days left up there, and there might be another week—end that my friend's family wouldn't be using it. So, who knows, maybe it'll work out for another time ..."

She'd already moved halfway to the closed door. She reached for the knob, saying, "I really have to get going now, you know get a head start on all that studying. Thanks for your time, professor."

There flashed across Martin's mind the thought ,"But I didn't give you my *real* time," but by then she was through the door and had already shut it, with, unless Martin's ears were getting even more unreliable than he was aware, just the slightest hint of a slam.

"November_____

"Cutting right to the chase—I was propositioned by Jenny Hauser. Formally, Ms. Hauser, student of my Contracts class. She invited me to a week—end tryst in a secluded cabin in Wisconsin. Just for accuracy's sake—while she did this she looked positively physically irresistible. She'd dressed up like a very desirable woman who most definitely wanted to be sexually noticed, rather than like a young girl dedicated to being a diligent law student. She succeeded. Big time!! I certainly more than noticed. She showed off an extraordinarily shapely, very, very, provocative body in *extremely* tight clothing. Let me tell you journal, just between you and me, not to put too fine a point on it—she's a magnificent, hugely luscious piece of ass, as we boys of fifties Brooklyn were so fond of saying.

"But, even if I wanted to take her up on her enticing proposition, so to speak, (and, as I've indicated here before, there're some devastatingly cogent reasons not to,) it wasn't all that simple since she's going to be in my class until May. I've got very sound reason, in addition to my substantial endemic inferiority complex, to doubt that she wanted me for myself. I smelled a flagrant catch. Before she asked me to accompany her she made it patently clear that her purpose in going up there was to get some quiet time for a solid start on studying for exams, now less than a month away. I've got to think that there was a very distinct possibility, (probablilty,) that she was willing to prostitute herself for 'help' with her exams. Who knows, maybe she thinks I could fix her grades in other courses, as well as Contracts. A l'autre main, on the other hand that is, maybe I'm just too negative about myself, perhaps her motives were at least mixed. Maybe she likes me a little and doesn't find it all that difficult to prostitute herself in behalf of her grades and that all important career she'd previously spoken to me about. Maybe if she had no positive feelings at all toward me, or found me actually repellent, she wouldn't have been able to bring herself to suggest it, even to assure (a) good grade(s.) Maybe her motives are really mixed—she likes me a bit just as a man, wouldn't mind helping her grades along and, moreover, would love to notch the experience of fucking one of her professors so that she could regale all her friends, acquaintances, fellow students, anyone she meets, with the tale of her triumph— endlessly. 'And then Professor Steen, I called him Marty the main man, started licking my left nipple … ' Etc., etc. ETC.!!!!!

"I'd love to flatter myself and seriously think that a sensational looking thing like her was really somewhat interested in me qua man. But I'm not that delusional—yet. It had to be a quid pro quo deal. But as far as reporting her to the Honor Committee at school, or anything like that, I can't prove a thing , can I? She was just chatting with me, student to teacher, and merely casually suggested that I might like to join her in something she was planning to do—she didn't mention a thing about sleeping arrangements or such or insinuate any double entendres or suggestive remarks. Students are always asking teachers to share their activities with them—a cup of coffee with a group of them, come to a class party, go to a school basketball game, what not. I mean there was the way she was dressed—to show off to the very best possible advantage an absolute knockout body— but that's hardly , or 'admissible' proof that she was documentably bribing me, illicitly, by asking me to join her at the cabin to admire Fall foliage. After all, she also mentioned that there'd be a very quiet place for me to read and do research, (as though I'm positively yearning, every single moment, to do research,) and that there were some decent restaurants in the area. She was presenting, (in the sense of 'present,') me with the opportunity for a pleasant, but quiet, sedate, entirely Platonic week—end, just a token of her appreciation of my kindly counseling with her, would be her story.

"As someone born considerably before yesterday I can't believe it for a minute. But I'm still a sufficiently practical lawyer to sense that I can't actually *prove* a thing to the Honor Committee. It could all come out looking like the assertion of a sexual bribe is an absolutely ridiculous fantasy generated by the warped mind of a horny middle—aged law professor who hasn't gotten near a woman, not to mention laid, in several years. No, I don't think I'm on the hook of ethical repsonsibilty to report her here ...

"Damn, there goes the phone ..."

"Hello."

"O.K., who started the fifth game of the '55 World Series for the Dodgers? If you need a hint, fecal—matter for brains, I'll throw you one."

It was Michael Goldston, Martin's lifelong friend- he'd met him in the Brooklyn junior high school they'd attended in the early fifties- calling from Manhattan where he was a busily practicing psychologist. Typically they called each other once or twice a week and often quizzed each other on common minutiae and trivia from their common past. Very frequently the pertinent subject matter was the history of the Brooklyn Dodgers, 1947—1956.

"Of course I don't need a hint, boob—brain. You need a hint—on life. It was Roger Craig, currently manager of the San Francisco Giants. That was going to be your grudging hint—wasn't it? Something like 'He currently manages a major league team.' I not only do not need your hint, ignorant ass—hole, but I chuck it right back at your pathetic self."

"Alright, schmuck, so you were able to nail a simple ..."

"Here's one for you pellet—mind. How many innings did Craig go and who relieved him? You're so abjectly stupid you probably think he went all the way …"

"No, putz—head, I know that Labine finished up. I just can't remember whether he came in in the sixth or seventh …"

"I can't either. But I asked you the question and you flubbed it up dementia brain. Mark one in the 'L' column for you, and in the 'W' column for me. Then again, there are so many 'L's racked up against you that one more hardly matters. The whole thing is beyond you because, as I recall, you never learned to count too high. A number was like Sanskrit to you. You probably don't even remember what grade Mr. Zamore gave you in seventh grade Math … Mind you, I'm not asking you to remember what magnificent grade I got, just your own , feeble—mind."

"Of course I remember—ninety seven it was …"

"Exactly!! Practically a failing mark!! Remember what I got?"

"I know what you should have gotten. Around forty—one. Who knows what you cheated your way to. What did you really get, sixty—five, passing by the skin of your teeth?"

"Horse shit that you think I got sixty—five. You *know* that I got a hundred on every test and you are fully aware of the fact that Zithead Zamore, as we so imaginatively dubbed him, because his complexion wasn't perfect, told me I was the only pupil who he ever had who he even had to consider giving one hundred to on the report card. But he said he just didn't believe in doing that, because it implied perfection and no one, not even he himself, was perfect. So he said he decided to give me ninety—nine which he said he'd never given before, either. Therefore, QED, as I said before, your ninety—seven was like an amoeba turd."

"I did so poorly because I was intelligent enough to spend most of my time in that class ogling Michelle Lasky's budding-by-the-day chest, in the enormous variety of sweaters she pranced around in , day after day, to verify that she, indeed, was the first in her class to have certifiably significant tits."

"Which only goes to show how gross your taste was back then. All Lasky had was a major rack, not true beauty or style. I spent my time, and it was just as much time as you spent, because I didn't need to pay any attention at all to Zamore's halting lessons, since I was so inherently brilliant, I spent my time gazing at the delicate, fine—featured, authentic beauty of Emily Geller who was crossing over the threshold from pre—adolescence to devastating femme fatale."

"A lot of good her fatale did you. You didn't have the guts to get close enough to her to catch a sniffle."

"Yeah, well I don't seem to recall you wining and dining Michelle Lasky into a bed of ravishment either."

'That's the amusing part, isn't it Marty? Even if we'd had the courage to try for and had actually succeeded in getting the slightest access to any of these enchanting young ladies, whom we obviously still remember so longingly, we wouldn't have had the slightest idea of what to do."

"Well, there are some things you got right. Not many, but a few. Anyway, here I am, almost fifty, although not quite as close to it as you, and still chasing skirts."

"You're chasing the feminine gender? Glad to hear it. But what do you mean 'still'? You're just catching up for a mis—spent youth when you were absolutely and totally petrified of going near the fair damsels. If not for the enticing charms of Anna you would have remained a monk. Not even you could pretend obliviousness to, or resist, *her*. So, anyway, you're chasing. So, are you catching?"

Martin told Michael about the encounter with Mary Hanks, concluding by asking, "So, since you're a maven of human nature and sundry allied things, what do you think happened?"

"Well, first of all, although from the way you describe her she sounds very charming and perhaps even more beautiful, I'm deeply suspicious of her taste because I think she set up the zoo appointment because she liked you and I think, from the way you describe how the day went, that she got to like you more and still likes you; another serious negative reflection on her acuity and powers of observation. I think she left the way she did because, just exactly like she said, she suddenly realized she was late for an appointment that she felt she just had to keep. I further think that you should ring up the young middle—aged siren and ask for an authentic date."

"You may think so, in your august professional opinion, but who's got the courage?"

"I don't know who has it, but maybe you'd better find out. If you don't have it I advise getting it. Otherwise you'll be cheating yourself.

Nothing ventured ... You'll always wonder ... Report back to me in three days."

"You may be right doctor, probably are, but I don't know if I've got the fortitude to follow your prescription. I'll take it under advisement, as we lawyers say, see if I can sort things out.To change the topic from me, or as Bette Midler playing a self—absorbed actress in that pretty good flick, 'Beaches,' said:' Let's talk about you for a while; what did you think of my performance?'How's your woman—of twenty- seven years now, isn't it? How's Rita doing?"

"Just goes to show how bad at math you really are. We're only married twenty—six years. It's not twenty—seven until March. She's doing pretty well. Had some good students start to take lessons in the last few months. Restored her faith in the vocation of piano teacher."

"Let me know when she comes across the next Serkin. Rudolf, I mean—but even a Peter, the son, will be o.k."

"She'll probably tell you right after she lets me know. That's if she lets me know. Anyway, I have to get off soon, so that I don't blow her entire weekly earnings on this call. However, the next time we palaver I do want a report from you on when your next date with the lissome Professor Hanks will be. Or, better yet, has been."

"With your always encouraging remarks and barbs I'll work on the necessary gumption. But I just don't know if I can come through on this one. In the meantime, here's one for you to work on for the next time we talk. Obviously, shit—head, no fair consulting reference sources such as THE BASEBALL ENCYCLOPEDIA, etcetera, etcetera. O.K., what was the final score of the second game in the 1951 Dodger—Giant play—off and who were the starting pitchers? Also, name three players who homered in the game."

"Fair enough; I'll work on that one, you work on Hanks. Alright, take care and keep pitching."

"Very punny. That's *punny*, I said."

"O.K., journal, here I am back from the phone. As always it was nice to talk to Michael G. But he, in his professional and friendship wisdom, thinks it's a good idea for me to pursue Hanks and I just don't think

I really can. My spirits simply aren't in a hale enough state to absorb an outright rejection from that lovely gal. Yes, the cliché is 'Nothing ventured, nothing gained,' but nothing lost either. I don't have too many reserves left from which to pay losses.

"Damn it—I haven't done either the exercise bike, or, speaking of Rita Goldston, as I was just doing with Mike, my piano practicing yet. And it's almost eight. I'm perched on the precipice of delinquency …

"Back again, just about an hour later, after doing both my biking and my piano practicing. Sometimes, maybe even frequently, I think about giving up one of them—or both. I suppose I don't have a realistic option with the biking. Good for the heart, circulation, lungs, etc., etc. But it' so thunderingly BORING!! They say you have to do it at least twenty to thirty minutes for it to be 'aerobic,' and, therefore, beneficial to the heart, blood pressure and so forth. But to just keep pedaling in place for that amount of time is not at all an easy thing. At first I tried listening to my music to divert me and make the time go faster. But, for some reason, that just didn't work. Maybe I just resisted mixing something I love so much with the hateful tedium of relentlessly pushing down on one pedal after another, after another, after another, after the other, after the other … I just couldn't seem to concentrate on the music as I normally would. I couldn't borrow oblivion, for the tightening sensation in my calves and thighs, from the sweep of lush melody, the drive of pulsating rhythm.

"Television, and its plethora of cable channels, worked better for a while. Holding the remote control device in one hand, the handle bars with the other , pedaling away, I had almost fifty possible sources of distraction. Under such circumstances I was better able to focus on a mildly amusing sit—com than I could on a Haydn symphony. But then things started getting very irritating when, just as I was getting absorbed enough in the sit—com episode to want to see how things would evolve and turn out, a flurry of commercials would assault me. At first it was almost perversely amusing to see how many different products would be successively advertised before the resumption of the program itself. I'd think that the fourth ad had to be the last, or surely the fifth, certainly the sixth. But always there seemed to be one more. One additional inane, irritating, infuriating provocation to any reasonable sensibility or intelligence. How could there be endured one more paean to self—indulgence insisting on how incontrovertibly entitled to this or that beer, or depilatory, each of us hard—working pillars of respectability, salts of society, was. And frantically pushing the buttons on the remote, wildly jumping from one channel to another, only accentuated the frustration since most of the time it seems that you just run into another commercial—or even the very same one you were fleeing. In fact, several of the channels seem devoted exclusively to shopping. They keep on displaying and chattering about products which can be ordered simply by dialing the oft indicated telephone number and telling the account number of one of your many credit cards. Others run half—hour self confessedly nakedly commercial programs; their entire length and content devoted to extolling something like a specific hand cream or lipstick. Sometimes the format is three or four well—known 'celebrity' women having a 'discussion' about the innumerable virtues of the magical cosmetic being huscksterred.

"The best T.V. alternative is to find a sporting event in which I can work up some interest, rooting or otherwise. Of course this too will be interrupted by a ceaseless string of commercials. Bu there I can cope by flipping through all the channels and when I've determined that there's nothing worth watching on any of those I can return to the game or match, whatever, and find that it's nearly ready to resume, the last or almost last of the muliple intruding commercials trailing off.

"Tennis matches are the best because I truly love the sport, having followed it for just about forty years now. (I remember Gardner Mulloy, Billy Talbert, Vic Seixias, [E. Victor Seixas,] Pancho Gonzales, Tony Trabert, et. al. Those were great, exciting days.) Its balletic movements are so graceful, they're absolutely beautiful sometimes. But an athletic event of any sort isn't always on and I like to bike whenever the moment of resolution effectively throws my guilt complex into highest gear. I'd better palliate myself with *some* solution, or better keep groping for one, since relinquishing this regular exercise routine is not a real possibility for my Calvinistic, duty—bound personality. And, in any event, I really do believe that it's beneficial to health since I definitely feel better after I do it. And, naturally, I'd like to stay as healthy as possible for as long as possible. Life, whatever its deficiencies and pitfalls, is good enough for that. Or, presumably, its possibilities are.

"But the piano is something different—I don't *have* to do it. It's supposed to be for pleasure. But I'm so inept that it all can be enormously frustrating. It's simply beyond me to execute so much of the beauty I'd like to be able to express. My fingers are leadenly uncontrollable. Vladimir relishes repeatedly telling me that I'm the worst student he's ever had. ("Fingers should be like steel pistons; yours like wet spaghetti.") I distinctly sense that he's only partially jesting. I've been taking lessons from him for ten years now and am not as accomplished as students who haven't been playing for more than a year or two. I have to assiduously and laboriously practice a relatively simple piece, like Schumann's "Traumerei" or a Chopin Prelude, for months and months, before it sounds even 'recognizable,' –the highest accolade Vladimir has ever conferred on me. (Sometimes he'll add—'But not very.') Occasionally after my desperate, strained, mightily effortful rendition of some such composition Vladimir will mumble 'it goes something like that.' And on some days my practicing turns out woefully, even for me. (Like tonight.) I just can't seem to even find Middle C, much less make anything that even remotely resembles music, with a line, shapely phrases and accurate, elastic rhythms. Why not just spend the (almost) daily half hour I spend practicing listening to great music performed and interpreted by world class artists on recordings? No!! I should keep on with my own lessons because it's a discipline I should maintain. It's good for me, just like biking. I have to keep struggling to do the best I can and shouldn't let myself slide off the hook into another passive 'intake' activity, e.g. sitting in a chair and reading or listening to music, neither of which makes any demand on me to put *out* anything. I have to persist in trying to satisfy Vladimir's standards, every two weeks, within the framework of my capabilities, howsoever limited they may be, (VERY!!) by preparing as conscientiously and effectively as I can. I'm not entitled to dispense with another requirement, (give myself another dispensation, as it were,) to which I should hold myself. I have to hold myself together. I must, you know."

The phone started ringing again. Martin had no idea who it could be this time. Especially since it was shading toward later in the evening. Not late, as such, yet. But headed there.

"Hello?" Martin's voice held a tinge of fatigue and irritation.

"Hi, ... I hope I didn't get you away from anything ..."

"No … no … that's alright …" he muttered equivocatingly, straining for recognition of the voice.

"It's Mary … How are you?"

He did finally realize who it was, simultaneously with her telling him, and was taken aback. Also confused as to whether pleasantly or not.

"I'm surviving, getting by. What about yourself?" He almost added something like, "Did you make it in time to your appointment on Saturday?" out of desperation to generate some fluent continuity. But he was able to pull that back.

"I had such a nice time on Saturday. The weather, the elephants, the company, were all so fine."

Martin had a fleeting temptation to ask her which part of her Saturday she'd most enjoyed—before or after she left him. He reined this in also and decided that he was very glad that she'd called, that he was again getting pleasure out of hearing the mineral water sparkle in her voice. "Yeah, I enjoyed myself, too. What a bonus day, in November, in Chicago. " What he wasn't going to do was put himself on some emotional limb and wax on and on about just how much he'd loved her company and how much he appreciated their plentiful laughs together, their discussion and exchanges about music …

"Thanks for the personal compliment," she teased.

"No, I … I'm sorry … Of course I …"

"I'll tell you why I called."

'Yes, justify your intrusion," Martin teased back, trying to sprinkle his voice with some sprightliness.

"Well, incredibly enough, I'm actually going to cook some food with nutrients in it for dinner tomorrow night. I don't know about you, but that activity doesn't occur very frequently around here …"

"Rest assured—you're not being outclassed in this kitchen."

"So much the better then. You'll appreciate the very fact of preparation involving a flame, irrespective of the quality or tastiness of the final product. So how about sharing the eating of the eggplant parmagiana, healthy too, you see, with me?"

"Do I hear a formal dinner invitation?" Martin tried to maintain some reserve, exhibit less than utter eagerness.

"Actually I was trying for as much informality as possible , so as to lower, rather than raise expectations about culinary matters … But you definitely did hear an invitation."

"That's good, very welcome, indeed, because it's already been established how famished we are around here, where cooking and culinary are virtually foreign words."

"Great, then we're on for tomorrow evening. How about if I say around seven? Is that a good time for you?"

"I'll be weak from want of food, my mouth a waterfaill of salivary anticipation by then."

"O.k., o.k. I'm certainly feeling the pressure. I'll try very hard to cook good. Let me give you the directions."

Martin wrote them down on a hurriedly turned up scrap of paper, with the merest stub of a pencil which he also was just barely able to reach while talking.

"Well then, faithful journal, the night has not closed without a decidedly unexpected turn of events, as they say in the newsreels, or somewhere: Mary Hanks called me, (I didn't have to screw up my courage to do the reverse,) to invite me to dinner tomorrow evening. Now I can worry and agonize over whether she *really* wants to have me over at her place for a meal, or (with tenure politics, too, perhaps in mind,) is just trying to soften the brusqueness of nixing on my dinner invitation Saturday and the generally abrupt way that whole thing ended up. She sounded a bit tentative and defensive, a negative thinker like myself could speculate, but basically warm and friendly. And she seemed to get more so when she perceived that I wasn't irretrievably irked at her. So why don't I just completely forget about the disappointing, unsatisfactory conclusion of Saturday's adventure and enthusiastically embrace Dr. Michael Goldston's analysis that she liked me to begin with, got to like me more during our time together, and is trying to show that she increasingly likes me. Sounds good, doesn't it?

"Well, I'm certainly glad that for once, (maybe, more accurately, just one of the few times,) I wasn't conclusively judgmental and that I didn't act cold, unforgiving, to her. Maybe this is all just cosmetic—she knows Saturday didn't end well and she needs to resurrect good feeling between us because I will eventually be one of those voting on tenure and promotion for her. So, then, maybe it's all just a showy, yet mechanical, peace offering. But, looking on the bright side, maybe not. Maybe it's much more interesting and inviting than that. Like Hemingway wrote in THE SUN ALSO RISES; "Wouldn't it be pretty to think so?" Or something close to that.

"Words are also sounds and rhythmic components. I took a poetry course in college and had a wonderful professor whose voice I can still hear reading from a poem entitled "Weathers" by the great nineteenth-early twentieth century English novelist, Thomas Hardy. The line I keep hearing, have heard repeatedly, since the very first time this outstanding teacher read it is 'This is the weather the shepherd shuns/ And so do I.' I'll never forget, I mean *never*, the way his voice, the very quality, the sound, the nasality, the inflection of it, expressed the sadness, lamentation, longing, memory, etc., etc., etc. in those eleven words. Forget the words, except as the bringer of his voice. He made music without singing. The voice was an instrument. Naturally, there's content there too. How many times have I repeated those words to myself, to my very soul, when in, or trying to fortify myself for, an unpleasant or difficult situation. 'This is the weather the shepherd shuns, and so do I.' They do give fortitude, and courage and resolution. But it's the sound of his voice, especially as it subtly dropped on "And so do I,' as an independent phenomenon, whichhaunts always. I've regaled, perhaps bored, it doesn't stop me, many friends, colleagues, family with the impact this aural magician, combined with Hardy, made. His voice, as well as Hardy's writing, will sound forever.

"But maybe I'm overemphasizing the discrete vitality of the rhythm and sheer sound of the phrase. The effect created, enhanced by the beautiful mien of the reader's voice, was supplemented by the meaning of the words. Their sadness, resignation, eternal greyness. Undeniably, there's an inextricable linking of substance with form, so that impressive as the latter is 'alone' it nevertheless gains from the connotations of the words. In truth, it stands not alone. Words are never totally alone. Form and substance meld into comprehensive meaning.

"I think, for now, I'll just luxuriate in non-speculatively waiting and seeing what will happen. *Que sera …*"

Chapter Eleven

Mary's condominium was further downtown, nearer the law school, yet still only a five or ten minute's drive from Martin's two bedroom on the solidly upper middle class block of 6000 Sheridan Road North. He found street parking, less than a block from her twenty—four storey building and felt good walking over in the cold, but not yet intimidatingly frigid, November night air. The fierce cold of winter seemed to be stealthily lurking in the challenging bite of the high 20s—low 30s temperature but it hadn't yet deployed its most formidable weapons. This was enough to cause the skin to tingle and make you look forward to being immersed in the warmth of inside, but it didn't yet crash icy, implacable despair against your body—and soul.

Her apartment was on the fourteenth floor and since it was only two doors down on the right Martin smelled the enticing aroma as soon as he emerged from the elevator. It got more and more inviting as he went down the corridor and when she opened the door the smells blended into urgent mouthwateringness.

She'd also blended herself perfectly. Perfectly. What every indescribably sexy woman law professor should wear. A starkly white blouse, with just the slightest shiny, clingy quality to it and a longish black woolen skirt, bottomed off by what even Martin could tell were most elegant medium—heeled black leather shoes. Her hair was swept into somewhat of a bun effect, but a good deal of it still hung fairly long and loose in its honey—blonde glory. Each and every time that Martin became explicitly aware of Mary's hair there flashed into his mind the biblical observation that a woman's hair was her crowning glory.

The silky effect of her stockings, on those Miss America legs, perfectly complemented the silken effect of her blouse. "Elegant" was an obvious, really mandatory adjective as she held the door open and smiled the infinite waatage smile. Even if Martin had still been nursing any flickers of resentment over the abrupt termination of the cellophane wrapped Saturday afternoon, they'd surely have been swept conclusively away by the sight of her and, particularly, by that brilliant smile which surely could raze the stoniest resistance conceivable. Martin was glad that he'd reverted to form and had decided that, since it was a mid—evening dinner, he'd appear in a tie and jacket. Specifically, his all Ivy League garb of thick woolen blue blazer, soft light wool grey slacks, cordovan loafers and red, blue—dotted tie on sparkling white Oxford shirt. Anna would sometimes call his sartorial choices a "throwback," or "antediluvian" …

"I was hoping that those aromas were coming from here," he said, as, trying for his own best smile, he handed her a bottle of wine, (he'd settled on a California white,) which after laborious thought he decided to bring.

"Did you doubt it?"

"Neither doubted nor believed; just hoped fervently." Then he let impulse overwhelm caution. "But, if you'll permit a chauvinist from the old school … now … looking at you … I've quite forgotten food, smell, taste or whatever. May I make so bold as a 'WOW!'?"

'Oh, a man is always permitted that type of comment," she responded, in a way that could have been characterized as coy, if they both did not know that each was thinking exactly that, as she gestured Martin in with the hand that wasn't on the door knob.

"But the effect isn"t complete yet," she warned, motioning him past a glass dining table, surrounded by four thickly upholstered armchairs, two of which had full dinner settings in front of them, and into a living room area with a deep beige carpet and almost glaring, stark white walls, hung with two Morrocan tapestries. There were also a very dark coffee brown sofa and matching armchairs. "I waited until you got here to put the music on."

She walked slowly,(sinuously flitted past Martin's mind), over to floor to ceiling cabinets set against the wall opposite the one behind the intensely dark brown sofa, and pushed buttons to activate a compact disc player. The ineffably haunting theme of one of the Impropmtus from Schubert's Opus 142 floated through the room in a densely sonorous, yet, at the same time, delicately sensitive, piano tone.

Martin's grin was immense. "If we had perfection before now we have supra—perfection. Is this what the French mean by the pluperfect tense? I see, or rather decidedly hear, that since our last chat about music you've gotten interested in Schubert Impromptus."

"You're a very compelling teacher, a super professor," she said, bending a very slight bow in Martin's direction.

"A teacher's teacher, no?" Martin returned, holding his arms partially out before him and shrugging slightly, to emphasize the point.

"If you like."

"Yes, I do like teaching whatever little I know about musc. And I especially enjoy teaching it to someone like you who really appreciates great music."

"Well, thank you for the good grade," she acknowledged, waving toward one of the easy chairs.

"Actually," Martin quickly remarked, as he settled into the chair, allowing himself to start sinking down into it, "I not only particularly like teaching it to someone like you, but, if the whole truth be told, I like to teach it to you, particularly." He had to fight averting his eyes from hers when he got this out, and he partially lost.

"It seems my grade gets better and better," she laughed, as Martin inclined his head at the speakers, just off to his right, one hand to an ear, his brow furrowed in an expression of someone listening with intense concentration.

After about thirty seconds, with Mary sitting at one end of the long sofa, Martin, hesitatingly, said: " I'm definitely not absolutely certain, I could be making an enormous fool of myself, but I think the pianist is Radu Lupu. It sure could be Murray Perahia, or even the too often clinical Barenboim, but reserving the right of you not thinking less of my music appreciation acumen if I 'm disastrously wrong, I'm going to go with Radu Lupu."

"You really are too much!!" she exclaimed, raising hands, palms upward, over her shoulders. Very impressive! How'd you know that? I'd barely even heard of Lupu, and didn't really know his work, but the kid helping me in the record store insisted that he's in the very top echelon of the younger pianists and that he's to die for, supreme, in these impromptus. And so it is; this is just unspeakably beautiful. I can't imagine anyone playing them more transcendentally, ethereally … But how can you just come up with something like that …"

"First of all, remember, I was by no means sure. I thought it was Lupu, but I could for sure have been wrong, embarrassingly so, actually. Stretched on my face in the mud, in front of you, my damsel. Secondly, because, it chagrins me to say, of the number of years I've been around, I've had a lot, that's a *lot* of listening experience. When you've heard a lot, you get to recognize a lot. Individual styles and touches, mannerisms in certain types of phrases. And there's even more you think you recognize. Which is how it's so easy to be wrong. So, basically, I lucked out."

"Well, I'm impressed, nevertheless."

"Oh, certainly don't let me inhibit you, not in any way, from being impressed with me. Feel totally free to to let yourself go, as expansively as you like, in that respect, anytime."

"O.k., I will," she said quietly, (was it a bit huskily, too?) smiling, directly at him; that knockout smile with, it seemed, an added dollop of sweetness thrown in.

Their eyes met solidly this time and they sustained the mutual gaze, as Schubert, plumbed, all the way down, by Radu Lupu, conferred serenity, poignancy, hope. Each stayed silently rapt for the twenty more minutes that the magical, trans—ethereal melodies were spun out effortlessly by Lupu's fingers.

"There's nothing that anyone can say that's apposite after that" she said, shaking her head in admiration and pulling herself off the sofa, "so I won't try."

"Even someone as voluble as yours truly won't ," Martin replied, looking up at her.

"But I do know when I smell a meal that's ready to be eaten," Mary remarked, smiling again, "and I also know that I, personally, am ready to devour it. I sincerely hope you are too."

"I've had a voracious appetite since the elevator door opened and those fantastic aromas rendered me helpless with desire."

"Oh, if there's desire we don't want it to be helpless, do we? Wasn't it Henry James who once wrote, somewhere, in some autobiographical fragment or something, 'Where there is emotion there am I.' Well, desire, clearly an emotion, should be expressed, acted upon, shouldn't it? Where there is desire there helplessness should not be, no?"

Martin, now also standing just a few feet away, looked at Mary, smiled a trace smile and barely said, practically whispered, "I suppose so."

"Then let's eat!" she commanded, pointing to the set table and turning to the brightly lit kitchen area connected to the dining alcove by a sliding door, now open.

The lights were dimmed over the table which could comfortably seat six. They sat across from each other, at either end. There was a dry, but not too dry, Italian wine, (not the bottle Martin had brought,) which was very satisfying. Martin, almost invariably, never had more than just several sips of any type of alcohol during the few social occasions where civility demanded he attend, but now he felt himself really appreciating the actual taste of the wine. He even came close to drinking enough so that a re—fill would have been in order. (Was she now making him into a oenophile too?) But not quite. Nevertheless, Mary tried to pour him some more, when she re—filled her own glass. But he shook his head, telling her he just wasn't much of a drinker.

She'd made a tasty feta cheese salad, with home made, exceedingly crunchy, croutons, on a thick bed of very crisp romaine lettuce, to go with the not overly salted egg plant parmagiana cooked to just the right consistency. They both ate most heartily. Martin, in fact, coyly asked for thirds, on the grounds that it was a vice he was entitled to indulge since he drank so sparingly.

While delighting in the food, which Mary said she'd pay the supreme compliment by admitting that it made her feel that she should cook more often, they also actually got around to discussing Martin's conversation with Dean Weymouth. Martin reminded her that it was the subject of his original phone call to her while Mary commented that, therefore, it "had brought them together." They laughed genuinely, richly, secure in wine, warmth on a wintry night and full stomachs. Mary opined that it didn't seem as though Weymouth was trying to be very oppressive, that he was probably just going through motions he'd promised the student complainers he'd go through. Under the circumstances of excellent cheer and easy, genial companionship Martin readily agreed. Weymouth was dismissed.

The sense of well being was accentuated, if possible, when Mary brought out the extravagantly creamy appearing chocolate mousse dessert. The coffee was decaffeinated, but deliciously flavored amaretto and each had a second cup to wash down the second servings of mousse—which they generously congratulated themselves on holdng to moderate size.

They lingered around the table, chatting amiably and animatedly about certain students they'd each had, focusing with some satisfaction on some of the very best ones and trying to restrain themselves from unduly savage humor about some of the most inept.

As the anecdotes petered out Martin started clearing the table and offered help washing the dishes. They got all the dishes, pans and pots in the sink and were starting to scrape and rinse to prepare them for loading in the dishwasher.

"Did it ever occur to you," Martin said, "that dishwashers are somewhat of a fraudulent invention because, basically, you have to wash the dishes so that the dishwasher can wash them effectively?"

"No, because a woman, as differentiated from you frivolous men, knows how much effort you'd have to put into truly sanitizing the dishes without a dishwasher to sterilize them."

Starting to verge on feeling quite giddy, Martin deadpanned," So you mean that these dishes won't be able to have little pitchers and saucers?"

Mary looked confused for a moment, but, after a few seconds, remonstrated, "That is just absolutely terrible, Martin, terminally grotesque in fact." She giggled appreciatively, tilting her head back, as they faced each other at the sink, each with dinner plate and sponge in hand.

Her neck and throat were delicate, yet young, skin firm, and with the slightest tinge of color. Martin, still holding the dish and sponge was impelled, it seemed almost involuntarily, to suddenly lean over, while her head was back, and softly kiss, for the merest moment, the cavity of her throat. When she realized what had happened she brought her head upright and looked, solemnly almost, directly into his eyes for several seconds. Then, still holding dish and sponge , she leaned forward and brought her lips to meet Martin's. Both had eyes closed as she exerted pressure against his lips and he returned the pressure. In a few seconds she pulled back and again holding Martin's eyes with hers she put the plate and sponge on the adjoining counter area, over the dishwasher. Martin, never taking his eyes from hers, gently placed the dish and sponge into the sink, and, outstretching his arms completely eliminated the three or four feet which had separated them. In one another's arms their open mouths met and then Martin gripped her shoulders and kissed her throat several times, before taking his right hand from her left shoulder and gingerly touching her eyelids closed. His lips making the very barest contact he kissed each lid, murmuring, "You're so very beautiful …"

He took her shoulders again and pressed his mouth back on hers. She emitted the slightest sigh, her hands loosening his tie away from his collar. Their tongues caressed and Martin dropped his hands to the irresistible silk of her blouse where her full, assertive breasts pushed. He sensed the nipples taut under the layers of blouse and brassiere netting. Then his right hand slid around her back and, clutchingly, it went down her skirt to her buttocks while his left hand began fumbling with the top buttons of her blouse. She used both hands to unbutton his shirt under the flapping tie. He reached down with his right hand so that he could lift her skirt enough to get his hand under it and move it gently upward along the exciting sheerness of her stockings until the thrilling full curve of her buttock was flush against the palm of his hand.

She leaned her lips against his right ear and blew softly into it.Then she whispered, "Not to change the subject, or anything … but you've seen the whole apartment except the bedroom … It seems like it's time …"

They dropped their hands, looked at each other for a few seconds and broke into chuckles.

"Why?" Martin retorted, do you object to being savagely taken right here on the kitchen floor?"

"No, not at all; sounds spicy. But I just wanted your opinion on the bedroom décor."

They laughed some more as Mary held out her hand for his and, as they continued to gaze and smile at each other , pulled him gently toward the bedroom, just off the living room. They did speak of its décor—but only some hours later.

"February 15th

"I can't believe that it's something like three months since I've written in here. The last time the fall semester was still going on and, now, we're already more than a month into the second semester. And that's after about five weeks of intersession for the holidays and so forth.

"But, of course, I really can very well believe it's been that long since I've scribbled here. Easy to believe because in the past the more unhappy I was the more I tended to wallow in written despair. Catharsis and all that, I suppose. But for the last three months I've been pretty darn happy , hardly ever even tinged by discouragement. Mary's changed all that –I think I have a notion of what bliss is now—and, hereby, I give her credit, in writing. I'll sign it if anybody wants.

"It turns out, my good luck, that a brief marriage of a few years ago didn't work out for her. I don't know what the doctor, that's who she was married to, a doctor, wanted, but she found out, after they were married less than a year, that he'd started dallying with his nurse. She suspected some substance abuse also. Mary concluded it all wasn't the basis of a lasting, lifetime relationship.

"As I say, I don't know what the man wanted. She's very interested and adventurous sexually and has "brought me out" in certain ways. We have a great time in that area. But, most importantly, we have a wonderful time in general. She's very mature and sensible for her thirty odd years, wise in ways that most people don't reach until they're a decade or so older. So the true gap between us isn't as great as the brute chronology suggests. That fifteen years is also minimized by her solid education and self—education, how widely read she is. Well versed on a variety of topics. When I happen to mention something that happened before she was born, or when she was a very young child, she's often familiar with the reference and doesn't stare at me with that blank confused expression which, for example, one of my students, (or some younger colleagues, for that matter,) might project in such circumstances. Also her values are admirable. Getting more isn't what she thinks the paramount, not to mention sole, objective in life. She's essentially service oriented, as I like to think I am. It's not that she wants to take a vow of poverty, but acquiring more and more materialistically, buffing up the bank account more and more, indulging herself with ever more creature comforts are not the motivations that make her get up in the morning. Getting and spending, in Wordsworth's immortal phrase, do not define every contour, every cranny, of her life.

"But, bottom line, we just have good times, fun, contentment, satisfaction and, to resort to an over—used phrase, sense of well being, together. I eagerly look forward to seeing her again after each time I've seen her. We haven't moved in with each other, and we agree that no one at school, including our colleagues, not to mention gossipy staff and students, should be told about our relationship, but we do spend a great deal of time with each other. She cooks tremendous meals, both qualitatively and quantitatively, (I devour a vastly greater portion of each one,) and I happen to be a very proficient dishwasher and general cleaner—upper. We watch selected t.v. programs, (alright—so sometimes they're not *that* selective,) curled up with each other on a couch. We natter about these programs or anything else we feel like BSing about while they din on. We eat out, too, at ethnic restaurants, ones at which we're pretty sure that no one either of us knows will be. (Not an overly difficult constraint to accommodate—especially for me.) Sometimes we argue and debate "lawyerlike" about current affairs. But we're usually in accord in a mellow, liberal sort of way, while we bemoan the very scant likelihood of our positions actually prevailing in the cynical, power—crazed, corrupt, rough and tumble universe of real world politics. Realpolitik, as they, (or atleast the Germans,) say. We also often listen to music together—again curled up on a couch with me stroking her luscious hair and as much of the luscious rest of her I can reach.

"We also tell each other about our respective research projects , criticize each other's ideas and approaches and make suggestions that might be helpful. On this I try to help Mary as much as possible, because she needs some solid papers in a reasonable amount of time to advance in her career. Actually she needs one or two in the pretty immediate future to keep her job, while I, a tenured professor, am under no time pressure to publish—or publish any more, at all, for that matter. (The need to keep at this sort of research now, in a quite intensive way, is one of the few things that will occasionally make Mary cranky.) Each nags about things the other should do, things on which a jostle is needed from time to time. Like making sure that Mary calls her folks in Massachusetts at least once or twice a week. And like making sure I stay faithful, in my fashion, as they say, to my exercise regimen. (My motivation is much stronger now that there's all the more reason to stay fit and toned.) We take substantial walks when it's not laceratingly cold and if we find something on which to disagree during conversation we may wind up flinging a snowball or two at each other, (she has a formidable pitching arm for her gender,) and/or dropping snow down each other's sweater collar, etc., etc. And all topped off by an exquisitely delicious hot chocolate in a cozy coffee shop. Or the even more cozy, casual, genial atmosphere of the kitchen Chez Mary. We've played tennis a few times at an indoor club and are close enough in competence levels to have had some exciting, crisply executed, close sets. (Also, the last time we played, after our hour was up, Mary said we should defer our showers until we got back to her place because she was in a hurry to get something into the oven in time for our dinner. She took care of that the second we arrived back and then immediately suggested that we should shower together. Frankly, I'd never had sexual intercourse in a bathtub before—but I can't wait for a repeat; her body is so welcomingly soft. Plush.)

"During the height of the holiday season, when we didn't think that too many people who knew either of us would be around, we hazarded an expedition to Orchestra Hall to hear the incomparable Radu Lupu, "our" pianist, play the Beethoven Piano Concerto No. 3, C—Minor, Op. 37, with the Chicago Symphony conducted by that great, spontaneous Beethovian, Klaus Tennstedt. Another hero worth worshipping. Our expectations were impossibly high but Lupu more than met them. He played with incisive verve and rhythmic intensity in the outer movements and tender sensitivity in the aching slow movement. And Tennstedt cajoled the band, as symphony musicians like to refer to their group, into being a perfectly attentive and supportive partner. He also led Schumann's "Rhennish" Symphony with superb elasticity and emphasis. Both of us were exalted when we left the hall. We then had an absolutely, obscenely, enormous dinner in a tiny Indian restaurant and afterwards went back to my apartment where we virtually devoured, incinerated each other with totally abandoned passion.

"I don't know quite what else to say, except that this has been going on for several months now and it feels *very* good. In fact, just splendid, *terrific*. I wake up after a solid night's sleep full of energy and pretty well bursting with plans, purposes, objectives of all sorts. I look forward to seeing, again, Mary's freshness and quiet beauty, to experiencing renewed sexual joy with her, to making plans with her. Is this leading anywhere? It sounds like it is, but I simply don't know. Nothing's been plotted out future—wise. We're having a good time and feel like we're going to keep on having a good time for a long while. That's enough for now, n'est-ce pas?"

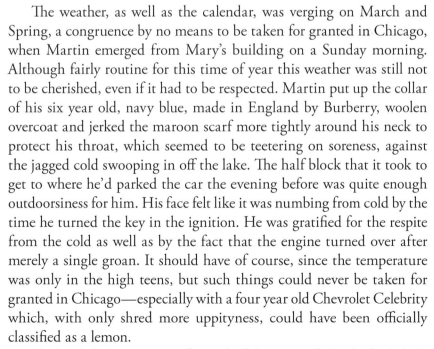

The weather, as well as the calendar, was verging on March and Spring, a congruence by no means to be taken for granted in Chicago, when Martin emerged from Mary's building on a Sunday morning. Although fairly routine for this time of year this weather was still not to be cherished, even if it had to be respected. Martin put up the collar of his six year old, navy blue, made in England by Burberry, woolen overcoat and jerked the maroon scarf more tightly around his neck to protect his throat, which seemed to be teetering on soreness, against the jagged cold swooping in off the lake. The half block that it took to get to where he'd parked the car the evening before was quite enough outdoorsiness for him. His face felt like it was numbing from cold by the time he turned the key in the ignition. He was gratified for the respite from the cold as well as by the fact that the engine turned over after merely a single groan. It should have of course, since the temperature was only in the high teens, but such things could never be taken for granted in Chicago—especially with a four year old Chevrolet Celebrity which, with only shred more uppityness, could have been officially classified as a lemon.

He headed the car away from the lake, towards I-94, the Eden's

Expressway. That would get him up to the Northern suburbs and his regular visit to the retirement home, euphemistically so—called, in heavily Jewish Skokie. That's where his aunt Sadye had lived for the last four years. His mother's sister and the only surviving child of his maternal grandparents. Only eighteen months after convincing Sadye to enter this facility Sadye's daughter and son—in—law, for career reasons, (his,) had to move to Cleveland and their visits to the eighty—six year old had now petered out to two or three a year. Martin had made it a point to see her at least once a month, sometimes, when he could muster the resolve, twice, to maintain some semblance of continuity for the severely arthritic woman.

The wind reminded Martin that it worked the suburbs too once he'd parked the car in the lot of the home and was making his head down way toward the lobby entrance. When he entered, identifying himself to the not overly amiable desk clerk, there were the usual three or four octogenarians nodding off in wheel chairs in the general lobby area. Every time he encountered this scene Martin was puzzled as to why they were positioned quite apart from each other rather than in much closer proximity so that they would have been able to chat with each other. He usually "resolved" his wondering by concluding that, in any event, it didn't matter since all of them were dozing. But then he moved to the next step of curiosity and wondered whether they'd all be dozing if they'd been situated so that there was a realistic chance to converse.

He got into the elevator to go to the fourth floor, the level for the "moderately incapacitated" residents. It had come up from the basement carrying its cargo of two very old men, each with a cane, and accompanied by some sort of aide or nurse. Both men were hunched over their canes in almost question mark figures, but when Martin got in to the elevator both raised their heads from staring at the floor mode, as much as could possibly be managed, to see who had gotten on. Martin smiled and nodded at each man and also met the eyes of the helpers. As the elevator ascended Martin commented, "It looks like a pretty raw day out there. In fact I can tell you, it is a pretty raw day out there." Both nurse types nodded, smiling slightly, but neither replied, while one of the old men, his head back to its customarily deeply bent over position, signified no response at all. But the other man again brought his head up as far as it could go, just to the point where he could look into Martin's eyes. Then he practically spat out, "But I'd still rather be out there than in here—you shouldn't know from it!"

The elevator stopped and each elderly resident, one hand on cane, the other under the arm of his aide, in house slippers, flannel shirt with large checkered pattern and baggy pants belted closely to wispy waist, shuffled off the elevator, while Martin kept the "Open" button pushed in, in agonizingly, almost insufferably slow steps.

Martin got off and headed for 409, Sadye's room. He passed two or three other rooms on each side of the corridor. They had neatly made—up beds and looked clean and tidy. In every one there was an aged man or woman sitting in a wheelchair, next to a large window. Most were looking straight out the window, a blanket across their laps. But some, heads on chests, were dozing. Martin conjectured that the doors to these rooms must be left open so that staff people could frequently check to make sure that nothing untoward had happened to anyone—or, perhaps more accurately, so that they could tell when something had.

On reaching Sadye's room he saw that she, too, was seated in her wheelchair by the window. As Martin approached her he noticed that while she seemed to be gazing out the window it was only through the daze of quickly on and off again naps. Once he was right at her chair she looked up. But, then, only stared wordlessly.

"Hi, Aunt Sadye. How are you?"

She continued looking at him blankly.

"It's me Aunt Sadye, Marty; your nephew, Martin."

Her eyes retrieved a dash of life. " Yes, yes, yeah, sure, yeah, Martin. Marty, Marty, yeah, sure. How are you Marty?"

"I'm o.k., Aunt Sadye. How are you doing?"

"How'm I doing? Well, to tell you the truth, a lot's happened in the many years since I saw you last, Marty. You were much younger then, you know."

"No, Aunt Sadye, I was here only three weeks ago. I was here then and I come to see you every two or three weeks. It's never that so much as a month goes by without my coming to see you."

"What's today? Wednesday? On Wednesdays I go to play Bingo in the rec room. You were here when we played Bingo last Wednesday?"

"No, Aunt Sadye, today's not Wednesday. It's Sunday. I come to see you every two or three weeks on Sunday."

"It's Sunday, today? O.k., let it be Sunday. That's right, it's Sunday. But, still, it's been such a long time, so many years, since I saw you the last time. I can remember your Bar Mitzvah day, you looked so serious and handsome."

"That was a long time ago, a very long time ago. A long time for all of us, Aunt Sadye."

"Why? Not so long ago. How old are you now, Marty? In your early thirties, no?"

"No, I'm afraid not, Aunt Sadye. I wish that were true, but I'm actually almost fifty years old."

"So, if you're fifty, Marty, so how old does that make me? How old am I, Marty?"

"Well, Aunt Sadye, you're young in spirit. That's what counts. But on the calendar you're eighty six, Aunt Sadye."

"Eighty—six? No, can't be. Go on! How could I be eighty—six. When was I born?"

"You were born in 1903, Aunt Sadye. So that makes you eighty—six years young. Congratulations.GAY GAZINTER HITE." (Martin had resorted to one of the few Yiddish phrases he still remembered—"Go in good health.")

"Why, what year is this? How could I be eighty—six? What is it? Nineteen—seventy? Or, maybe nineteen—seventy one, or two … ?"

"No, actually it's nineteen …"

'What day did you say it was today? Yeah, that's right Wednesday, you before said it was. It's Wednesday, right?"

"No Aunt Sadye, it's not …"

"So, if it's Wednesday, I have to go to Bingo. My memory's failing but some things I remember. When Bingo day is … I remember some things …"

Martin had been told by the professional staff that the official diagnosis wasn't Alzheimer's but, rather, dementia. Her short-term memory was particularly bad, virtually non—existent. In a very brief period, as short as five or ten minutes, she could repeatedly ask, as many as six or seven times, what day of the week it was or what she'd eaten, a half an hour ago, for lunch. Yet her recollection of things that had occurred as far back as her early childhood could be scalpel precise. Through experience Martin had found that when she started becoming totally confused, as she now seemed to be, and began rambling incoherently , it was helpful to bring up the very distant past.

"Aunt Sadye, do you remember when, before you got married, before you married Uncle Morris, you worked as a legal secretary?"

"Sure, of course. I was out in the business world from the time I was a young girl. Before I met your Uncle Morris. We didn't even bother finishing high school in those days. We had to get out there and earn some money to help mom and pop feed all of us. Six children. Yes, oh yes, I was a legal secretary. I can still take dictation; I still remember my shorthand. I still write notes to myself—you know to help me remember things. In short hand. Yes, yes, I worked for Eisner and Lubin. They were very big real estate lawyers at the time. They handled a lot of real estate. A lot. I recall it very well. Very well. I bet I could still recite the words of some of the documents. I typed up so many of them. 'Know all men by these presents … ' Oh yes. At Eisner and Lublin …"

"What were their first names, Aunt Sadye? Do you remember the full names of Mr. Eisner and Mr. Lublin?"

"Whaddya mean what were their first names? Naturally I remember their first names. It was Murray Eisner and Solomon Lublin.They were very big, maybe the biggest real estate lawyers in New York. I mean, at the time. Sure, of course: Eisner and Lublin, 36 Pine Street, New York, New York. No zip codes then.That was down right in the Wall Street area. You would get off at the Wall Street stop on the IRT subway …"

"Which one did what? I mean between Eisner and Lublin? Did they each specialize in a particular area of real estate law?"

"What else; VOODEN? Sure, of course they specialized. They had a very big practice. The biggest. So each one had to handle what he was good at, what he did best. I remember, very well, that Eisner did mostly commercial real estate. He would draw up the papers when an office building or restaurant or store was being bought or sold, you know turned over. Depending on which end his client was on. And Lublin took care of the rest—you know, personal transactions, like when one person sold a house to another person , or when a client bought a new home. Mostly he represented people buying homes and such, you know. Some very expensive I might add. Maybe twenty, twenty—five thousand."

The old woman was accelerating in animation as she reminisced. The only thing Martin had to do was to ask her about specific details on which she could then elaborate.

"Did you work nine to five then?"

"Oh, no, we had to be there at eight—thirty, definitely not a minute later, because court calls were at nine, and just in case a lawyer needed something before he went to court … Oh, no, it was definitely no later than eight—thirty sharp that you had to be in. And, what five? No five! No, no, you didn't leave a second earlier than five—thirty and, if necessary, later. Could be quite a bit later. You had to make sure that everything that had to be taken care of was taken care of, that everything was all set for the next day. And you know, of course, Marty, that we had to work Saturdays then. Except there were two other girls and, so, every other Saturday you only had to work half-a-day, until one o'clock. You could go and enjoy yourself on Saturday afternoon. Maybe go for a bite, and a little shopping, or something, if all your work was finished by one o'clock. But on the other two Saturdays you had to be there until five—thirty, like any other work day. And I remember, we'd go to lunch at Jenkins, I can still see it, it was a cafeteria on John Street, you know, where all the insurance companies were, a block or two from the office. You could get a complete meal, soup, a hot dish like meat or fish or something, with vegetables, potatoes or peas or string beans, and then your coffee with a nice thick slice of pie, they had delicious blueberry, or apple, all for maybe a quarter, or thirty cents, if you had something fancy like roast beef, you know something deluxe like that. And if you were a real sport, or in a special good mood, you would leave something like three cents or a nickel, on the table, after you were all through, and by the way you could sit there for as long as you liked, for the boy who cleaned up. Yes, believe me, a whole hot lunch for a quarter. And at Jenkins, yet, a very nice, airy, bright place. And the food was delicious."

"Lunch for a quarter, that's really something Aunt Sadye. But, then again, you didn't make very much back in those good old days."

"No, whaddya mean? We made a very nice living. I started at eight dollars a week and you'd get raises if you were a good worker. By the

time I met your Uncle Morris I think I was making , already, nine—
fifty a week. A quarter lunch, so you spent maybe a dollar and a half,
two dollars a week for lunch; a nickel carfare, so not much more than a
half—dollar a week on that. So then you had left over to pay some rent
and to give a little money to your mother and pa …"

"Those were certainly the good old days, eh, Aunt Sadye"?

"Yes, Marty, things were different then … We didn't expect
everything … The world owing us …"

The old woman's voice trailed off and silent tears began forming in
glistening eyes. Martin, who'd been sitting, leaning forward, hands on
knees, on a wooden chair he'd pulled close to her wheelchair, got up and
reached for a small wad of Kleenex he carried in the left front pocket of
his slacks. Peeling one off he dabbed dry his aunt's cheeks and eyes.

"Aunt Sadye, why're you crying? We were having such a nice time
talking about the past. You know, the good old days, when you were
still working, when you hadn't even gotten married yet …"

"Why I'm crying? I'll tell you why I started crying. I started crying
because I can remember so clearly, it's such a sharp picture in my
mind, every detail of things that happened seventy years ago … I can
remember all of that … And I can't remember what I had for lunch,
half an hour ago, or what day today is, even though I asked you time
after time already … That's why … I …"

She started shaking this time, as the tears seeped again and
began falling on the woolen robe she was wearing over a plain, pale
blue nightgown which looked like it couldn't absorb too many more
launderings. Martin left—handedly reached for the Kleenex again while
he put his right arm around the bony shoulders and hugged her to
him.

After he'd gotten her to quiet, and the heaving had stopped, he
started talking about how he'd spoken with her daughter, Frances,
just a few days ago, and how she'd told him that she and husband Mel
would be flying in from Cleveland , in only another few weeks, to
visit with Sadye for the week—end. He detailed their plans to stay at a
downtown hotel on Friday and Saturday nights but to spend a good part
of Saturday and Sunday with Sadye, at the home, before flying back on
Sunday evening. At first Sadye acted a bit puzzled and confused at this

information but then seemed to understand who Frances was and that she'd soon be visiting.

Martin, having promised Mary that he'd be back at her apartment by early afternoon, so that they'd be able to make the three o'clock showing of the latest Woody Allen film, prepared to go. After he had put the six year old blue coat back on and was leaning over to kiss Sadye good—bye, she, holding her cheek out towards him, suddenly said:

"But you know, Marty, at my stage and age another couple of weeks is a long time. Maybe a very long time."

As Martin, simultaneously disconsolate and eager, strode across the parking lot the wind seemed to have become steelier and more penetrating. He got very cold just walking to the car. And, although he set the heater at its maximum level, he couldn't seem to warm up at all until he'd driven practically all the way back to Mary's.

And the chill didn't completely leave his body until Mary opened her door, arms wide apart, and he fell into her embrace, clamping his own arms around her softness as tightly as he possibly could.

———————————— ⁓ ————————————

"Well, now I have a real problem. A *real* real problem. It's especially real because it actually requires a solution.I .e. a decision has to be made. I've got to go one way or the other. And the decision will be extremely significant in terms of the impact it'll have on the rest of my life. Yes, exactly, the route of the rest of my life, I believe. Maybe, just maybe, by writing about it here I can start to sort things out.I don't really think so, but no harm in trying right? That's what they say at least. It's better than just brooding and brooding about it and perhaps by writing I'll feel I'm gaining some control over it.

"Anyway, after coming back to Mary's from the Woody Allen, (another of the mediocre, barely amusing ones—the only type he seems capable of turning out for the last few years,) we were settling down on her couch for some pre—dinner palaver, additional Woody Allen re—hash, and who knows what physically stimulating activities, when suddenly Mary more or less sat bolt upright and solemnly intoned 'There's something we have to talk about.'

"It's been my experience that not many enjoyable conversations start off with those words. In any event, that was certainly the end of stroking her hair, her back and her thighs—and whatever joys might have followed. What we *had* to talk about was her having been told by Weymouth and, also, Samuel, (Sam What Am,) Levy, Professor of Constitutional Law and Chair of the Tenure and Promotion Committee that when faculty consideration of Mary being retained for the next academic year came up in about a month each of them would feel more favorably, much more comfortable about urging the faculty at large to act positively on her retention, if she, by that time, had had a substantial article accepted for publication in a solidly respected law review. Then she told me that she'd written about a third to a half of what she thought was a decent enough article on some new developments, in tort law, on product liability of manufacturers. But she added that she still had a considerable amount of research to do before she could complete it and that, anyhow, there was absolutely no way she could finish it up and get it accepted for publication within the month. (She correctly pointed out that sometimes more than a month can go by before you even get any response, whatsoever, to a submitted article, from a law review editor. And even then the response can merely say that while they received it and looked it over preliminarily they'll still require an indeterminate, usually longer rather than shorter, amount of time to seriously evaluate it for publication. So, she concluded, by this time she was pretty agitated,, that there simply was no way of giving Weymouth and Levy what they said they wanted and on which, apparently, her job depended.

"She said that she'd been cogitating intensely and doing mental manipulation, mental gymnastics and mental gyrations for days but that the only thing she could come up with was to say that she'd had an entire article on her computer , just a day or two short of completion, but that being technologically naïve she'd never backed it up on a floppy disk or by printing out a hard copy, (as she since found out she should have,) and that, suddenly, the computer had just crashed wiping out the whole thing. That, then, she'd feverishly tried to reconstruct from scratch as much of it as she could but that, since the crash had happened only a few days ago, she'd only been able to recover to the point at which, in truth, she really was. So she'd be able to show the third to half of the article, maybe a little bit more now, which she'd actually written.

"I started breaking in, right here, with misgivings. But she help up her hand, rather imperiously, in fact, and continued on. She remarked how it would be very helpful to this plan of hers if someone who had as much of a reputation for honesty and integrity with the rest of the faculty as I did would vouch unreservedly for her story of the computer crashing and thereby destroying the virtually completed article. She said that as far as she and I knew no one on the faulty had even the merest glimmer that she and I were particularly friendly, much less lovers, with a passionate, and generally deep, all—over relationship. So there'd be no question of my support being looked upon as tarnished with self—interest, conflict of interest, etc., etc. She even suggested that I could testify, as it were, that she'd asked me to come into her office to discuss a particular point in the paper, one she'd been right in the midst of writing up right then and so that I'd been directly on the spot at the exact time, and seen with my own eyes, that the computer had suddenly flagrantly mal—functioned and wiped out the whole paper in a moment. Truly the blink of an eye.

"I gave her credit for a high degree of resourcefulness, not to mention sheer creative writing cleverness, but I did mention the slight additional fact that her scenario required both of us to positively lie through our teeth in more than one respect. But my saying this caused her to become exercised to a degree I'd never seen before. She started fulminating that this wasn't any abstract, ethereal philosophical, or ethical debate but, rather, the very harsh concrete reality of her job being at stake. The extreme agitation continued and she started arguing, just as though she were presenting a legal brief, that the powers that are at the law school were holding her to particularly stringent standards which she doubted would be applied quite so rigorously were she a male with the same background and achievements. Then she added that additional animus toward her, from a not inconsiderable faculty faction, might well stem from her obviously liberal political orientation, perhaps most graphically indicated by the very strong support she'd given my proposal to hire a qualified minority faculty member. She continued gesticulating emphatically, almost fiercely, the softly beautiful features now seemingly hardened, as she practically yelled that there also could be some ill-will, in general, toward her, from various faculty members, because she hadn't been overly energetic in ingratiating herself with other professors on the trivial, bullshit level of 'Was the bagel you had with your coffee this morning garlic or onion and did you like it as much as the cinnamon ones, and which is your top favorite, etc., etc.?' She went on, still heatedly, that she tended to be a loner, just like me, and that such a mien just didn't sit well with many of the established faculty who seemed to feel that a recent hire ought to curry favor, at least to some extent, with those who controlled her career trajectory and advancement. At the very end of the diatribe she threw in a line about how she might have actually finished the paper in time if she hadn't spent so much time with, I think the phrase might even have been 'taking care of,' me, none other than moi.

"Naturally, I became pretty shook and didn't know quite how to begin answering or reasoning with her, whatever. But I did strongly know that, because her own personal, selfish interests were on the line, she was trying to justify doing something which she'd strongly, amost glibly, condemn someone else for attempting. And not only seeking to justify herself in doing something like that but also trying to get me to agree that she was, indeed, justified. Putting aside trying to get me to believe it was justified for me to participate in her concocted scheme—lie outrightly in a way I'd certainly condemn in others—on the grounds that I, too, should put her (our?) personal selfish interests above my normal moral scruples.

"Finally, while having gotten hold of her hand, and trying to be as soothing as possible, I did say that what she was proposing was something she'd normally castigate vociferously and that loyalty to important general, deeply believed principles sometimes required the sacrifice of expedient, personal, self—interested considerations. I went on that the very worst thing that could happen in these circumstances was that she'd have to look for another job and that even then she'd have a year and a half to find one. Maybe, I speculated, she might even feel worse about keeping her job if it meant betraying long-held ideals and beliefs and her powerful sense of integrity than she'd feel about being told that she wasn't being retained.

"She really heated up at this, pulling her hand violently from mine, and vituperatively calling it something like 'high falutin, abstract, ivory tower nonsense' which someone could pontificate only about somebody else losing her job. I responded that I really didn't think I was being cavalier and insensitive, that I sincerely thought that I would take the same tack, feel the same way, if my own job were at stake. She riposted with a truly nostril flaring, curt, whiplike really, 'Bullshit.' Well this agitated me, inflamed me really, to the point of asserting that lying was lying, especially where misleading others to feather your own nest is involved. I added that to claim you hated lying, deception and dissembling in general, only to suddenly resort to them when your selfish interests were involved was nothing but rank hypocrisy.

"Naturally this lit her fuse to sputtering, practically incoherent bursts and, finally, she said, making her voice as cold, icy rather, and 'dispassionate' as possible, that she had thought that she and I had something solid and very likely indefinitely durable, (sounded like verging on marriage to me, something which had certainly crossed my mind,) but that if I didn't back her up on the story she'd concocted, for the presentation of which she wanted my participation, I could just damn well forget about continuing with her as we had been. In fact, she screamed, (shrieked is really more like it,) I could just forget about her, period. Period, the end. The absolute end.

"Trying to divert her from this particular track a bit, slow down the express train of rupture, I mentioned that even if I supported her in her fabrication of why she hadn't yet produced a publishable article, the faculty,might, nevertheless, be sufficiently skeptical about her scholarly talents and productivity potential, or otherwise ornery or persnickety enough, to vote not to renew her contract. And I further pointed out that if some of the real animus which she sensed was arrayed against her was caused by her political views or unwillingness to kowtow to the entrenched guard, then papers and articles, their states of completion, quality, quantity, ad infinitum, really wouldn't matter. If she had one published paper they'd claim that two, or even more, were necessary, the norm. If she had two they'd evaluate one or both as below the acceptable par. So, even if she convinced them, by the joint scam she was proposing she and I pull, that she'd just completed an article it might all be to no avail. And then she'd have also betrayed, in a fundamental way, her true self and have coerced me into doing the same. I did manage to resist quoting Polonius's pietistic 'To thine own self be true,' from 'Hamlet.'

"With utter iciness still the predominant meteorology of her voice she said that all of that would be another thing, that if she went down after her best shot then she went down. She could accept that. But disloyalty and lack of support from me were another story entirely. One which her self—respect and her reasonable expectations wouldn't permit her to tolerate. Or, more to the point, live with.

Now I screamed. 'Self—respect,' how did that have anything to do with whether you could get another person to lie for you by emotional, physical blackmail etc.? Her response in the still, (if not more so,) frigid, clinical, (calculating?) voice was that I could adorn it in as much' horsecrap' and all the phony philosophical principles I could delude myself into thinking apposite, but that her position was unequivocally, unmistakably, once and definitely for all time, non—negotiably clear: either I backed up her story pretty much just as she'd scripted it or we were definitively, completely, no doubt about it, whatsoever, 'through.' She wouldn't be able to go on, as we had been going on, with someone who placed philosophical abstractions above the real human emotions of a person he presumably loved. (She, I suddenly recognized, was certainly completely right about how I'd come to feel about her.)

"At that point I got up saying I'd have to think about all that, but right then, at that precise moment, it was surely time for me to go home. I got the old navy blue overcoat, slowly put it on, opened the front door and walked through toward the elevator. I heard, the very hard, slam of the door."

Martin got up from his desk and slowly went to the hall closet to get his old, navy blue, English wool overcoat. He distractedly put it on, threw the red woolen scarf around his neck, slapped a beret on his head and made for the elevator. As soon as he opened the lobby door, to begin what he knew would be a long, extremely pensive, agonizingly contemplative walk, a sharp blast of fiercely cold Chicago winter twilight wind sliced at his face.